A Spinster's Folly

COURTING *the* UNCONVENTIONAL

LAURA BEERS

1

England, 1814

Lady Eugenie Drayton found newlyweds to be utterly insufferable. At present, she was trapped in a cramped coach across from her brother, Niles, Earl of Westcott, and his new wife, Elsbeth. She had no means of escape, which meant she was forced to endure their endless exchanges of tender looks and whispered sentiments.

Lifting her book as a barrier between her and the couple, she hoped for some reprieve. Instead, it seemed to encourage them further. Elsbeth leaned in for another kiss. Eugenie groaned inwardly. Did they think she was invisible? She decided to test her theory and pinched her arm.

"Ouch," she muttered under her breath.

Niles, glancing up, raised an eyebrow. "Why did you pinch yourself?"

"I was checking to see if I was invisible," Eugenie retorted.

Niles tilted his head in confusion. "And why would you think that?"

Lowering her book, Eugenie fixed him with a dry stare.

"Because neither of you bother to acknowledge my presence. You're carrying on as though I don't exist."

Elsbeth offered a contrite smile. "I'm sorry, Eugenie. We have been terrible company, haven't we?"

"I don't think so," Niles interjected, sliding his arm around his wife's shoulders. "In fact, I think it's good for Eugenie to witness such a loving marriage. Isn't that right, my love biscuit?"

Eugenie made a gagging noise. "I think I just threw up a little in my mouth," she mocked.

Niles chuckled. "You are being overdramatic."

"And you are being unbearable," Eugenie countered. "Can you two please stop touching for two seconds? Is that even possible?"

Elsbeth removed Niles's arm from her shoulders, her eyes holding compassion. "Eugenie has a fair point. We should be more mindful."

"Should we?" Niles asked, leaning closer to his wife. "Perhaps we should go on another wedding tour. I rather enjoyed being alone with you."

Eugenie rolled her eyes. It was like talking to a brick wall. Why did she even bother speaking up?

Quite frankly, she was happy for Niles and Elsbeth. Her brother had been so unhappy before he had met Elsbeth. But his wife had brought him alive in so many ways. Now he was the brother that she had always hoped would reemerge once more.

Turning towards the window, she decided to let Niles and Elsbeth have their moment. It wouldn't be long before they arrived at their townhouse in London. She wasn't particularly excited about the upcoming Season, but she enjoyed being in Town. There was so much to participate in, including the circulating libraries. She could read to her heart's content.

Niles's voice broke through her thoughts. "We're nearly there."

"Thank you for stating the obvious," Eugenie muttered, not bothering to look his way.

Elsbeth leaned forward. "Eugenie, is it true what Niles says about your family's library? He speaks of it so fondly."

Eugenie's lips curved into a small smile as she met her sister-in-law's gaze. "It's true. Our father was an avid reader, like me. There are more books than one can count; many of them are rare first editions. It's like having a collection of old friends at my fingertips."

"That sounds enchanting," Elsbeth replied. "Perhaps I'll take up reading myself."

Niles smirked. "Why?" he asked. "If you are looking for something to entertain yourself, I would be more than happy to offer my services." He waggled his eyebrows.

"I know you would, but I want to take an interest in what Eugenie is doing," Elsbeth said. "It is the duty of any good sister-in-law."

"You don't need to read—you are a countess," Niles remarked, a playful edge in his voice.

Eugenie knew that her brother was goading her, but she couldn't help but take the bait. "People who read are far more interesting than their counterparts who don't," she insisted. "Do you want a boring wife?"

Niles shook his head. "Elsbeth is far from boring. I find her the most intriguing person that I know."

Elsbeth shifted in her seat to face her husband. "That is so sweet of you to say," she murmured, leaning in for a kiss.

Good heavens! These two were incorrigible. Perhaps she was unrealistic about her expectations of them. They were young and in love.

Thankfully, the coach came to a halt in front of their townhouse. Eugenie wasted no time in stepping out and inhaling the crisp London air. She was home, and free from the cramped coach.

Elsbeth joined her, gazing up at the whitewashed façade. "What a beautiful home," she remarked.

Niles reached for his wife's hand. "I hope you love it," he said. "It was redecorated by my mother shortly before she passed."

"I am sure I will love it, then," Elsbeth assured him.

"Come, let me introduce you to the household staff," Niles said as he helped his wife up the townhouse steps.

Eugenie followed behind, feeling like an interloper in her own home. The main door opened and the tall, white-haired butler stood to the side to allow them entry.

"Welcome home, my lord," Tanner greeted.

Niles came to a stop on the black-and-white marbled floor of the entry hall. "Tanner, this is my wife, the Countess of Westcott," he shared proudly.

Tanner bowed, his movements stiff. "It is a pleasure to meet you, my lady. As requested, the main bedchamber has been prepared for your arrival."

"Very good," Niles said.

Eugenie headed towards the grand staircase. "I do believe I will take a nap now. Do try not to smother each other in the meantime."

"Before you go," Niles's voice called out, halting Eugenie mid-step.

Drat. She had almost escaped.

Eugenie turned back, schooling her expression into one of reluctant patience. "Yes?"

"Bedford will be joining us for supper," Niles informed her, a faintly smug smile tugging at his lips as though he anticipated her reaction.

Eugenie fought to suppress a grimace. Lord Bedford. Of course. "Wonderful," she muttered. "Now I have something to look forward to." Without waiting for a response, she spun on her heel and ascended the staircase.

Reaching the sanctuary of her bedchamber, she opened the door to find her lady's maid, Alice, unpacking the last of her trunks.

Eugenie crossed the room and flopped unceremoniously onto the bed. "I don't think I'm going to survive this Season," she declared.

Alice laughed. "You'll manage just fine, my lady. You always do."

Rolling onto her side, Eugenie propped herself up on one elbow. "Did you manage to retrieve the newssheets?"

"I did." Alice turned, wiping her hands on her apron. "There's a lecture at Oxford tomorrow on the optics and principles of Newton, Plato, and Aristotle."

Eugenie straightened. "When?"

"Tomorrow morning, in the great lecture hall," Alice replied, her tone tempered with caution. "But it's for gentlemen only."

Eugenie's excitement dimmed, replaced with a familiar frustration. "Of course it is," she sighed. "Anything of intellectual value is always reserved for men." She slumped back against the pillows. "Are there any lectures I can attend?"

"There are a few next week on religion and poetry," Alice offered.

Eugenie groaned. "Poetry again? How dreadfully uninspired. Last time I attended a poetry lecture, the most thrilling moment was when I accidentally dropped a lozenge and watched it roll all the way to the front of the hall."

Alice grinned. "I'm sure Lord Westcott wasn't pleased."

"No, but what could he do about it?" Eugenie pushed herself off the bed and moved towards her trunk. "Have you unpacked my trousers yet?"

Alice's smile faltered, replaced by a look of wary resignation. "No, but I fear I know where this is going."

Eugenie crouched, rummaging through the trunk until she retrieved a pair of neatly folded trousers and a matching waistcoat. "If I dress the part of a gentleman, I can attend the lecture," she declared, holding the garments aloft triumphantly. "I've done it once before."

Alice's expression darkened with concern. "What if you're caught? You'd be ruined."

"Then I won't get caught," Eugenie said, pulling out a cravat and jacket to complete the look. She laid the clothes out on the settee, her determination evident.

"My lady," Alice began, her tone tinged with warning, "you were lucky last time. I wouldn't tempt fate again."

Eugenie waved off the concern with a dismissive hand. "Oxford is only six hours away and my dear friend, Alexandra, lives nearby. I'll simply tell Niles I'm going to visit her for the day. We will leave before first light and return home right after the lecture. He's so preoccupied with Elsbeth these days, he won't even notice."

The sharpness in her tone didn't escape Alice, who softened instantly. "Your brother cares for you."

"I know," Eugenie admitted as she straightened the jacket. "But he's understandably distracted right now."

Alice hesitated before responding, "Even so, he'd want you to be safe."

Eugenie nodded absently, her mind already spinning with plans for tomorrow. "I'll be safe. It is just one lecture. No one will even give me heed."

"I think this is foolish," Alice said, her voice tinged with both concern and disapproval.

"Duly noted." Eugenie crossed the room and dropped onto the bed. "Now, if you'll excuse me, it's time for me to rest before dinner."

Alice let out a soft sigh, clearly dissatisfied but knowing better than to argue further. She moved towards the window and drew the heavy drapes, plunging the room into darkness. "Perhaps a nap will help you realize that no amount of clever dressing could make anyone believe you're a man."

Eugenie laid her head onto the pillow and closed her eyes. She understood Alice's apprehension, but the truth was, she was tired. Not just of the day's journey or the constant charade of pleasantries expected of a lady of her standing, but of the stifling constraints that seemed to define her existence. The endless whispers of what she could and couldn't do. What she should and shouldn't want.

It wasn't foolishness that drove her to such extremes—it was defiance. A quiet, stubborn insistence that her life could be more than Seasons filled with dull poetry lectures and tiresome suitors. She wanted to expand her mind, push boundaries, and feel the thrill of stepping into a world that unequivocally told her that she didn't belong.

Charles Ellsworth, Earl of Bedford, felt utterly exasperated as he trudged through the foul-smelling streets of a disreputable part of Town. The mission to retrieve his wayward cousin had long since worn thin, and all he wanted now was to be home poring over estate accounts.

Beside him, Richard, Marquess of Wilton, cast a doubtful glance at their surroundings. "Are you certain we're in the right place?" he asked, his tone betraying skepticism.

Charles nodded stiffly. "*The Rabbit and the Fox* gambling hell is supposed to be on this street," he said, his eyes scanning the dilapidated structures. Some had roofs caving in, others were barely held together by rotting beams. The few figures loitering in the shadows paused to observe the two well-dressed gentle-men, their eyes sharp and curious, as if they knew these men didn't belong here.

Wilton pointed towards a narrow door from which a man had just emerged, wiping his nose on his sleeve. "Perhaps that's it."

Charles pulled a crumpled slip of paper from his pocket and glanced down at the address. "It's worth a try. None of these buildings seem to have numbers anyway."

"Frankly, I doubt people live in these buildings at all," Wilton muttered.

As if to prove him wrong, the wail of a baby pierced the air. Charles grimaced. The sound was a harsh reminder that, even in the filthiest corners of London, life stubbornly persisted. He steeled himself and approached the door, testing the handle. Locked. With a sigh, he pounded his fist against the wood.

After a long pause, a narrow slit at the top of the door slid open, revealing a pair of suspicious eyes. "What's your business?" the man behind the door growled.

"Is this *The Rabbit and the Fox*?" Charles asked.

The man's gaze narrowed further. "What's it to you?"

"I'm looking for my cousin, Mr. Philip Ellsworth," Charles responded.

"Don't know him. Now shove off," the man snapped and moved to close the slit.

Charles thrust his hand into the opening, halting the move-ment. His voice dropped, low and dangerous. "I was told my cousin was here, and I don't intend to leave without him. If you'd prefer, I can return with the constable."

The man let out an irritated sigh, clearly weighing his options. Finally, he muttered, "Fine. But you get your cousin and you get out."

"Thank you," Charles said, withdrawing his hand.

The slit slammed shut, and a moment later, the sound of

multiple locks being disengaged echoed in the dim street. The door creaked open, revealing a burly man with a bald head. He stepped aside, motioning for them to hurry. "Come in, before anyone notices."

Charles and Wilton stepped into the dark corridor, the door slamming shut behind them. Their silent escort led them deeper into the building, past flickering lanterns and the thick scent of cigar smoke. They entered a large room filled with haze and the low hum of conversation. Men hunched over card tables, coins clinking as they changed hands. Scantily clad women lounged nearby, some draped over men's shoulders, and others watching the game intently.

The burly man pointed towards a table in the back corner. "There's your cousin. No doubt losing at cards."

Charles spotted his lanky, dark-haired cousin seated at the table with cards in hand and an air of false confidence about him. His irritation flared. "Wait here," he said to Wilton before weaving his way through the crowded room, ignoring the stares of the women and the gamblers alike.

When he reached the table, he placed a firm hand on Philip's shoulder. "Let's go," he commanded.

Philip turned, his eyes wide with surprise. "Charles? What are you doing here?"

"I've come to take you home," Charles said bluntly.

Philip turned back to his cards with an air of dismissal. "There's no need. I've got a winning hand."

Charles glanced at the cards and instantly saw how slim his cousin's chances were. "I doubt that," he stated. "Besides, your mother is worried about you."

Philip snorted, not bothering to look at him. "I am eighteen years old. I do not need a nursemaid."

"Apparently, you do," Charles shot back. "You're squandering your money on cards in a place like this."

One of the other men at the table, a short and stout fellow

with a sneering grin, chuckled. "Go home, Boy. You're out of coin anyway."

Philip's shoulders stiffened. "I can win it back," he insisted.

"Unlikely," the man mocked. "Run along now before you embarrass yourself further."

Shoving his chair back, Philip shot to his feet. "You have no right to speak to me that way!"

"I have every right," the man countered coldly. "You owe me money. Until you pay up, I'll speak to you however I like."

Charles stepped between them, placing a restraining hand on Philip's chest. "Enough," he said sharply. "We're leaving. Now."

Philip glared at him. "You have no right to dictate what I do."

"I have every right," Charles responded. "If you don't come with me, I'll cut off your allowance."

The stout man snorted. "Must be nice to have an allowance, eh?"

Philip faltered, his defiance wavering. After a tense moment, he shoved past Charles, brushing his shoulder as he stormed towards the exit. "Fine. But I'll find my own way home," he snapped.

Charles followed as he responded, "I assured your mother I'd bring you home, and I intend to keep my word."

Philip said nothing, his pace quick and angry as they stepped back out into the night air. Standing on the filthy pavement, Charles inhaled deeply, trying to steady his fraying patience.

"Where is your coach?" Philip demanded.

Charles gestured down the dimly lit street. "Not far. Just around the corner."

Without waiting for them, Philip stormed off in that direction, his shoulders stiff with indignation.

Wilton stepped up beside Charles. "Your cousin seems to be in an exceptionally pleasant mood," he quipped.

Charles sighed, rubbing a hand over his face. "I don't know why I bother," he muttered. "Philip is never going to change. He's determined to squander every opportunity handed to him."

Wilton tilted his head thoughtfully. "You don't know that. We all had our rebellious streaks when we were young."

Charles began walking, falling into step with Wilton. "True," he admitted begrudgingly. "But I've never been foolish enough to chase every vice like Philip. When I was young, I knew the limits of what I could afford. And frankly, I didn't have the funds to indulge in nonsense. Even now, my estate's profitability hinges on careful management and investments."

Wilton cast him a sidelong glance. "So what's the plan? What will you do?"

"As of now, Philip is still my heir," Charles said, his tone grim. "But if he continues down this path, I may have no choice but to reconsider giving him an allowance. He needs to grow up, take responsibility, and stop acting like an insolent child."

"Did he really get kicked out of Oxford?" Wilton asked.

Charles's jaw tightened. "So it seems, though I plan to confirm that with the Master tomorrow. With any luck, I'll be able to convince them to reinstate him."

"You might need to sweeten the deal with a donation," Wilton suggested.

"Wonderful," Charles muttered. "Just what I need—another expense caused by Philip's poor decisions."

They reached the coach, where the footman was already opening the door. Charles climbed inside first, taking the seat directly across from Philip, who was sprawled against the cushions with a sulky expression, his arms crossed tightly over his chest. Wilton followed and settled beside Charles as the coach jerked forward.

"You made a fool of me in there," Philip growled, his gaze fixed out the window. "You had no right to interfere."

"It's time for you to grow up and start focusing on your responsibilities," Charles replied.

"Responsibilities," Philip scoffed, his lips curling in disdain. "Like you? Spending your days buried in estate accounts and ledgers?"

"Precisely."

Philip let out a dramatic sigh and tilted his head back, staring at the ceiling of the coach. "You want me to be boring."

"There is nothing boring about managing an estate," Charles countered. "It's meaningful, necessary work."

Philip barked a humorless laugh. "Meaningful? Sitting in a chair all day? Counting numbers? That sounds dreadful. I'd rather do anything than end up with a flat bum like yours."

Charles bristled. "My bum is not flat. And this isn't about me. It's about you and the fact that you have responsibilities as my heir."

Philip sat up straighter. "Responsibilities? Only until you get married and your wife starts popping out sons. Then I'll be conveniently discarded, won't I?"

Charles's lips pressed into a thin line. "You don't know what the future holds," he said evenly, though there was a faint edge of tension in his voice.

Philip leaned back again, his gaze hard. "Neither do you. But don't expect me to sit quietly in the corner while you play lord of the manor."

"You seem to forget that I *am* the lord of the manor and I can act however I see fit," Charles defended.

Wilton pulled out his pocket watch and studied it. "Do you not have plans to dine with your cousin and her family this evening?"

Charles hesitated. "I did, but perhaps it's best if I forgo the dinner," he said, glancing towards Philip. "Someone needs to keep an eye on him."

At this, Philip let out a derisive snort, but remained quiet, seemingly perturbed by anything and everything.

Wilton snapped his watch shut and tucked it back into his waistcoat pocket. "Nonsense," he said firmly. "Go to dinner. I'll ensure Philip is returned home properly and doesn't wander off again."

Charles considered the suggestion for a moment. It would be intolerably rude to send his regrets at this late hour. And there was another reason—a far more personal one—that made him reluctant to cancel. Lady Eugenie. She had been in his thoughts far too often for his liking. It was that blasted kiss. It had been a moment of weakness, but one that had unsettled him deeply.

"Very well," Charles said. "I shall take you up on your offer, but make sure Philip goes straight home. No detours."

Wilton gave a wry smile. "You wound me, Charles. Do you truly think I'd let him out of my sight?"

Charles raised an eyebrow. "Yes."

Wilton chuckled. "Fair enough," he conceded. "But I give you my word. The boy will be delivered home intact."

Philip shifted in his seat, clearly annoyed. "I'm not a parcel to be delivered," he muttered under his breath.

Ignoring the boy, Charles adjusted his coat and leaned back against the bench, his mind already drifting to the dinner ahead. He would be a dutiful guest and hope that the evening wouldn't bring more complications than he already had in his life.

2

Eugenie sat in the drawing room, elegantly poised in a dark blue gown that complemented her fair complexion. A book rested in her hands, but her attention was far from the printed words. This was unusual since reading had always been her greatest solace, her refuge from the world. And yet, tonight, she found herself rereading the same sentence over and over, unable to focus.

Her gaze flickered to the long clock in the corner, its polished brass pendulum swinging in a steady rhythm. She had checked the time at least five times in the last few moments, telling herself it was simply out of habit. Certainly not because she was anticipating Lord Bedford's arrival.

Not that she cared. At least, that was what she kept trying to tell herself.

But, heaven help her, she did.

Why had she let him kiss her? It had been sheer madness on her part. The moment his lips had met hers, the world had ceased to exist. It had been more than what she had ever imagined a kiss could be. And that was precisely the problem.

There was no future in entertaining such thoughts, no

logical reason to allow herself to be distracted by a man she had no business thinking about. She was perfectly content being a spinster. A marriage would only shackle her, limiting the freedoms she so fiercely cherished.

She tried to convince herself that the kiss meant nothing. It had been a stolen moment in the library of Lady Britton's townhouse during a ball—nearly six months ago. And at the time, she had no idea who Lord Bedford was. Had she known, she would never have let him kiss her. Not that she gave away her kisses. No. Lord Bedford was the only person she had ever kissed. They had been arguing and it had just happened.

The chime of the long clock echoed through the room, jolting her from her wayward thoughts. Lord Bedford would be here any moment. The thought made her heart race, which was utterly ridiculous. She was not some love-starved debutante waiting for a suitor's call.

She needed to compose herself.

Just as she was taking a steadying breath, the butler stepped into the room. "Lord Bedford has arrived, my lady," Tanner announced.

Eugenie forced an expression of nonchalance and raised her book as if wholly engrossed. "Send him in, please," she said, feigning disinterest. It would not do to appear as though she had been waiting for him.

From the corner of her eye, she saw Lord Bedford enter. He was tall, broad-shouldered, and his dark hair was impeccably brushed forward. Clad in a fine black jacket and matching trousers, he exuded effortless confidence. Worse still, he looked far too handsome for his own good.

Or hers.

Lord Bedford strode across the room with his usual surety, stopping just before her. She could feel his gaze on her, but she kept her eyes fixed on the pages before her, lifting a finger as if she were in the midst of an utterly engrossing passage. "One moment," she murmured.

She read precisely three lines—none of which she comprehended—before finally snapping the book shut and lowering it to her lap. "My apologies," she said. "I had to finish the chapter."

Lord Bedford inclined his head. "Understandable. May I ask what you were reading?"

Drat.

It was a simple enough question, but in his presence, she found that recalling even the most basic details became unreasonably difficult. She glanced down at the book as if seeing it for the first time. "*Roxana: The Fortunate Mistress* by Daniel Defoe."

A flicker of something—interest? amusement?—crossed his face. "Ah, a story about a woman who rises through Society using her intelligence and charm but ultimately faces the weight of moral dilemmas."

Eugenie arched a brow. "You've read it?"

Lord Bedford grinned. "You sound surprised."

"I am," she admitted. "Most gentlemen of the *ton* do not waste their time on fiction. They consider it beneath them."

His grin widened. "You will find that I am not like most gentlemen." He winked.

Oh, dear. A slow warmth crept up her neck, and she quickly averted her gaze, tracing idle patterns along the spine of her book in a desperate attempt to appear unaffected.

Lord Bedford took a seat beside her, his proximity sending an unwelcome flutter through her stomach. "I'm surprised Westcott and Elsbeth aren't down yet."

Eugenie exhaled, grateful for the change in topic. "I'm not. They can't seem to keep their hands off one another."

Lord Bedford visibly shuddered. "That is an unfortunate thought."

"You should try riding in a coach with them. It was truly dreadful. I even pinched myself to see if I had become invisible."

He laughed. The rich, deep sound was entirely too intoxicating. "You poor thing."

The dinner bell rang in the distance, its chime echoing through the house.

Eugenie turned towards the doorway. "Well, they should be down shortly," she remarked, immediately chastising herself for stating the obvious.

Lord Bedford relaxed against the settee, regarding her with an amused expression. "What shall we talk about while we wait?"

Before she could think better of it, she blurted, "Do you like the weather?"

The moment the words left her lips, she nearly groaned aloud. The weather? Good heavens, what was wrong with her? There was nothing remotely interesting about the weather. It always rained in England. That was a simple, indisputable fact.

Lord Bedford smirked. "I do," he said, clearly humoring her.

"So do I." Eugenie shut her eyes in mortification. *Why, why, why?*

His smirk widened. "I was hoping for a slightly more intellectually stimulating conversation."

"Of course," she said hastily, wishing the floor would open up and swallow her whole.

He studied her for a long moment before asking, "What do you think of the Luddite Movement?"

"You truly wish to know?" Eugenie asked, utterly surprised by the question.

Lord Bedford leaned forward slightly, his expression earnest. "I wouldn't have asked if I didn't want to hear the answer."

For the first time that evening, Eugenie felt herself truly

relax. Perhaps she had underestimated Lord Bedford after all. He was actually engaging her in real discourse, a rarity among men of his social standing.

"Well," she began, leaning slightly forward, "I find that I sympathize with the Luddites. Their livelihoods are being stripped away, replaced by industrial machines that can produce goods faster and cheaper."

Lord Bedford studied her intently, his sharp gaze never wavering. "But should we not embrace industrialization? Progress is inevitable."

"Not at the expense of people's livelihoods," Eugenie countered, a note of passion creeping into her voice. "These workers already endure grueling hours for meager wages. To have their only source of income taken from them—without any alternatives—how can that be justified?"

Lord Bedford tilted his head. "However, the Luddites do not merely protest. They break into factories and destroy expensive machinery. Surely, that level of destruction cannot be condoned."

Eugenie set her book aside, folding her hands in her lap as she met his gaze with unwavering conviction. "What other choice do they have?" she asked. "Their pleas are ignored by the very people who profit from their misfortunes. They have families to feed and roofs to keep over their heads. Desperation makes men act in ways they might not otherwise."

"I understand their plight," Lord Bedford admitted, "but industrialization also makes textiles more affordable for the masses. The economy grows, and, in theory, new jobs emerge."

"Perhaps," Eugenie conceded, "but that does not change the fact that breaking machinery should not be a crime punishable by death. The Frame Breaking Act of 1812 is barbaric. Execution for damaging a loom? Surely you cannot defend that."

Lord Bedford opened his mouth as if to formulate a

response, but before he could say anything, a soft, familiar voice interrupted them from the doorway.

"Cousin," Elsbeth greeted warmly.

Both Eugenie and Lord Bedford turned towards the entrance, where Elsbeth stood with a radiant smile. Her dark curls were pinned elegantly, and her gown was a soft shade of lavender that flattered her delicate features.

Lord Bedford rose from his seat and crossed the room, taking Elsbeth's hands before leaning down to press a light kiss to her cheek. "I see that marriage agrees with you," he observed, a genuine note of affection in his voice.

Elsbeth beamed. "It does," she admitted. "It is far better than I ever imagined it could be."

"Where is Westcott?" Lord Bedford asked.

"He should be here in a moment. He is reviewing the accounts," Elsbeth shared. "I do apologize for interrupting your riveting conversation."

Eugenie offered a small, knowing smile. "We were simply engaging in an intellectual discussion, that is all."

Lord Bedford, still standing beside Elsbeth, glanced back at Eugenie, his lips twitching. "An engaging one, indeed."

Just then, Niles appeared in the doorway, his arm slipping around Elsbeth's waist. "Shall we adjourn for dinner?"

Eugenie rose from her seat. "Yes, please." Then leveling her brother with a look, she added, "And need I remind you that we have company? Do try to keep your hands to yourself this evening."

Niles didn't so much as feign remorse. Instead, his lips curled into a smug grin. "I'll try," he said. "But I can't promise Elsbeth will do the same. I simply can't get her to stop kissing me. Not that I blame her, of course. I am quite the catch."

Elsbeth, to her credit, did not blush or scold him, but merely smiled, entirely undeterred. "Yes, you are, my love," she murmured, placing her hand over his.

Eugenie rolled her eyes, but before she could respond, Lord Bedford stepped beside her. Leaning in slightly, he lowered his voice so only she could hear. "You did try to warn me."

"Trust me. It only gets worse," Eugenie said. "Wait until he calls her his 'love biscuit.'"

Lord Bedford shook his head as he offered his arm. "May I escort you into dinner?"

Eugenie hesitated for only a moment before placing her gloved hand lightly on his arm. "You may," she said, her voice composed—though her heart was another matter entirely.

The last time she had been this close to him, he had kissed her.

The kiss.

Why, *why* couldn't she get it out of her mind? It had been impulsive, reckless. So why did the memory linger, insistent, playing on an endless loop in her thoughts? The way he had held her. The way he had looked at her afterward, as if he wanted more.

She needed to stop thinking about it.

As they followed Niles and Elsbeth out of the drawing room and towards the dining hall, Lord Bedford glanced over at her. "Are you looking forward to the Season?"

Eugenie sighed. "That is a difficult question," she admitted. "I'm looking forward to being in Town again, taking in the sights, indulging in the circulating libraries. But I am dreading the social events."

"As am I," Lord Bedford admitted.

She arched a brow at him. "But you are an earl."

Lord Bedford furrowed his brow as if the thought had never occurred to him before. "And you are the daughter of an earl," he countered. "Does that mean we were bred to enjoy social events?"

"Point taken," Eugenie acknowledged. She was secretly pleased that—like her—he merely tolerated social events.

They stepped into the dining room and Lord Bedford moved to pull out the chair for her.

"Thank you, my lord," she said as she lowered herself into her seat.

Lord Bedford took the seat beside her as Niles and Elsbeth settled into their own seats across from them.

Eugenie exhaled softly, forcing herself to focus on the meal ahead rather than the man sitting so close that she could feel the warmth of his presence.

This was going to be a long dinner.

Charles sat at the long, polished mahogany table in the grand dining room, the vast space echoing with the occasional clink of his silver spoon against the delicate porcelain teacup. The morning sun poured through the tall windows, illuminating the intricate crown molding and the gilded sconces that lined the walls. He unfolded the newssheets, scanning the printed words with practiced ease, though his mind was only half-engaged. The estate's affairs, the financial reports, the latest political happenings—none of it seemed to hold his attention for long.

Despite the grand setting, he was alone, or at least as alone as one could be in a house teeming with servants. The ever-present footmen and housemaids moved silently through the corridors, attending to their morning duties with quiet efficiency. Still, solitude was a luxury he seldom enjoyed, and this morning, he found himself yearning for something even more elusive than peace. He missed the days of his youth, the simplicity of a life unburdened by titles, estates, and expectations.

Not that he had a right to complain. He had inherited a

title, secured entailed properties, and, thanks to Mr. Stockton's generous intervention, had the financial means to ensure the estate's prosperity for many years to come. By all accounts, he should have been content. And yet, he wasn't.

An image of Lady Eugenie flickered in his mind and he banished the thought. There was no reason for him to think of her. He had no intention of pursuing anyone at present and his attention needed to remain on his accounts.

His mother swept into the room. Her maroon gown emphasized her slender figure, while the morning light caught in the strands of her fading blonde hair. The fine lines on her face, deepening with time, did nothing to diminish her regal presence.

"Good morning," she greeted.

Charles lowered the newssheets. "Not that I am complaining, but do you not usually request a tray to be sent to your bedchamber?"

"I do," his mother replied, settling into the chair across from him. She unfolded a white linen napkin onto her lap. "But I was lonely this morning."

The admission took him by surprise. His mother was not one to openly express sentimentality. She continued, her eyes keen as she regarded him. "How was dinner last night with Elsbeth?"

"It was eventful," he answered, setting the newssheets aside. "Why did you not join us?"

She waved a delicate hand dismissively. "You did not need an old woman there. Besides, I wanted to finish my book."

"You sound just like Lady Eugenie."

A pleased smile curved her lips. "I simply adore Lady Eugenie. She reminds me so much of myself when I was younger."

Charles shook his head. "Westcott thinks she reads entirely too much and is caught up in what he calls 'reading mania.'"

"Is there such a thing?"

"Apparently so," he said, a smirk tugging at the corner of his mouth. "Do you have any plans for today?"

At that, his mother straightened, a glint of excitement in her gaze. "I was invited by Elsbeth to join her sewing circle. Did you know she makes clothing for the orphans in the workhouses?"

"Yes, she has mentioned it to me a time or two," Charles said. "Elsbeth has a good heart."

"You should have married her when you had the chance," his mother teased.

Charles huffed. "I was trying to do the honorable thing when I offered for her, but it was a good thing she declined."

"I couldn't agree more," his mother admitted. "You two are far too similar—or should I say, stubborn."

Folding the newssheets, Charles placed them on the table. "I am happy for Elsbeth and Westcott. They make a fine pair, and their love is evident."

His mother's gaze softened. "That is what I want for you."

He frowned. "I am only five-and-twenty. I need to focus on my accounts, not the marriage mart."

"You can do both."

"Not well enough, if you ask me," he said, taking a sip from his teacup. "It is a tremendous amount of pressure to be responsible for so many livelihoods."

His mother leaned forward and patted his hand. "You are more than capable of managing the estate."

"Only because of Mr. Stockton and his generous gift of fifteen thousand pounds," Charles said. "Without that, I would be dealing with a nearly bankrupt estate."

His mother's expression grew solemn. "Mr. Stockton is a good man."

"That he is. And it is evident that Aunt Isabella loves him very much," Charles added. "They behave like newlyweds."

"I am happy for Isabella," his mother said. "She endured much at her late husband's hand."

Charles nodded. "But it is over. My uncle can't hurt her—or anyone else—anymore."

A footman stepped forward, placing a plate before Charles's mother. She picked up her fork and knife before asking, "What do you intend to do today?"

"I must go to Oxford to meet with the Master of University College," Charles replied.

His mother lifted a brow. "Do you intend to earn another degree? Is your Bachelor of Arts not enough?"

Charles chuckled. "My degree is sufficient," he replied. "I need to speak to the Master on Philip's behalf."

All humor left his mother's expression. "What has Philip done now?"

"He was expelled from Oxford."

His mother pursed her lips. "When is that boy going to learn?"

"That *boy* is eighteen and is my heir," Charles said. "If I do not have my own heir, Philip will inherit my title one day."

"I shudder at the thought."

"As do I," Charles admitted. "I had to call in favors to get him admitted, and he is squandering it."

"Perhaps he might thrive at a different college," his mother suggested. "University College is the oldest and, in my opinion, the most prestigious at Oxford."

Before Charles could respond, the butler stepped into the room, his black hair slicked neatly to the side. "Mrs. Adam Ellsworth has come to call."

His mother's face lit up. "Please send her in."

Moments later, his Aunt Phoebe entered, her brown curls bouncing with each step. She approached the table with an exasperated sigh. "I am giving Philip away. Would either of you like him?"

"I already have a child that doesn't entirely listen to me," his mother quipped.

Charles looked heavenward. "You love me."

"I do," she replied, amusement in her eyes. "But it took years to train you to ensure I liked you as well."

Charles rose from his chair and gestured towards the empty seat across from him. "Please, Phoebe, join us for breakfast."

A footman stepped forward without hesitation, his gloved hands carefully pulling back the chair for her. Phoebe offered a weary smile as she lowered herself onto the seat. "Thank you, Charles," she said, her voice carrying the weight of exhaustion. "Philip was gone when I woke up this morning."

Charles stiffened. That was not the news he had hoped to hear. "Do you know where he went?"

"I don't," Phoebe admitted, her lips pressing into a tight line. "But I fear he has returned to that gambling hell. With what money, I know not."

"I will speak to him... again." He had tried countless times to steer Philip in the right direction, but the young man refused to heed his counsel.

A footman silently approached, setting a delicate cup of rich chocolate before Phoebe. She leaned slightly to the side and reached for the cup. "His father wouldn't have wanted this life for him," she murmured, her gaze distant.

"No, he wouldn't have," his mother agreed. "But you should know, Phoebe, that you are doing the best you can under these circumstances."

Phoebe's shoulders sagged. "I feel like I am failing. With Philip. With everything."

"You mustn't think that way," his mother asserted.

"How can I not?" Phoebe asked, her voice cracking slightly. "If Adam were still alive, he would never have let Philip act this way. He would have put him on the right path."

Charles met her gaze. "We will get through to Philip," he assured her, though the certainty in his voice was more for her benefit than his own.

Phoebe sighed, her fingers tightening around her cup. "I heard he was expelled from Oxford."

"That is the rumor, yes," Charles responded. "But I am speaking with the Master today to sort this all out."

Phoebe's hands trembled as she lifted the cup to her lips. "My son is a fool," she said quietly. "I only hope he learns his lesson before he throws away his future."

"Philip is still young," his mother attempted.

Phoebe, however, did not look convinced. "He is old enough to fight in the war, to attend university, and even to marry," she countered. "That is hardly a child, is it?"

"I think you need a distraction," his mother declared. "Join me this afternoon at Elsbeth's sewing circle. We are making clothing for the orphans in the workhouses."

"Do you think that is wise? I might not be the best of company," Phoebe said.

"I do," his mother affirmed with an encouraging smile. "It will be enjoyable, and I know that Elsbeth is always looking for more people to participate."

Phoebe still seemed unsure. "It would be nice to see Elsbeth again," she admitted after a pause. "I haven't seen her since she was a child."

Before the conversation could continue, the butler stepped into the room with a silver tray in his gloved hands. "A messenger just delivered a note for you, my lord," Hagen announced.

Charles accepted the note and carefully unfolded it, scanning the words quickly. With a quiet sigh, he crumpled the paper in his fist. "The Master of University College, Mr. Griffith, has agreed to meet with me regarding Philip's expulsion from Oxford."

His mother sat straighter in her chair. "That is good, is it not?"

"It is," Charles replied, though his tone carried little enthusiasm. "But we must not get our hopes up. These matters can be difficult to reverse. That said, I promise that I will do everything in my power to get him reinstated."

Phoebe offered him a small, appreciative smile. "I know you will, and I cannot thank you enough for your efforts."

Charles rounded the table, coming to stand beside her. "I should go," he said, adjusting the cuffs of his jacket. "I will send word as soon as I have spoken with Mr. Griffith."

"I wish you luck," his mother called after him as he strode towards the door.

As Charles reached for his top hat, he knew with certainty that luck had nothing to do with it. Mr. Griffith was a pragmatic man, one who responded only to logic and influence. Charles would have to rely on both if he hoped to change the Master's mind.

3

As the coach rumbled along the uneven road, Eugenie adjusted the cap over her dark-haired wig, her pulse quickening with anticipation. The mere thought of attending a lecture at Oxford felt like stepping into a dream. The idea of sitting among scholars, listening to some of the greatest minds of the time, filled her with an exhilaration she had rarely known.

Her lady's maid, Alice, was far less enthusiastic. "That wig looks ridiculous."

"It will suffice," Eugenie replied.

Alice's gaze roved critically over her attire. "Where, pray tell, did you even find that gown?"

Eugenie adjusted the sleeves of the black academic robe, smoothing the fabric over her slender frame. "I purchased it from a young man who dropped out of university. I need to blend in with the other students."

"But you aren't a student."

"Well, I certainly look like one," Eugenie countered, her lips quirking into a mischievous smile.

Alice frowned. "No one is going to mistake you for a gentleman. Your skin is too fair, and your features are far too delicate."

"That is why I will keep my head down and refrain from speaking to anyone," Eugenie assured her. "No one will pay me any heed."

"And if they do?" Alice pressed.

Eugenie waved a dismissive hand. "You worry too much. I am attending a lecture, not enlisting in the Royal Army."

Alice's frown deepened. "If you are caught, you will be ruined."

"Which is why I will not be caught."

"You make it sound so simple—"

"It is," Eugenie interjected before Alice could finish. "I know no one at Oxford, and thus, no one will recognize me." She hoped that she sounded more confident than she felt. She fully understood the risks of what she was about to do. If she were caught, she would be ruined. Utterly ruined. But she had to at least try to attend this lecture.

Before Alice could protest further, the coach slowed and came to a halt. Eugenie peered out of the small window, her breath hitching as she caught sight of the grand entrance to University College. It was glorious and beautiful. "Wish me luck," she said, reaching for the handle.

Alice hesitated. "Perhaps I should go with you."

"If you did, I would surely be caught since lady's maids do not accompany students," Eugenie said. "Remain in the coach, and all will be well. I promise."

"Very well," Alice conceded, though she looked far from convinced. "I shall take you at your word."

Eugenie stepped out of the carriage, inhaling deeply. She could do this. Yet, even as she formed the thought, a cold wave of apprehension tightened around her chest, making her rethink everything. Was she being reckless? Had she underestimated the risk?

Her gloved fingers clenched at the robe as she cast a hesitant glance over her shoulder at the waiting coach, its presence a silent invitation to turn back before it was too late. The sensible choice would be to retreat, to preserve her reputation before she did something she might come to regret. But then what? She would spend the rest of her life haunted by uncertainty, forever wondering what might have been.

No. She straightened her shoulders, steeling herself. The path ahead was uncertain, but the regret of not taking it would be far worse.

A footman approached, dipping his head slightly. "Good luck, my lady," he murmured under his breath.

"Thank you, Bryan," she replied. She had discreetly slipped both him and the driver a generous portion of her pin money—an unspoken pact sealed with coin and trust. Their silence was essential.

With deliberate calm, she walked towards the entrance, blending seamlessly into the throng of students. The lecture was to be held at Radcliffe Quadrangle, and she needed to find her way there unnoticed.

Keeping her head down, she followed the flow of students, her heart pounding with a mixture of nerves and excitement. The first step was complete—she had gained access to the college without drawing suspicion. With each passing moment, her confidence grew. She could do this. She would listen to the lecture and return home as if nothing had happened.

As she entered Radcliffe Quadrangle, she noticed a group of students animatedly discussing Newton's Laws of Physics. The temptation to linger and listen was strong, but she knew better than to risk unnecessary attention. However, she was so absorbed in their conversation that she failed to notice where she was going and collided with a solid wall.

No. Not a wall. A man's chest.

She staggered back, quickly ducking her head. In the deepest voice she could muster, she muttered, "My apologies."

She attempted to brush past him, but a voice—deep, familiar—stilled her.

"Lady Eugenie?"

Her breath caught. Dread pooled in her stomach. She would know that voice anywhere.

Lord Bedford.

Her mind raced. She had two choices. She could keep walking and feign ignorance, or acknowledge him and accept whatever consequences followed.

Before she could make her decision, Lord Bedford stepped in front of her, his keen eyes locking on to her face. He leaned in slightly, his voice barely above a whisper. "It is you."

Knowing her ruse had been discovered, she lifted her gaze. "What are you even doing here?" she demanded, keeping her voice low.

His brow arched. "Me? What are *you* doing here?"

She squared her shoulders. "I am attending a lecture."

"Dressed as a man and impersonating a student?" he asked incredulously, his voice rising slightly.

"Shh!" She gestured frantically for him to lower his voice.

Lord Bedford cast a quick glance around them before grasping her arm gently, steering her towards the shadows of the building. "Explain yourself," he ordered.

Eugenie thought it was best just to tell him the truth and hoped that he would understand. "I wanted to attend the lecture series, but women are not permitted. So, I simply dressed up as a man. Please do not make a big ado about nothing."

His jaw tightened. "Do you understand what will happen if you are caught? Your reputation would be in tatters."

"I will not get caught," she insisted.

He let out a dry chuckle. "And yet, I caught you."

"That was purely coincidental," she argued. "What are you doing here, anyway?"

A shadow passed over his features. "I am here to speak with the Master about my cousin, Philip. He was expelled from University College."

"That is unfortunate," Eugenie murmured.

"It is," Lord Bedford agreed. "But I cannot, in good conscience, go speak with the Master while knowing you are traipsing around Oxford in disguise."

Eugenie smoothed the fabric of her black academic gown. "You need not concern yourself with me. I will be perfectly fine."

Lord Bedford crossed his arms. "Does your brother know you are here?"

She shifted uncomfortably. "No. He believes I am visiting with a friend and shopping on High Street."

"I will escort you back to your coach, and you will return home at once," he said firmly.

"No."

His brows furrowed. "No?"

Eugenie lifted her chin defiantly. "I am going to attend the lecture."

Lord Bedford muttered a curse under his breath before fixing Eugenie with a pointed stare. "Why is this lecture so important to you?"

"I tire of the lectures reserved for women," she replied. "They are dull, uninspired, and wholly unchallenging. I want to be engaged, to be tested."

"At the risk of your reputation?" he pressed, his voice edged with concern.

Eugenie knew she likely sounded foolish, taking such a risk, but she wanted more than a life spent idly in a drawing room, awaiting suitors and discussing embroidery. "Yes," she admitted at last. "I do."

Lord Bedford's lips pressed into a thin line. "And what of Elsbeth's reputation?"

"What does that have to do with me?"

He unfolded his arms, stepping closer. "If you are caught, it won't be just your reputation at stake. Your actions will reflect poorly upon your brother and Elsbeth as well," he stated. "Society has only just begun to welcome her back into its good graces. Do you truly wish to jeopardize that?"

Eugenie knew that he had a point, though she hated to admit it. Risking her own name was one thing, but putting her family in the line of scandal was another entirely. Drat. Why did Lord Bedford have to be right? It was maddening.

"You make a good point," she conceded begrudgingly. "I will return home."

Lord Bedford's shoulders eased, and relief flickered across his face. "Allow me to escort you."

She shook her head. "There is no need. I am more than capable of returning to my coach unaccompanied."

"I have no doubt," he replied, "but it would ease my conscience."

"All right." With that, she turned on her heel and started towards the exit.

Lord Bedford matched her stride, falling into step beside her. As they walked, he cast her a sidelong glance. "Dare I ask if you have done this before?"

"I have attended a lecture before, dressed as a man, but this is my first attempt at Oxford," she confessed. "It seemed like a simple enough feat."

"And what if the professor had been at the door to greet each student personally?"

Eugenie bit her lower lip. "I suppose that was a possibility I hadn't considered."

He let out a short chuckle. "You are far too beautiful to ever be mistaken for a man."

A rush of warmth crept up her neck, and she quickly ducked her head to hide the blush forming on her cheeks. She chided herself for having such a reaction. Surely he was merely attempting to flatter her.

They arrived at her coach, where the footman immediately stepped forward and pulled open the door. Eugenie paused, one hand resting on the frame as a thought occurred to her. "Do you intend to tell my brother or Elsbeth about this?"

Lord Bedford studied her for a moment before responding. "Your secret is safe with me," he said. "But on one condition."

She narrowed her eyes warily. "And what is that?"

He leaned slightly closer. "You will allow me to call you by your given name."

Eugenie looked at him in surprise. "That is your condition?"

"It is," he said, rocking back slightly. "Take it or leave it."

A smile played at her lips. "I suppose that is only fair," she said, secretly pleased by the request. "Does this mean I may call you by your given name?"

He nodded. "I would prefer it, Eugenie."

The way he spoke her name, effortlessly and naturally, sent an unexpected thrill down her spine. It sounded comfortable, intimate even.

"All right, Charles," she replied, savoring the sound of his name on her tongue.

A bright smile broke across his face. "I rather like the way you say my name."

Her gaze flickered to his lips, and she remembered how much she had enjoyed their kiss. Clearing her throat, she quickly looked away. "Good day," she said briskly.

"Good day," he echoed, extending a hand towards her.

Eugenie glanced down at his outstretched palm before whispering, "What are you doing? Gentlemen do not assist other gentlemen into carriages."

Realization dawned on his face, and he swiftly withdrew his

hand, a sheepish smile tugging at his lips. "You are right. My apologies."

She stepped into the coach, settling onto the plush seat across from her lady's maid. The footman closed the door behind her with a solid thud. A moment later, the carriage lurched forward, the rhythmic clatter of hooves against cobblestone filling the space between them.

Alice watched her intently, a knowing look in her eyes. After a brief silence, she finally spoke. "So..." she drawled. "I see that Lord Bedford saw through your ruse."

Eugenie exhaled, tilting her head back against the cushioned interior. "He did," she admitted. "But he has graciously agreed not to tell my brother or Elsbeth."

"That is rather kind of him."

"It is," Eugenie agreed with a slight nod. "But this isn't over. I will try again."

Alice's expression held a mixture of exasperation and resignation. "I was afraid you were going to say that, my lady."

Eugenie reached up, unpinning the cap and peeling off the scratchy wig that had made her scalp itch. Today had not gone according to plan, but that did not mean she would give up. She couldn't. Her desire to learn and be challenged was too great to let one failed attempt deter her.

No, this was only the beginning.

Charles stood on the pavement, watching as Eugenie's coach disappeared down the cobblestone street. A sigh escaped him as he pondered the risks she had taken to attend a lecture. He couldn't bring himself to fault her since he understood all too well the thirst for knowledge. He had been on the path to becoming a professor before his uncle and father had died suddenly, leaving him to inherit the title. Now, instead of lecturing eager students, he pored over estate accounts and managed the endless duties of an earl.

Eugenie reminded him so much of his late sister, Mary. She had always defied societal expectations, preferring trousers to gowns and books to needlework. But unlike his feelings for Mary, his feelings for Eugenie were far from fraternal. No, there was an undeniable pull towards her that left him wondering what it would be like to kiss her again.

Shaking off his thoughts, he turned and strode towards the entrance of University College. The stone buildings loomed with an air of solemnity, their ancient walls steeped in knowledge and tradition. As he reached the building that housed the Master's office, he stepped inside, immediately noting the musty scent of old books and parchment. A lanky clerk sat at a desk, his nose buried in an open ledger.

The man didn't bother looking up as Charles approached. "State your business," he muttered.

Charles halted before the desk. "I wish to see Master Griffith."

"I'm afraid he is unavailable," the clerk said dismissively, flicking a glance at Charles before returning his attention to the book. "Try again later, if you don't mind."

Charles wasn't about to be turned away so easily. Clearing his throat, he stood straighter and spoke in a commanding voice. "Will you inform Master Griffith that the Earl of Bedford wishes to speak with him?"

The clerk's eyes widened, his complexion paling slightly. "You are Lord Bedford?"

"I am," Charles confirmed. "And Master Griffith sent word that he would meet with me this morning."

The clerk practically tripped over himself as he pushed back his chair and rushed towards the inner office. "Yes, my lord. Please remain here, and I shall inform him of your arrival."

Within moments, the man returned and held the door open. "Master Griffith will see you now."

"Thank you," Charles said, stepping inside.

The office was stately yet functional. A large desk sat in the center, with two chairs positioned before it. Bookshelves lined the back wall, brimming with books, while a warm fire crackled in the hearth. Seated behind the desk was Master Griffith. He was an impeccably dressed man with dark hair and long sideburns. He carried an air of refinement, precisely the image one would expect of a Master.

Gesturing towards a chair, Master Griffith said, "Please, have a seat."

Charles settled into the proffered chair. "Thank you for agreeing to meet with me."

"The pleasure is mine, my lord, but I fear we do not have much to discuss," Master Griffith replied. "I expelled your cousin for a myriad of reasons."

"Can you be more specific?" Charles asked.

Master Griffith reached for a thick file stuffed with documents. He opened it and read aloud, "Cheating, plagiarism, vandalism—just to name a few."

Charles stiffened. "I beg your pardon?"

"I am unsure what your cousin told you, but he scarcely attended his classes," Master Griffith revealed. "We took into account that he was your heir, but the Fellows and I unanimously decided to expel him."

Frowning, Charles asked, "Dare I ask about the vandalism?"

Master Griffith flipped to another page and picked up a paper. "Ah, yes. Here is the bill for the removal of paint Philip so generously left on the inner wall of Radcliffe Quadrangle. It was quite the artistic endeavor."

Charles accepted the paper and scanned the sum. He

resisted the urge to groan. Why had his cousin done something so inexcusably foolish?

Master Griffith leaned back in his chair. "I understand this is not what you wished to hear, but we are an institution of higher learning, not a refuge for misfit boys."

"I understand," Charles replied, though disappointment churned within him. He hesitated. "Would a generous donation ensure Philip's re-enrollment?"

"I'm afraid not," Master Griffith said firmly.

Charles sighed. "I had to try." Rising from his chair, he added, "Thank you for your time."

As he turned to leave, Master Griffith spoke again. "If I may, my lord..." he began. "University College has a reputation to uphold, as do all Oxford's colleges. Your cousin's antics would be better managed elsewhere. Perhaps buying him a commission in the Royal Army would provide him with the discipline he so desperately needs."

Charles winced. "I am not certain the Royal Army is prepared for someone like Philip."

Master Griffith gave a wry smile. "It is well known that Wellington was once a gambler and got into some trouble because of it. Perhaps there is hope for your cousin yet."

"I certainly hope so," Charles muttered. "Good day."

Exiting the office, he walked aimlessly until he reached a stone bench in the courtyard. He sat down heavily, running a hand through his hair. What was he to do with Philip? Perhaps he should simply marry a wife who would bear him sons, and then he could wash his hands of his cousin's antics entirely.

A familiar voice interrupted his thoughts. "What brings you here?"

Charles glanced up to see Professor Addington—a tall, broad-shouldered man dressed in his academic robes, his cap perched neatly atop his dark hair.

"I came to speak with Master Griffith about Philip," Charles admitted.

"Ah," Addington said, lowering himself onto the bench beside him. "I take it that it did not go well."

"No, it did not," Charles admitted.

Addington tilted his head. "What will you do?"

Charles leaned forward, elbows on his knees. "Master Griffith suggested I purchase Philip a commission in the Royal Army."

"That would be highly unorthodox, given that he is your heir."

"I know," Charles replied. "But we cannot continue as we are. His mother will be devastated when she learns there is nothing that can be done about Philip being expelled. Their family has upheld a long-standing tradition here. She won't take it lightly."

"What of Cambridge?" Addington suggested after a pause.

Charles shook his head. "Philip would be expelled just as swiftly," he remarked. "Did you know he defaced Radcliffe Quad?"

Addington blinked. "That was him?" A chuckle escaped him. "Perhaps he has a future as an artist."

"I hope not," Charles stated. "Few artists make a decent income."

"It could be a hobby," Addington mused.

Charles rubbed his temples. "What he needs is a purpose. And I haven't the slightest idea how to give him that."

Addington stood. "Come, let me buy you a drink."

"It isn't even noon."

"When has that ever stopped you?" Addington grinned. "Besides, you look like you could use one."

Rising, Charles conceded, "You're not wrong."

Addington clapped him on the back. "I've missed this," he said. "I barely see you now that you're a high and mighty earl."

"That's because you're busy trying to secure your fellowship."

"Which is precisely what you would be doing now if you hadn't inherited an ancient title," Addington remarked.

As they started down the well-trodden path, Charles took a deep breath. "Is it odd that I miss the smell of musty books?"

"Yes, it is," Addington retorted with a smirk. "But I do understand, considering how much time we spent in the library when we were studying here."

Charles glanced at his friend. "How is your mother?"

All traces of humor vanished from Addington's expression. "She is alive, for now," he revealed, his gaze shifting towards the overcast sky as if searching for answers among the heavy clouds.

Charles nodded solemnly. "That is most fortunate."

"I suppose I am working so hard to become a Fellow before she passes. I want her to be proud of me."

"I don't think you need to become a Fellow for that," Charles said. "You have already accomplished so much. Anyone would be proud."

A small smile spread across Addington's lips, but it faded quickly. "Thank you for saying so, but being the younger son of an earl carries certain expectations," he said, his tone laced with quiet frustration. "I am expected to make something of myself, despite not inheriting a title."

"Which you have," Charles insisted.

Addington let out a humorless chuckle. "My father is not too impressed that I am a professor of history," he shared. "He believes he wasted his money on my education."

Their conversation was momentarily interrupted as they stepped inside a grand hall, its vaulted ceiling and towering stained-glass windows casting an almost reverent atmosphere over the room.

Finding an empty table near the hearth, they took their

seats at one of the round tables, the flickering glow of the fire offering a welcome warmth.

A short man with a neatly pressed waistcoat approached them, bowing slightly. "Would you care for something to drink, gentlemen?"

"We would," Addington said. "Two brandies."

As the man disappeared into the bustling hall, Charles turned towards his friend. "Just ignore your father," he advised, his tone more earnest than before. "He has never been the most supportive of you anyway."

Addington ran a hand over his face. "No, he hasn't been," he agreed. "Which is why it will be difficult when my mother passes."

Charles regarded him with sympathy. "I can only offer this —treasure the time you have left with her," he said gently. "I miss my father every single day. He always knew the right thing to say and the right course of action to take."

"Your father was a good man."

"He was," Charles responded, growing pensive. A familiar ache settled in his chest as he thought of his father's wisdom, the quiet strength that had steadied him in uncertain times. If only he were here now. He would know exactly what to do about Philip.

The short man arrived, bearing a tray with two glasses. He moved with practiced efficiency, setting their drinks down on the polished wooden table before stepping back. "Will there be anything else?"

"No, thank you," Addington replied, reaching for his glass. He held it up slightly. "I propose a toast."

Charles picked up his own glass. "And what exactly are we toasting?"

Addington's lips curled into a faint smile. "To our friendship," he declared. "Since that fateful day we were assigned as roommates at Eton, we have found ourselves in all manner of scrapes, yet we always managed to remain friends."

"That, I can drink to." Their glasses met with a satisfying clink, the sound echoing softly in the hall.

Addington took a thoughtful sip before lowering his glass to the table. "Don't worry, Charles. You'll know what to do with Philip when the time comes."

Charles scoffed lightly. "I wish I had your confidence."

Addington smirked. "If we survived having Arthur Drake as a roommate, we can survive anything."

A genuine chuckle escaped Charles's lips. "Do you remember how he used to leave notes for us around the room?"

"How could I forget?" Addington groaned, though amusement flickered in his eyes. "He took particular issue with me not hanging up my clothing. I daresay I received a note reminding me every single day."

Charles grinned. "You did start hanging up your drawers just to irritate him."

"And it was worth every moment just to see the sheer outrage on his face," Addington said. "The man even had the nerve to report me to the headmaster."

Charles leaned back in his chair. "I wonder what Drake is up to these days."

Addington shrugged, lifting his glass once more. "Quite frankly, I neither know nor care. He aggravated me to no end."

Charles laughed again, savoring the rare moment of lightness between them. Amidst all the burdens and uncertainties, it was good to remember that, no matter what trials lay ahead, some things—like friendship—remained constant.

4

E ugenie emerged from her bedchamber, the soft folds of her pale blue gown whispering against the polished wooden floor as she stepped into the corridor. With measured steps, she made her way down the grand staircase, her hand grazing the iron banister.

Just as she reached the last step, a sharp knock echoed through the entry hall. The sound reverberated through the quiet house, halting Eugenie's descent for the briefest of moments.

Tanner crossed the room in a few brisk strides and unlatched the heavy door. The hinges groaned slightly as the door swung open, revealing two figures silhouetted against the daylight.

From the doorway of the drawing room, Elsbeth's voice rang out. "Aunt Mariam and Aunt Phoebe," she greeted as she stepped forward.

The women stepped into the entry hall with warm smiles on their faces.

Elsbeth turned slightly, gesturing towards Eugenie. "Are you acquainted with my sister-in-law, Lady Eugenie?"

The fading blonde-haired woman's gaze settled on Eugenie. "I'm afraid I haven't seen you since you were young. My, how you've grown into a beautiful young woman."

Eugenie returned her smile, dipping her head politely. "Thank you, Mrs. Ellsworth."

"Mariam, Dear," she replied. "There is no need to stand on formalities with me."

The other woman spoke up. "I am not sure if you remember me, but I am Phoebe."

"Yes, of course, you are Philip's mother," Eugenie remarked. "Please, you must call me Eugenie."

With a graceful pivot, Elsbeth gestured towards the drawing room. "Shall we adjourn and begin the sewing circle?"

As the ladies filed into the room, Eugenie's gaze fell upon the neatly stacked fabrics arranged on the long mahogany table.

Elsbeth moved towards the table and lifted a piece of fabric. "I thought we could make frocks for the girls. The maids have already cut the fabric; we just need to stitch the pieces together."

"What a worthwhile endeavor," Phoebe remarked approvingly as she took a seat.

Eugenie selected a piece of fabric and a threaded needle, settling into place beside the others. Just as she did, Tanner reappeared in the doorway, addressing Elsbeth. "Lady Jane has come to call, my lady."

Elsbeth, who had just reached for her own sewing materials, froze mid-motion. "Lady Jane?" she repeated, her voice laced with surprise.

Eugenie gave her a curious look. "Did you not invite her?"

"No," Elsbeth admitted, a shadow crossing her features. "She was one of the friends who turned their backs on me after my father died. I haven't spoken to her since then."

Eugenie studied her sister-in-law's expression, sensing the

unspoken weight behind her words. "What do you intend to do?"

Coming to a decision, Elsbeth straightened. "Please, send her in."

Moments later, a young woman with blonde hair entered hesitantly, her gaze darting around the room as though expecting to be turned away. She cleared her throat before speaking. "I was hoping—assuming it is all right with you—that I could join your sewing circle once more."

Elsbeth remained seated, her expression giving nothing away. "I am surprised you are lowering yourself to speak to me again." There was a curtness to her words.

Lady Jane offered a weak smile, though it faltered at the edges. "I was wrong to give you the cut direct after your father's passing. My father insisted I do so for the sake of our family's reputation."

"And now?" Elsbeth asked.

With a quiet yet resolute tilt of her chin, Lady Jane replied, "I have decided that it is my choice whom I associate with."

A knowing look passed over Elsbeth's face. "Your father doesn't know you are here, does he?"

Lady Jane's hesitation gave her away before she even spoke. "No. He thinks I am shopping."

Elsbeth exhaled slowly, then gestured towards an open seat. "Take a seat," she said graciously. "I could always use your help."

Relief flickered across Lady Jane's face as she moved to sit across from Elsbeth. "Thank you," she murmured.

Eugenie picked up her sewing once more. The room gradually settled into a quiet rhythm, the gentle sounds of fabric being handled and needles piercing cloth filling the air.

But the moment of peace was short-lived.

Mariam, seated comfortably with her own work in hand,

glanced up and met Eugenie's gaze. Her eyes twinkled with curiosity. "How do you occupy your time, Lady Eugenie?"

"Eugenie," she corrected softly. "And I suppose I engage in the usual pursuits expected of a lady."

Before she could elaborate, Elsbeth interjected with a knowing smirk. "Do not let her modesty fool you. Eugenie is an avid reader—so much so that she practically devours books. She finishes one a day."

Mariam's brows lifted. "Is that so? A most admirable habit," she said approvingly. "There was a time I could always find a book in Charles's hands as well. He would disappear into his reading for hours, sometimes forgetting his own meals. But now..." She exhaled wistfully. "Now, he is much more focused on running his estate."

"Is that not a good thing?" Eugenie asked, her needle pausing mid-stitch.

Mariam smiled, though there was something wistful in the curve of her lips. "Oh, it is, of course. But I know how much he once longed to be a professor at Oxford. That was all he talked about when he was younger. He dreamed of lecturing about philosophy, of shaping young minds."

Eugenie's fingers resumed their work, her gaze fixed on the delicate thread weaving through the fabric. "Dreams can change," she murmured, her tone thoughtful.

"Yes, they can," Mariam agreed. She shifted slightly, then asked, "And what do you dream about, Eugenie?"

The unexpected question gave Eugenie pause. Her sewing slowed as she considered her response. It was rare for anyone to ask what she wanted—not in the manner of idle conversation, but as a genuine inquiry into her ambitions.

Finally, she spoke. "I have always wanted to write articles for the newssheets," she admitted.

"And why don't you?" Mariam asked.

Eugenie let out a small, wry huff. "For starters, I am a

woman, and as everyone knows, women cannot possibly be intelligent enough to write for the newssheets," she said, her voice tinged with dry sarcasm.

"That is poppycock!" Phoebe declared, shaking her head in indignation. "'A Lady' has written many books, and she is rather clever indeed."

Eugenie smiled faintly at Phoebe's spirited response but sighed. "Even if I truly wanted to, I wouldn't even know where to begin."

Across the table, Lady Jane, who had been quietly listening, suddenly spoke up. "My uncle works for *The Morning Post*," she offered. "Perhaps I could ask him to read a sampling of your work."

Eugenie's needle slipped in her hand as she turned, staring at Lady Jane in astonishment. "You would do that?" she asked, scarcely able to believe the offer.

"I would," Lady Jane affirmed. "But even if he were to consider your writing, you would have to publish under a pseudonym."

Eugenie nodded, her mind already racing with possibilities. "Of course. I would not expect otherwise."

Lady Jane gave an encouraging smile. "Let's not get ahead of ourselves just yet. What would you even write about?"

Without hesitation, Eugenie answered, "Political and social reform."

Lady Jane let out a soft laugh. "That is quite a heavy topic," she remarked. "Why not start as a gossip writer?"

Eugenie wrinkled her nose in distaste. "I want to do more than write about the latest scandals on the Society page."

Lady Jane shrugged. "Many authors get their start writing for the Society pages," she pointed out. "I would not dismiss the idea so quickly. A few well-placed pieces could establish your name—well, your *pseudonym*—and once you have the editor's favor, you may be able to branch out into more serious topics."

Eugenie considered this, mulling over the idea as she resumed stitching. The notion of writing gossip felt frivolous, but if it could be the start to something great... perhaps it was worth considering, after all.

"That is rather kind of you," Elsbeth acknowledged.

Lady Jane offered a sheepish smile, tucking a loose strand of blonde hair behind her ear. "I know it can't erase the past or make up for what I have done," she admitted, her gaze dipping momentarily to the embroidery in her lap. "But I hope it can serve as a stepping stone to renewing our friendship."

Elsbeth's expression softened. "I would like that."

A flicker of relief passed over Lady Jane's features. "Wonderful," she murmured, almost to herself.

Seated beside her, Mariam shifted slightly in her chair, her gaze appraising as she turned her attention to Lady Jane. "And what do you dream of, my lady?" she asked, her tone laced with genuine curiosity.

"I don't know," Lady Jane said, surprise etched on her features. "No one has ever asked me that question before."

Mariam gave her a pointed look. "Well then, I'd say it is about time that someone did."

Lady Jane lowered the fabric she had been sewing into her lap, her fingers smoothing out the delicate material as she gathered her thoughts. "I suppose my dream is to have a voice," she finally said. "Especially around my father and brother. They can be... overbearing at times."

"Just a little," Elsbeth teased.

Lady Jane let out a soft laugh. "My father is so consumed with our family's reputation that I daresay he cares for little else. That is why I am twenty and unwed. He has yet to find a suitor worthy enough to marry into our family."

"Do you not wish to marry for love?" Phoebe asked.

"Love? That is what fools aspire to, or so my father tells me," Lady Jane said. "He has made it clear that I will not have a say in the matter. When the time comes, he will arrange a marriage for me."

Elsbeth frowned. "Is that what *you* want?"

"No," Lady Jane admitted. "But what choice do I have? I am merely a woman, after all. What do I know about marriage?"

Elsbeth set aside her needlework. "When you find the right person, they make you forget about yesterday and dream about tomorrow."

Across from her, Eugenie pressed her lips together, suppressing a smile. "You'll have to excuse Elsbeth. She is a newlywed and, as such, has a terribly skewed way of looking at things," she said. "You can remain a spinster with me."

Lady Jane let out a soft gasp of protest, shaking her head adamantly. "Oh, no, I do not wish to be a spinster," she declared.

"Well then," Eugenie said, threading her needle with renewed purpose. "We may have to find you a way to outmaneuver your father."

"One can only dream," Lady Jane murmured, lowering her gaze.

Eugenie couldn't help but feel a pang of sympathy for Lady Jane. The thought of having one's future decided by another, with no regard for personal desires, was a fate she could not imagine enduring. Her own brother, for all his faults, would never dare attempt to arrange a marriage for her. He knew better than to try.

Not that it mattered. She had no interest in marriage. The very notion of tying herself to someone, of relinquishing even a portion of her independence, felt suffocating. She answered to no one but herself, and that was a luxury she would not trade for anything.

Charles sat at his desk, the flickering candle casting long shadows across the worn pages of his ledger. The dim light danced over the carefully inked numbers and transactions, but he barely saw them. This was his life now. It was an endless column of figures, and the weight of responsibility pressed down on him like an iron shackle. He would review the accounts until he died, and though he knew his perspective was grim, he couldn't summon the will to change it.

Once, academia had been his life. Numbers had fascinated him, and the pursuit of knowledge had given him purpose. But that life had been ripped away from him in an instant. Now, he was an earl, burdened with an inherited title, an expansive estate, and countless obligations. By all accounts, he should be grateful. His family no longer wanted for anything. He had the means to do good things, to better the lives of those under his care. And yet, deep within, he longed for something more—something he couldn't quite name.

With a weary sigh, Charles closed the ledger and ran a hand over his face. What right did he have to complain? Others would kill for his position, wealth, and security he could provide his family. And yet, what was the purpose of it all if he could find no joy in it?

Before he could dwell further on his discontent, his mother swept into the study, dressed in a dark purple gown. "Why are you not ready?" she asked, her sharp gaze scanning him with barely concealed disapproval.

Charles rose from his chair, stretching out his stiff limbs. "I'm afraid I got rather preoccupied with the accounts," he replied. "But I am ready now."

His mother's expression softened, if only slightly. "Wonderful. The coach is out front. Shall we depart?"

He moved around the desk, straightening his waistcoat. "Why, pray tell, did you agree to have dinner with Elsbeth this evening?"

His mother looked at him as if he were a simpleton. "Because I did not get to dine with her last night."

Charles frowned. "We do not need to dine with them every evening. What if she grows tired of us?"

"I highly doubt that, considering it was her idea."

"That doesn't surprise me, since I doubt it was Lord Westcott's idea. There is no love lost between us."

His mother reached up, adjusting his cravat with the careful precision of a woman who had done so for years. "Which is a shame, really, since you two are very much alike."

Charles scoffed, mock horror on his face. "How dare you!" In truth, while he and Westcott had started off as adversaries, their relationship had grown into something resembling mutual respect. Perhaps even reluctant friendship.

His mother merely spun on her heel. "Come. We don't wish to be late."

Resigning himself to the evening, Charles caught up to her, escorting her to the waiting carriage. As they settled onto the bench inside, he glanced at his mother. "How was the sewing circle?"

Her face lit up with a bright smile, a clear sign that he had asked the right question. "It was delightful," she said with enthusiasm. "I particularly enjoyed conversing with Lady Eugenie."

At the mention of Eugenie's name, an image of her sprang unbidden to his mind—golden curls, eyes alight with intelligence, a soft smile that could charm even the most hardened of hearts. But he shoved the thought away. It would do him no good to dwell on her.

His mother studied him closely. "You are smiling."

He quickly schooled his features. "Was I?"

Her knowing look made it clear she was not fooled. "That is an odd reaction to me mentioning Lady Eugenie."

"I was thinking of something else," he said too quickly.

She arched a brow. "And what do you think of Lady Eugenie?"

Charles hesitated. "She is a... woman." The moment the words left his mouth, he inwardly cringed. That was, without a doubt, the most idiotic thing he had ever said.

"That she is," she agreed, amusement dancing in her eyes. "A very beautiful young woman."

Feigning disinterest, he turned to look out the window. "Is she? I hadn't noticed."

"She is also quite clever."

He turned back to her, exasperated. "Is there a point to this conversation?"

His mother raised a hand innocently. "No, not at all. Just making conversation."

Charles knew better. If she were attempting to play match-maker, she would be sorely disappointed. He had no intention of marrying Eugenie—or anyone, for that matter. Not yet. There was too much he needed to accomplish first.

Thankfully, the coach came to a stop in front of Elsbeth's townhouse, and Charles wasted no time stepping out onto the pavement. He turned back, assisting his mother down before leading her up to the main door.

The butler opened it promptly. "My lord. Mrs. Ellsworth."

Charles inclined his head in acknowledgment before stepping into the entry hall. Out of the corner of his eye, he caught movement. He turned slightly—and there she was.

Eugenie descended the grand staircase, clad in a deep blue gown that accentuated her fair complexion. Her blonde hair was arranged in an elegant chignon, with delicate curls framing her face. But it wasn't just her beauty that held him captive. It was something deeper.

She was beautiful in the way she saw the world and in the way her eyes lit up when she spoke of something she loved. She was beautiful in the sharp wit that danced on her tongue and in the kindness she showed to those around her.

For a fleeting moment, Charles forgot himself. And then, just as quickly, he forced the thoughts away. It did not matter. It could not matter. He had far too much to do to be distracted by thoughts of Lady Eugenie. Even if she was utterly captivating.

His mother nudged him gently with her elbow, her voice lowered to a whisper. "Remember what I said about smiling earlier?"

Charles snapped his gaze to her. "My apologies. I was just…"

"Thinking about something else," she finished for him. "And I have a strong suspicion as to what—or rather, who—that 'something else' is."

Charles cleared his throat, casting a warning glance at his mother. "Drop it, Mother," he muttered under his breath before turning his full attention to Lady Eugenie. With practiced precision, he bowed. "My lady."

Eugenie dipped into a curtsy. "My lord," she murmured before lifting her gaze to his mother. "Mrs. Ellsworth."

His mother tsked. "Mariam, my dear," she corrected with a patient smile.

"Yes, of course. Mariam," Eugenie said.

A voice rang out from the grand staircase, drawing their attention. "Cousin. Aunt Mariam," Elsbeth greeted, descending with effortless poise, her hand resting lightly on her husband's arm.

Charles turned towards her. "Cousin. Westcott."

Westcott came to a stop in front of him. "Bedford. What an absolute delight to see you two nights in a row," he said dryly.

Beside him, Elsbeth gave his arm a playful swat. "You promised to be nice," she chided lightly.

"This is me being nice." Westcott softened the quip with an easy, knowing smile.

Before Charles could respond, the dinner bell chimed through the main level.

"Shall we adjourn to dinner?" Elsbeth asked.

"What a wonderful idea, Wife," Westcott replied, leaning in to press a kiss to her lips.

Charles could practically hear Eugenie roll her eyes. He turned towards her. "May I escort you to dinner?"

Eugenie glanced down at his proffered arm, hesitating only a fraction of a second before delicately placing her gloved hand upon it. "Thank you," she replied.

He moved to offer his other arm to his mother, only to find that she had already taken it upon herself to follow Elsbeth and Westcott towards the dining room. With no need to rush, Charles took his time escorting Eugenie. He rather enjoyed having her this close.

He stole a sidelong glance at her. "How was shopping?" he asked, though they both knew he was inquiring about something far more particular—her recent excursion to Oxford.

A small smile curved Eugenie's lips. "It went well. At least... until the very end."

"That is most unfortunate," he responded. Then with careful deliberation, he added, "I was thinking—if you would like to go *shopping* again, I may have found a way for you to do so."

Eugenie arched a brow. "Is that so?"

He nodded. "I happen to have a friend who teaches at a shop," he said, deliberately vague. "I could inquire whether he would allow you to visit on occasion, assuming, of course, that you dress appropriately for such an outing."

She stopped abruptly, her hand tightening ever so slightly on his arm. "Do you think he would mind?"

Charles offered a small shrug. "No, though I should warn you that it is a history class," he said. "I am not entirely sure if that would interest you."

Eugenie let out an incredulous laugh. "Of course it interests me! It is far preferable to the poetry and religious lectures I have been subjected to."

"Very well, then. I shall ask him."

Her expression brightened instantly, her smile so brilliant that it nearly stole his breath. For a brief moment, he simply stared, utterly entranced.

"Thank you, Charles," she said, her voice brimming with sincerity. "This means so much to me."

He exhaled a short chuckle. "My friend has not agreed to it yet."

"He will," Eugenie declared with unwavering confidence. "Because if anyone can convince someone to do something, it is you."

Charles couldn't stop the grin that pulled at his lips. "You are rather easy to please."

"You will find," Eugenie said, a playful lilt in her voice, "that I would do just about anything to go *shopping*. It is, without question, my favorite pastime."

Charles considered her for a moment. "That is something we have in common, then."

For a brief moment, he held her gaze—longer than what would be considered proper. There was something disarming about her, something that made it impossible to look away.

The spell was broken by a voice from the doorway of the dining room.

"Did you two get lost on the way to dinner?" Westcott drawled.

Eugenie turned towards her brother. "We were just discussing shopping."

"Shopping?" Westcott sounded genuinely appalled. "How dreadfully dull. I hadn't taken Bedford for a man who does much shopping."

Charles smirked. "Shopping is rather enjoyable, assuming you do it right."

Westcott snorted. "And how, pray tell, does one 'do it right'?" He raised his hand before Charles could answer. "No, never mind. I do not want to know. Just hurry along before Elsbeth comes to fetch you herself."

"We wouldn't want that," Charles said before leading Eugenie into the dining room.

5

Eugenie lay beneath the canopy of her four-poster bed while her cat, Shadow, sat next to her. A smile spread across her lips as excitement bubbled within her. The monotony of her life—predictable, orderly, and shaped entirely by societal expectations—was finally giving way to something thrilling, something new. She had always longed for intellectual pursuits, for a taste of something beyond the carefully curated existence expected of a young lady of her station. And now, the possibility of attending lectures at Oxford dangled before her like the sweetest of temptations.

A giddy sound nearly escaped her lips, but before she could give in to the urge, a firm knock came at the door. It opened swiftly, revealing her lady's maid. "Good morning, my lady," she greeted.

"Good morning, Alice," Eugenie responded brightly, sitting up in bed with a newfound energy. "Today is going to be the most wonderful of days."

Alice arched a skeptical brow as she stepped closer. "Are you feeling unwell, my lady?"

Eugenie let out a light laugh. "Not in the least. I am simply looking forward to what the day has in store."

Still unconvinced, Alice pressed the back of her hand against Eugenie's forehead. "You're not feverish, but perhaps I should fetch the doctor just to be certain."

Shaking her head, Eugenie batted Alice's hand away playfully. "I assure you, I am in perfect health."

Alice pursed her lips, considering her mistress with a narrowed gaze. "Are you bottle-weary, then?"

Eugenie laughed again, shaking her head. "I am not drunk either, if that is what you mean." She threw the covers off and swung her legs over the side of the bed, her bare feet brushing the cold floor. "I am simply elated at the prospect of attending lectures at Oxford."

Alice stepped towards the wardrobe and pulled out a pale green morning gown. "If you say so, my lady," she said. "But before you get too lost in your scholarly ambitions, you should know that Lady Jane has come to call."

Eugenie furrowed her brows. "Lady Jane? She is here to see me, not Elsbeth?"

Alice nodded as she laid the gown on the bed. "Yes, my lady. Shall we dress you?"

"Yes," she replied. "I do not want to keep her waiting too long."

A short time later, Eugenie was dressed, and her hair was carefully swept up into a neat chignon, a few delicate curls framing her face. Her pulse quickened as she made her way through the grand hallways of the house towards the drawing room, anticipation making her steps lighter than usual.

As she stepped into the room, she immediately spotted Lady Jane in the center, clad in an elegant pink gown that complemented her fair complexion.

Eugenie decided to make her presence known. "Good morning, Lady Jane," she greeted warmly.

Lady Jane turned swiftly, her eyes alight with excitement. "Lady Eugenie, I must apologize for calling so early, but I bring the most delightful news."

Eugenie gestured towards the settees. "Would you care to sit?"

"Thank you," Lady Jane said, lowering herself gracefully down onto the settee. She barely waited for Eugenie to settle beside her before continuing. "I spoke to my uncle, and he was most impressed with the sampling of your work."

Eugenie's breath caught in her throat. "He was?"

Lady Jane nodded eagerly. "Indeed. So much so that he wishes for you to submit a full article for consideration to be published."

Eugenie's heart stuttered. For a moment, she could do nothing but stare. "Are you in earnest?" she managed at last.

Lady Jane's smile widened. "I am. My uncle, of course, requests that you submit an article for the Society page. I know that is not the subject you long to write about, but it is an opportunity—a first step."

Eugenie nodded, excitement and disbelief warring within her. "I could certainly do that."

"My uncle will contact you once he has reviewed your submission," Lady Jane added.

Eugenie exhaled sharply and leaned back against the settee, the weight of the moment sinking in. "Thank you," she whispered, the words barely containing her gratitude.

Lady Jane tilted her head, observing Eugenie with a mix of amusement and sincerity. "Have you considered a name to write under?"

"Not yet."

Lady Jane rose. "You should come up with one, and quickly."

Eugenie stood as well, still caught in the whirlwind of emotions. "How can I ever thank you for this?"

Lady Jane's expression softened. "Do not squander this opportunity," she said simply. "That is all I ask."

"I won't," Eugenie promised.

A flicker of something passed across Lady Jane's face—a shadow of longing, of wistfulness. "I wish I had the courage to do something like this," she admitted quietly.

"Why can't you?"

Lady Jane let out a soft, humorless laugh. "My father and brother would never allow it."

There was an unmistakable sorrow in her voice, a resignation that Eugenie recognized all too well. It was the feeling of being powerless with one's own destiny.

Eugenie's excitement dimmed slightly as she reached for Lady Jane's hand and gave it a reassuring squeeze. "Perhaps one day, things will change."

Lady Jane forced a smile, but the sadness in her eyes remained. "Perhaps," she murmured. "I should go."

Eugenie wished she could offer more than mere words, something that would banish the sorrow from her friend's face. But she was at a loss for words. "Thank you for coming by."

They walked together to the main door, their footsteps softened by the plush carpets. Lady Jane exited the townhouse and stepped into her waiting carriage. Eugenie headed towards the dining room and stepped inside.

At the far end, Elsbeth sat engrossed in the newssheets. A cup of tea sat before her, barely touched.

"I have the most wonderful news," Eugenie gushed, unable to contain herself.

Elsbeth looked up. She set the newssheets aside, folding them neatly. "What is it?"

Eugenie slid into the chair across from her. "Lady Jane came to call and informed me that her uncle enjoyed my sampling of work. He wants me to submit an article for consideration to be published."

Elsbeth's face brightened with delight. "That is wonderful news!" she exclaimed.

As if on cue, a footman approached and placed a cup of chocolate before Eugenie. She barely spared it a glance, too consumed by her excitement. "It would be an article for the Society page," she added, as though testing the thought aloud.

Before Elsbeth could respond, a voice rang sharply through the room.

"Absolutely not!"

The harsh declaration cut through the warm atmosphere like a blade, and both women turned towards the doorway where Niles stood, his expression thunderous. His broad shoulders were tense beneath his morning coat, his dark brows drawn together in clear disapproval.

"Oh, dear," Elsbeth muttered under her breath.

Eugenie did not cower under her brother's glare. Instead, she met his eyes with an unwavering resolve. "And whyever not?" she challenged.

Niles strode into the room. "Do you not understand the scandal you would create if you published an article in the newssheets?" he demanded, his voice edged with frustration. "A lady does not write articles for the public. It is wholly improper."

Eugenie willed herself to remain calm. "I do understand," she said. "Which is why I will write under a pseudonym." She lifted her chin. "I could write under Mother's surname —Wentworth."

Niles sank into the chair beside his wife, rubbing his temple as though the very idea exhausted him. "That is not good enough," he countered. "If anyone were to discover the truth—"

"They won't," Eugenie interrupted, her voice firm.

Niles narrowed his eyes. "And how can you be certain?" he asked. "You cannot predict the future."

"Exactly," Eugenie shot back. "Which is why I must seize this opportunity while I can."

His gaze flickered to his wife, as if hoping for reinforcement. "Elsbeth, will you talk some sense into her?"

Elsbeth merely smiled. "I would," she said, lifting her cup to her lips, "if I thought she was entirely wrong."

Niles stared at her, utterly incredulous. "You think Eugenie should write articles for the newssheets?"

Elsbeth tilted her head, regarding him thoughtfully. "What harm could it do?" she asked. "If she writes well and under a different name, who would be any the wiser?"

Niles exhaled sharply. "Eugenie..." he started. "This is a terrible idea. Surely you can admit that."

"I admit nothing," she responded.

His frown deepened. "Be reasonable."

She reached for her cup of chocolate, letting the warmth seep into her fingers as she considered her words. Then with quiet conviction, she said, "I need to do this, Brother."

Niles leaned forward, his gaze searching hers. "Why?" he asked, his voice no longer angry but bewildered. "Why would you risk ruination to do something so foolish?"

Eugenie held his gaze. "Because I need to prove to myself that I can do more than what Society expects of me."

Silence stretched between them.

Eugenie had always known what was expected of her—to marry well, manage a household, bear children, and never stray beyond the boundaries so carefully constructed around her since birth. But she had spent years watching men debate, challenge, and change the world through their words, while women were expected to sit quietly and observe. She was tired of watching.

She wanted to be heard.

Niles put his hands up in surrender. "Very well. But for the record, I think this is a terrible idea."

"Duly noted," Eugenie said.

"I know you have resigned yourself to spinsterhood, but I want more for you," he said, his expression softening. "I want you to find love. To have a family. To experience the kind of happiness that comes from sharing your life with someone."

"Not everyone is destined to have a perfect love story like yours," Eugenie stated.

Niles reached for Elsbeth's hand. "I never said it was perfect. I just wanted someone who would never give up on me."

A footman placed a plate of food down in front of her, and Eugenie reached for her fork and knife. She knew Niles meant well. He had always seen himself as her protector, the one who was supposed to guide her towards the life Society deemed appropriate. But what he didn't understand—what he could never quite grasp—was that she had no desire to follow the path that had been so neatly laid before her.

She needed to carve out her own future, one built on purpose, not expectation.

Charles sat in the back of the lecture hall, his hands folded on the polished wooden desk before him, as Professor Addington commanded the room with his booming voice. The professor's lecture on the fall of the Roman Empire held the students rapt, their faces alight with curiosity. Charles studied them with quiet envy. These young men had their entire academic lives ahead of them, free to indulge in endless discussions and debates and to lose themselves in pursuing knowledge.

That could have been his life.

He swallowed against the familiar knot of regret tightening in his throat. Had fate taken a different turn, he would have been among them—not merely an observer but an eager participant. But his path had been set the moment he inherited his title. There had been no choice, only duty. He told himself it was as it should be, that he had made peace with it. And yet, something gnawed at him. Something missing. The worst part was that he couldn't name what it was. That uncertainty infuriated him more than anything.

The polite sound of applause snapped him back to the present. The lecture had concluded, and students were rising from their seats, murmuring to one another as they shuffled towards the exits. Charles waited, watching them go, before finally standing and making his way towards the front of the room.

"Well done," he praised.

Professor Addington turned from gathering his papers, a wry grin lifting his lips. "To what do I owe the great pleasure of an earl gracing my lecture?"

"I needed to speak with you."

Addington stuffed the last of his papers into a satchel and slung it over his shoulder. "I have a meeting across campus, but we can talk as we walk."

As they stepped outside, Charles let his gaze wander over the familiar spires of Oxford, the grand architecture that had once felt like home. "I miss this," he admitted. "The lectures, the discourse, the life I once knew."

Addington chuckled, adjusting the strap of his satchel. "Oh, you poor lord. Forced to inherit a title while I scrape by as a mere professor."

Charles sighed, knowing full well that he would get little sympathy from his friend. "I won't deny that there are some advantages."

"Some advantages?" Addington repeated. "You have a townhouse, a country estate, and land. I have a cramped flat on the edge of campus."

"You do not live at your ancestral townhouse?"

"Good gads, no." Addington shook his head. "I refuse to live under my father's roof and abide by his rules. I need to make my own way in the world."

"And you are doing an admirable job," Charles said sincerely.

"I will be, once I secure a fellowship. Until then, I am in a constant state of proving myself."

Charles nodded in understanding. "How is that process going?"

"Long and arduous," Addington muttered. "I need to publish more if I even want to be considered."

"That is one part of academia I do not miss."

Addington shot him a knowing look before stopping in the courtyard. "Enough pleasantries. What do you need?"

Charles hesitated, pressing his lips together. Finally, he said, "I have a favor to ask."

Addington raised an amused eyebrow. "The last time you asked me for a favor, I ended up running through Eton's dining hall in nothing but my drawers."

Charles barked a laugh. "That was a dare, not a request."

"And what about the time I covered myself in butter and slipped through the headmaster's window to change our marks?" Addington challenged.

Charles grinned. "That was entirely your idea."

Addington scoffed. "The window was small. Butter was necessary. And, need I remind you, I succeeded."

"You did," Charles admitted. "Though you were promptly caught and punished for it."

Addington let out a chuckle. "Honestly, it's remarkable we weren't expelled."

"It would have been preferable to the thrashing we received," Charles mused.

"Deservedly so," Addington added. "Now, what favor do you seek this time?"

Charles decided it was best to say what needed to be said and be done with it. "I have a friend who wishes to attend your lectures."

Addington's brow furrowed. "Is this student enrolled at University College?"

"Not exactly."

Suspicion flickered across Addington's face. "What does that mean?"

"This person is not the kind Oxford would ever admit."

Addington lowered his voice. "Is he Irish?"

"No, he is not Irish."

"Then why the secrecy?" Addington demanded, pulling out his pocket watch and checking the time. "I don't have the luxury of standing here all day. Just say what you need to say."

Charles took a steadying breath. "The person in question... is a woman."

Addington snapped his watch closed with an audible click. "Absolutely not," he said, his voice firm. "Women cannot attend lectures at Oxford. You know that."

"I do," Charles conceded. "But if it helps, she would be disguised as a man."

Addington stared at him. "No, that does not help." He crossed his arms. "Who is this brazen woman?"

"That is irrelevant."

"I think it's quite relevant," Addington countered. "If I am caught with a woman in my lecture hall, I will be ruined. A laughingstock."

Charles lifted his hand in a calming gesture. "No one would know. I give you my word."

Addington studied him intently. "Why is this so important to you?"

Charles paused. Why was this so important to him? It shouldn't matter. Eugenie was merely a friend. Yet the thought of denying her this opportunity made something in him twist uncomfortably. He wanted this for her—more than he cared to admit.

Still, he kept his expression composed. "It would mean a great deal to me if you would consider it."

Addington exhaled sharply. "You do realize what you're asking of me?"

"I do."

"And yet, you're still asking?"

"I am."

Addington removed his cap, raking a hand through his neatly groomed hair as he muttered a string of curses under his breath. He glanced around, as if ensuring no one had over-heard their conversation, then fixed Charles with a hard stare.

"Fine," he muttered, though the reluctance in his voice was unmistakable. "Bring this young woman to my lecture tomor-row, but her disguise had better be as foolproof as you claim it is. If she's discovered, it won't just be her facing consequences —it will be both of us."

"It is. You have my word," Charles assured him. "And thank you, Addington."

"Don't thank me yet," Addington shot back. "I will meet her at the door, just as I do with all my students. If there is even the slightest chance that she could be unmasked, I will turn her away without hesitation."

"That is more than fair."

Addington narrowed his eyes. "And you will be accompa-nying her?"

Charles inclined his head. "Of course. I will see her safely in and out."

A long pause stretched between them as Addington tapped his fingers against the leather of his satchel, deep in thought. At last, he let out a resigned sigh. "I hope, for your sake, that this young woman is worth all this trouble."

"She is," Charles replied promptly.

Addington gave him a sharp look. "She had better be, because if anything goes awry, we are both risking far more than our reputations." He pulled out his pocket watch once more and clicked it open with an irritated flick of his wrist. "Speaking of which, I am now late for my meeting." He turned sharply on his heel and strode away.

"Thank you, Addington," Charles called after him.

Without breaking his stride, Addington simply raised a hand in brief acknowledgment before disappearing down the path, leaving Charles standing alone.

Satisfied with the outcome, Charles turned on his heel, making his way towards his waiting coach. His chest swelled with anticipation; he knew the risk his friend was taking, but this matter was of great importance to him. The mere thought of Eugenie's reaction sent a thrill through him. Would she smile in that beguiling way of hers? Perhaps even reward him with a kiss?

One could only hope.

As he passed through the towering gates of the university, a familiar figure strode down the path towards him. Charles recognized the long, purposeful gait of Guildford Winslow, Viscount Alcott. The man moved with the confidence of a soldier, though there was an uncharacteristic tension in his posture.

Charles raised a hand in greeting. "Good morning."

Alcott came to a halt in front of him, his dark brows pulled into a scowl. "Good morning," he muttered, his tone suggesting anything but.

Charles studied his dark-haired friend more closely. The rigid set of his shoulders, the slight downturn of his mouth— something was amiss. "What troubles you?"

Alcott exhaled sharply, glancing away for a brief moment before meeting Charles's gaze. "I've sold my commission in the Royal Army."

"You've resigned? Is that truly a problem, given your new station?"

Alcott shifted uncomfortably, his jaw tightening. "I didn't ask for this life. I was content with my old one."

"Neither did I," Charles said with a knowing look. "But duty must come before personal desires."

"Duty," Alcott scoffed, shaking his head. "I know my duty. It was on the battlefield, fighting for England, not parading about London in a bloody cravat."

Charles's gaze dropped to the black armband adorning Alcott's sleeve. His expression softened. "I am truly sorry about your father. He was a good man."

A muscle in Alcott's jaw ticked. "Yes, to some, he was." His voice was tight, clipped, the grief still raw beneath the surface.

Sensing the need for a change in subject, Charles asked, "And how is your sister faring?"

Alcott's expression darkened, his scowl deepening. "Charlotte? She's a menace."

Charles fought back a chuckle. Miss Charlotte Winslow surely couldn't be as dreadful as her brother made her out to be. Could she?

Alcott didn't wait for a response before continuing. "She is determined to be the diamond of the Season, and knowing her, she will stop at nothing to achieve that title."

"Don't most young women aspire to the same thing?"

"Perhaps, but Charlotte is cunning enough to succeed," Alcott admitted. "Life was much simpler when I was leading a charge on the battlefield."

Charles let out a short laugh. "I, for one, am glad to have you back in England, my friend. Come, we should share a drink at White's. Just like old times."

The corner of Alcott's mouth twitched in what might have passed for a smile—faint, fleeting, but it was there, nonetheless.

"I would like that, but not just yet. I am far too pensive to be pleasant company."

"Soon, then?"

Alcott exhaled, nodding. "I shall plan on it." He cocked his head. "What business brought you to Oxford this morning?"

"I went to see Addington."

"Ah," Alcott mused, his expression shifting to mild interest. "And how fares our dear scholar? I hear he is under consideration for a fellowship."

"That he is," Charles confirmed.

Alcott's brows lifted in approval. "Good for him. He always had the mind for it. We should invite him to join us at White's. It has been ages since I last saw him."

"I shall extend the invitation," Charles promised.

"Very good." Alcott gave a curt nod before a long-suffering sigh escaped him. "Now, if you'll excuse me, I have some brooding to attend to before I am forced to return home and suffer through another afternoon with my sister."

Charles chuckled. "I wish you luck."

He watched Alcott depart before turning towards his waiting coach. As he approached, he instructed his driver of his next destination. "To Lady Eugenie's residence," he ordered.

He climbed inside the carriage, settling against the plush interior, his body sinking into the well-worn cushions. A slow, eager anticipation curled in his chest. He could scarcely wait to see Eugenie and tell her the good news.

6

E ugenie sat in the library of her townhouse, a half-filled sheet of parchment before her. The writing desk was littered with crumpled attempts. She tapped the feather tip of the quill absently against her lips. What should she write about?

The Society pages thrived on gossip, but the very idea of indulging in such frivolity made her stomach twist. What did she truly know about the latest rivalries among the debutantes or which young lady was vying for the most eligible bachelor? She hardly paid attention at social events, preferring to disappear into the library instead.

She glanced at her paper once more. Perhaps an article on the quiet existence of a spinster? Would the *ton* have any interest in such a subject? It was worth a try. The worst that could happen was a rejection, and if so, she would simply try again.

Eugenie had just dipped her quill back into the inkwell when a soft knock came at the door, followed by the entrance of Tanner. He straightened his posture before announcing, "Lord Bedford has come to call, my lady."

Eugenie carefully placed the quill next to the inkpot and looked up. "Send him in."

Tanner inclined his head before disappearing through the doorway. Moments later, Charles stepped into the library. "Thank you for agreeing to see me," he said as he approached her, his lips curving into a devilish smile. "I have come bearing the most wonderful news."

Eugenie raised a brow, intrigued. He had her full attention now. "The most wonderful news?" she echoed. "What could possibly warrant such an introduction?"

Charles lowered himself into the chair opposite hers. "I spoke with my friend, Professor Addington, at University College, Oxford, and he has agreed to let you sit in on his lecture."

Eugenie's breath caught. "Are you in earnest?"

He held up his hands, palms outward as if to temper her enthusiasm. "There are conditions, of course. You will have to attend in disguise, and you must remain silent during the lectures—no questions."

A thrill shot through her. "That won't be an issue," she said quickly. "When can I go?"

"Tomorrow."

A bright, unrestrained smile spread across her lips. "This is extraordinary," she gushed, unable to contain her excitement. "Thank you! Truly, you are the best of men!"

Charles leaned back, looking immensely pleased with himself. "I thought this might make you happy."

Eugenie clasped her hands together, resisting the ridiculous urge to throw her arms around him. "It does. It truly does. And it means more to me than you could ever know. How can I ever thank you?"

A slow smirk tugged at the corner of Charles's mouth. "I was hoping for another kiss, actually."

Eugenie's delighted expression faltered as she pursed her

lips. "Shh..." She pressed a finger against them in warning. "You must not speak of that here."

Charles's grin widened. "Whyever not?"

She sighed, lowering her hand. "Because it was a mistake."

"I beg to differ," he said. "It was rather pleasurable."

"A mistake can still be pleasurable."

Charles tilted his head, considering her words. "Then shall we make another mistake? Maybe two?"

She rolled her eyes. "You are incorrigible."

"Thank you."

"That wasn't a compliment."

Charles leaned forward, elbows resting on his knees. "I took it as one."

Before Eugenie could reply, a maid entered, carrying a silver tea service. She carefully placed the tray on the low table between them and curtsied. "Would you care for some tea, my lady?"

Eugenie saw this as her opportunity to create a bit of distance between herself and the entirely-too-charming Lord Bedford. Rising from her seat, she replied, "I shall see to it, Nancy."

The maid curtsied again before taking a seat in the corner of the room, ensuring they were not alone. Eugenie reached for the teapot and asked, "Would you care for some tea, my lord?"

"I would," Charles said.

She handed him a cup before reclaiming her own seat, taking a small sip in an attempt to compose herself. Despite the lessons in propriety drilled into her since childhood, she found her thoughts rather unruly in Charles's presence.

Desperate for a safe topic, she grasped at the first question that came to mind. "May I ask what you are reading at the moment?"

Charles settled back into his chair. "I find that I have little time for reading for enjoyment. Between managing my estate and corralling my cousin, I have little time for anything else."

"That is a shame," Eugenie murmured. "May I ask how Philip is faring?"

Charles let out a weary sigh, rubbing a hand over his jaw. "Not well," he admitted. "He seems determined to squander every opportunity that has been placed before him. Oxford expelled him, and no amount of pleading, negotiating, or reasoning could change their minds. And truthfully, I am not certain I would have wanted them to."

Eugenie's brows drew together in concern. "I am sorry," she said, not knowing what else she could say.

Charles gave her an apologetic smile. "It is I who should be sorry. I should not be burdening you with my troubles."

"Nonsense," she replied, sitting up a little straighter. "We are friends, are we not?"

His lips quirked, the tension in his shoulders easing just slightly. "We are."

"Well, friends help one another," Eugenie said, setting down her teacup. "How can I be of assistance?"

Charles studied her for a moment. "I'm not sure there is anything to be done—at least, not where Philip is concerned. His greatest vice is gambling, and from what I have heard, he is rather dreadful at it. He does not know when to walk away."

"Perhaps I could speak to him," she suggested.

Charles gave a dry chuckle. "That would accomplish little, I fear. I have lectured him until I am red in the face, but he refuses to listen. If anything, he only grows more resentful."

"Then what will you do?"

A muscle in Charles's jaw ticked. "Eventually, I will marry," he said after a pause. "And I hope that union will produce an heir. My priority will be securing the estate's future, but I also wish to ensure Philip is cared for when the time comes. He is my cousin, no matter his failings."

Eugenie swallowed, an unexpected weight settling in her stomach. The thought of Charles marrying—it should not have affected her so, yet it did. She had always known he would have to take a wife one day. It was the natural course of things. However, she found herself dreading the answer to the question that formed on her lips.

"Are you pursuing someone?" she ventured.

Charles held her gaze for a moment before shaking his head. "Not at the moment," he admitted. "Right now, my focus is on the estate. I want to ensure it is profitable and thriving before I even consider taking a wife."

Eugenie released a breath she hadn't realized she was holding. "That is wise."

Charles arched a brow. "Do I detect relief in your tone, Lady Eugenie?"

She lifted her teacup to her lips, taking a slow sip to mask the warmth rising in her cheeks. "Not at all," she said. "I simply meant that it is admirable to place duty before personal matters."

A small smirk tugged at the corner of Charles's mouth. "Mmm."

She ignored the knowing glint in his eyes, setting her cup down with deliberate care. "So tell me, my lord—do you have any particular qualities in mind for this future bride of yours?"

Charles's smirk grew, but instead of answering, he leaned forward, resting his forearms on his knees. "Now that," he murmured, "is an interesting question."

"Is it?" Eugenie asked, feigning indifference.

Charles leaned back in his chair, a thoughtful expression settling over his features. "I suppose I would want a young woman who is kind, clever, and, if I am being entirely honest, one who possesses a respectable dowry."

A pang of disappointment flickered through Eugenie at his

words, though she kept her expression carefully composed. "So you are a fortune hunter, then?"

The amusement drained from Charles's face. "I am not," he replied, his voice firm. "But marriage is a business transaction. A woman brings her dowry into the union, and in return, her husband provides for her in the manner to which she is accustomed. It is a practical arrangement."

"You make it sound positively romantic," she muttered, unable to keep the bite from her tone.

"There is nothing romantic about marriage," Charles replied. "At least, not for members of the *ton*."

Eugenie lifted her chin. "If I ever did marry, I would want it to be for love."

The way Charles looked at her made her stomach twist. It wasn't amusement or even disdain—it was pity. And somehow, that was worse.

"I wish you luck, Eugenie," he said softly, "but life is far more complicated than the fairy tales you have read."

"Elsbeth and Niles married for love," she countered.

"That is true," he conceded. "But such matches are rare in our circles, and you know that. Most people marry for convenience. It is easier that way."

Eugenie pressed her lips together. "I disagree. I think it would be far more difficult to build a life with someone you barely know, someone you do not even care for."

Charles spread his hands in a gesture of resignation. "And when, exactly, would I have the time to pursue love? Between managing my estate and my duties in the House of Lords, I scarcely have time for anything else."

"That is rather sad," Eugenie said.

"No, it is pragmatic," he remarked. "My parents did not marry for love, and yet they were content. That is more than many can say."

Eugenie met his gaze. "You deserve love, Charles," she said. "I hope you know that."

Something flickered in his eyes, something almost unreadable. "As do you," he replied. "And I truly hope you find it."

She exhaled slowly, then gave a small shrug. "It hardly matters since I do not wish to marry."

Charles's brow furrowed. "Whyever not? You would willingly choose spinsterhood?"

She broke his gaze, looking towards the window where the sunlight cast golden patterns across the floor. "I want to live my life on my own terms," she admitted. "I have freedoms now that I would lose the moment I took a husband. I do not wish to be bound by expectations that are not my own."

Charles studied her for a long moment before saying, "The right man wouldn't ask you to change. He would love you as you are."

A wistful smile tugged at her lips. "And where, pray tell, would I find such a man?"

Before he could respond, a voice interrupted from the doorway.

"Cousin," Elsbeth greeted, stepping into the room with a knowing smile. "What a pleasant surprise."

Charles rose to his feet. "I came to speak to Eugenie about a private matter."

Elsbeth's gaze flickered between them, her grin widening. "Is that so?" she mused. "How very mysterious."

Charles chuckled. "You are reading far too much into it, but alas, I should take my leave." He gave them both a polite bow. "Ladies."

As soon as he departed, Elsbeth turned to Eugenie with a curious expression. "And what, pray tell, was that all about?"

"Nothing," Eugenie rushed out, standing before she could be further interrogated.

A teasing gleam came into Elsbeth's eyes. "Fine, keep your secrets. But the truth always comes out, you know."

"As delightful as this conversation has been, I do believe it is time for my nap."

"You can run, but you can't hide."

Eugenie strode towards the door, willing her heart to still. She would not dwell on Charles's words. She would not wonder what his answer would have been had Elsbeth not interrupted.

And most of all, she would not think about the possibility that she cared for Charles more than she dared to admit.

Charles stepped down from his coach and strode towards his grand townhouse. The polished brass knocker gleamed under the gray London sky, but he had no need for it since the door was already opening as he approached. Hagen stepped aside, inclining his head with the usual deference.

"My lord," Hagen greeted.

Charles merely tipped his head in acknowledgment and moved past him towards the study. He entered the room and rounded his desk, pulling open the heavy ledger that awaited his attention. If nothing else, he could attempt to make use of the afternoon by tending to matters that actually required his focus.

However, fate had other plans.

He had barely begun scanning the rows of figures when the study door opened. He didn't need to look up to recognize the familiar footsteps. It was his mother's firm, deliberate stride, followed by the softer, hurried steps of Phoebe.

"Good, you are finally home," his mother announced, not bothering with pleasantries. "We have a problem."

Charles closed the ledger with an audible thud. So much for getting any work done. "What is it now?" he asked, already dreading the answer.

Phoebe stepped forward, a folded piece of paper in her hand, her eyes clouded with worry. "Some young woman claims that Philip got her with child, and her brother—Mr. Kingston—has issued a challenge. A duel."

"A duel?" Charles repeated, rising swiftly from his chair. "When?"

Phoebe handed him the letter. "I don't know, but Mr. Kingston has given him the opportunity to choose his second."

Charles unfolded the paper and scanned the hastily written words. He exhaled sharply. "So there is no time or place set yet?"

"Not that I am aware of," Phoebe replied.

Charles frowned. "Where is Philip now?"

"Where else?" Phoebe said, her tone laced with exasperation. "His favorite gambling hell."

Charles let out a curse under his breath, dropping the letter onto his desk. "I need to speak with him."

Phoebe stiffened. "He cannot participate in a duel, Charles. He is a terrible shot. He will get himself killed."

"I won't let that happen," Charles vowed, though even he knew how difficult controlling Philip could be. He rounded his desk, heading for the door. "Try not to worry."

Phoebe wrung her hands together. "If that letter speaks the truth, then Philip has done more than put his own life in jeopardy. He has ruined a young woman's future. That is not how I raised him."

Charles paused beside her, his hands settling firmly on her shoulders. "Let's focus on preventing the duel first."

Phoebe hesitated, then conceded. "Very well."

His mother, ever pragmatic, added, "I had Hagen bring your horse around to the front."

Charles gave her a curt nod of appreciation. "Good thinking. That will save us a considerable amount of time."

Without another word, he left the study, his strides long and purposeful as he made his way towards the entrance. How could Philip be so reckless? A duel, of all things. What on earth was his cousin thinking?

Stepping outside, he mounted his horse with practiced ease and urged it forward, the bustling streets of London blurring past as he made his way towards *The Rabbit and the Fox*.

A short ride later, he slowed to a stop a short distance from the infamous establishment, securing his horse before striding towards the entrance. The heavy wooden door loomed before him, its iron studs glinting under the lantern light. He knocked firmly.

A small panel slid open, revealing a pair of narrowed, suspicious eyes. "What do you want?" the man behind the door growled.

"Let me in," Charles ordered.

The doorman's scowl deepened. "I don't take orders from you."

"Do you want me to waste my money here or not?"

There was a beat of silence, then the panel slid shut. A moment later, he heard the sound of locks being unfastened. The door creaked open, and the man stepped aside grudgingly. "I assume you know where to go, Mister."

Ignoring the doorman, Charles stepped inside. The thick haze of cigar smoke immediately assaulted his senses, mingling with the clinking of coins and the low hum of conversation. He navigated the crowded hall, his gaze sweeping the room until it landed on Philip.

There he was, seated at a round table in the back, a stack of cards in his hand, his posture relaxed as if he hadn't a single care in the world.

Before Charles could approach, a woman draped in a

revealing gown sidled up to him, her lips curling into a slow smile. "Looking for a good time?"

"I'm looking for my cousin," Charles replied, barely sparing her a glance.

He crossed the room and stopped beside Philip's table, clearing his throat.

Philip looked up, his expression twisting in irritation. "What are you doing here?"

"We need to talk."

"Not now." Philip's attention returned to his cards.

Charles's patience snapped. He reached out and clamped a firm hand on his cousin's shoulder. "Yes. Now."

Philip let out a long-suffering sigh and threw his cards down. "This better be important. I was about to win that round."

"You weren't," Charles countered, steering him away from the table.

They stepped into the corridor, the noise of the hall muffled behind them. Philip turned, crossing his arms. "Well? What is it this time?"

Charles fixed him with a hard stare. "Would you care to explain yourself?"

"That depends. What exactly am I supposed to explain?"

In a low voice, he asked, "A duel, Philip? Are you mad?"

Philip shook his head. "Let me guess—my mother has been snooping in my affairs again."

"She had every right to," Charles snapped. "Do you understand the risk you're taking? A duel is a good way to get yourself killed."

"I wasn't the one who issued the challenge," Philip countered. "Mr. Kingston did."

"Did you get his sister pregnant?"

With a slight shrug, Philip replied, "So she claims."

Charles's jaw tightened. "Did you or did you not sleep with her?"

Philip bristled. "I don't see how that's any of your business."

Taking a step closer, Charles lowered his voice and said, "Because actions have consequences. And because you are my heir."

Philip scoffed. "Heir *presumptive*, Charles," he corrected. "We both know you'll marry and have sons, leaving me in the dust."

"That's not the point," Charles said, forcing himself to remain calm. "You need to settle this matter before it goes too far."

"I was going to ask you to be my second, but clearly, that was a mistake."

"You cannot honestly be considering going through with this duel," Charles said, incredulous.

Philip lifted his chin. "I can. And I will."

Charles thought it was best to try to reason with his cousin. Surely that couldn't hurt. "Just apologize. Offer to care for the child. If you do that, Mr. Kingston may let this go."

Philip laughed loudly. "Why would I do that?"

"Because it's your responsibility," Charles snapped.

"I have no proof the child is mine."

Through clenched teeth, Charles threatened, "Philip, if you go through with this, I will cut you off."

Philip's expression faltered. "You wouldn't dare."

"I would."

His eyes grew wide in disbelief. "All this over some chit?"

Charles held his gaze. "Over a matter of honor."

Silence stretched between them. Charles could only hope that, for once, Philip would make the right choice.

Philip took a step back, his expression hardening with defiance. "You have no right to dictate what I can and cannot do,

Cousin," he said, his voice laced with both arrogance and frustration. "I am my own man. I will do as I please, when I please."

Charles didn't flinch. He held his cousin's gaze with unwavering authority. "Not on my penny, you won't."

Philip threw his hands in the air. "Fine! I do not want your money," he snapped. "I will make my own fortune, and I will prove you wrong. You will see."

"Philip—"

But before Charles could say another word, his cousin turned on his heel and strode back into the hall, disappearing into the haze of cigar smoke and the raucous laughter of drunken men.

Charles knew there was no point in going after him. He had already drawn enough attention—the murmurs of nearby onlookers told him as much. A few men were still lingering near the corridor, their eyes glinting with interest, having clearly eavesdropped on their conversation.

There was no point in pressing further. Philip had made his choice.

Turning on his heel, Charles strode out of the gambling hell. The cold air was a welcome contrast to the thick, suffocating atmosphere of the establishment. He pulled his coat tighter around him as he crossed the street to where his horse was tethered.

He mounted swiftly, gripping the reins with more force than necessary as frustration burned in his chest. He had come here in the hope of knocking some sense into his cousin, but once again, Philip had proven to be as reckless and stubborn as ever.

As he urged his horse forward, guiding it back towards his townhouse, the weight of the evening settled over him. He had tried—tried to reason with him, tried to make him see the danger he was walking into—but Philip was determined to be a fool.

And Charles feared it would cost him more than just his pride.

7

———

Eugenie adjusted the cap atop her head, making sure it sat snugly over her carefully pinned-up hair. Her heart pounded with an exhilarating mix of nerves and excitement. She was about to attend a real lecture at Oxford. She had only dreamed of stepping into this place as a student. And it was all thanks to Charles.

Across from her in the carriage, Alice sat with a decidedly less enthusiastic expression, wringing her hands in her lap. "Are you certain this is wise?"

"It is," Eugenie replied with a self-assured nod, though her own stomach fluttered with anticipation.

Alice's lips pressed into a thin line. "And what if you are caught?"

Eugenie gave her a reassuring smile. "You need not fret. Lord Bedford will be with me, and the professor is already aware of my circumstances."

Alice glanced nervously out the carriage window at the bustling streets. "We could still abandon this foolishness and actually go shopping on High Street as you told your brother we would."

"Where is your sense of adventure?" Eugenie teased.

With a slight huff, Alice responded, "I suppose I am simply interested in keeping my position."

"I promise you will never lose your employment with me, no matter what happens."

But Alice didn't look convinced. "I just hope you know what you are doing."

"I do," Eugenie said, lifting her chin with determination. "I will enter with Lord Bedford, sit quietly through the lecture, and leave with no one the wiser."

Alice regarded her skeptically. "Why is Lord Bedford helping you with this?"

Eugenie had wondered the same herself on more than one occasion. "I suppose it is because I am rather charming." Then, with a touch more sincerity, she added, "And because we are friends."

Now who was she trying to convince—Alice or herself?

Before Alice could respond, the carriage rolled to a jerking stop. Eugenie adjusted the long black academic gown that concealed the men's clothing she was wearing. She barely had time to steel herself before the door swung open.

Charles stood on the pavement, sunlight glinting off his dark hair. "Shall we?" he murmured, stepping back to give her room.

Eugenie inhaled deeply and stepped out, her heart soaring. The sun shone brilliantly overhead, casting a golden glow over the stately buildings of Oxford. The low murmur of students deep in discussion filled the street, and for a moment, she felt as though she truly belonged among them.

Then Charles leaned in, his voice low in her ear. "You are smiling far too broadly," he warned. "Remember, you are trying to blend in, not stand out."

"I find that I am in a grand mood," she replied, unable to contain her giddy excitement.

"Well, do try to curtail that emotion," Charles said, his tone amused. "Most students at Oxford are perpetually brooding."

Eugenie shot him a quizzical look. "How can one be gloomy when one is studying at university?"

Charles chuckled, shaking his head. "Trust me. It is entirely possible. To them, attending lectures is an everyday drudgery. And, if I were being honest, some are rather dull."

She gaped at him. "Do they not realize how fortunate they are? To study subjects they love? To have this privilege?"

"Wait until after Professor Addington's lecture," Charles mused, "and you might not feel the same."

His words were teasing, but something in his expression made Eugenie pause. There was a shadow in his eyes, a tension in his features that did not belong to his usual easy manner.

"Is everything all right?" she asked.

He answered too quickly. "It is."

Now she was certain something was amiss. "Out with it," she demanded.

Charles raised a brow. "Out with what?"

"What is troubling you?"

He let out the faintest huff of breath. "Why do you assume something is bothering me?"

Eugenie turned fully towards him, one hand resting on her hip. "Because I can see it in your eyes."

His lips quirked in the faintest smirk. "Should I be flattered?"

"You should," she said without hesitation.

But the humor in his gaze didn't last. Charles exhaled slowly. "Very well," he said at last. "Philip has been challenged to a duel. And he intends to go through with it."

Eugenie's breath hitched. "A duel? Over what?"

He winced. "He got a young woman pregnant."

"How awful," she said. "What if he were to apologize for his actions?"

"I don't think an apology will suffice in this instance. He needs to take responsibility—to care for the child. But I doubt he will."

Eugenie's heart ached for the poor woman caught in the middle of such a scandal. And for Charles, who bore the burden of his cousin's recklessness.

"There is still time," she said, placing a hand on his arm. "Perhaps, if the seconds intervene, a peaceful resolution can be reached."

Charles's jaw tightened. "Philip is as stubborn as ever. He refuses to see reason."

Eugenie gave his arm a gentle squeeze. "Then you must make him see reason."

The shadow in his eyes deepened. "I wish it were that simple."

She held his stare, her determination unwavering. "Nothing about life is simple. But that does not mean we stop trying."

For a long moment, Charles simply regarded her, his gaze searching hers as though trying to decipher something unspoken. Then, almost imperceptibly, he inclined his head. "Thank you."

Eugenie withdrew her hand. "For what?"

"For listening."

She flashed a knowing smile. "You will find that I am an excellent listener. One of my most admirable qualities, in fact."

Charles gestured towards the stone pathway leading into the courtyard. "I would ask what the others are, but we wouldn't want to be late to class."

As they started walking, Eugenie kept her shoulders squared and her back rigid, attempting to exude the quiet confidence of a young scholar.

Charles glanced over at her. "Relax your shoulders. You aren't having an audience with the queen."

"I am attempting to appear confident," she murmured through a tight smile.

"Confidence is one thing," he said. "You look like you're preparing to defend your family's honor in battle."

"And how, pray tell, does one adopt the air of nonchalance?"

Charles gave an exaggerated shrug. "Pretend that this is just another dreary lecture on poetry or theology—something guaranteed to put half the class to sleep. The sort you claim to be endlessly fond of."

She felt her shoulders loosen as she laughed. "So I must act as though I am bored to tears?"

"Precisely. Though I imagine you'll find that difficult. You look positively giddy."

"You are right. I must act as though nothing is out of the ordinary. I am merely an unremarkable student on his way to a lecture."

"Now you are catching on," Charles said. As they neared the entrance, he added, "You will like Professor Addington. His lectures can be rather intense, but his knowledge is unparalleled."

"I am eager to meet him."

Charles stepped ahead to pull open the heavy wooden door, allowing her to enter first. She stepped inside, drinking in her surroundings, her heartbeat quickening with exhilaration.

Before she could get too carried away, Charles fixed her with a pointed look. "Remember, you are not to ask any questions."

"I am aware."

"Good, because your disguise is barely passable, and your voice would fool no one."

She cleared her throat and dropped her voice to a deep, rumbling register. "Is this better?"

Charles snorted. "That is far, far worse. You sound like you are gargling gravel." He pointed towards the corridor ahead. "Professor Addington's lecture hall is just there. Are you ready?"

Eugenie pressed a hand to her stomach, willing herself to remain composed. "Yes. As ready as I will ever be."

"Your mediocre response does not bode well for me," Charles muttered under his breath.

They reached the open door, and Charles gestured for her to enter first. Stepping inside, Eugenie found herself face to face with Professor Addington. He stood with an air of quiet authority, his dark curls peeking out beneath his academic cap. He was younger than she had expected, with striking features and an observant gaze that immediately landed on her.

He studied her with interest before speaking. "Welcome to my class. And you are?"

Drat.

Eugenie's mind whirred. She needed a name—quickly. One that sounded believable.

Before she could open her mouth, Charles smoothly interjected, "This is Winston Plunkett."

A flicker of amusement passed over the professor's face. "Mr. Plunkett," he greeted. "I believe you will find the seats at the back most agreeable."

"Yes, I think—" she started.

Charles placed a firm hand on her shoulder, halting her words. "The back is more than acceptable. Thank you, Professor."

Professor Addington nodded, stepping aside, and Eugenie moved quickly towards the back of the room, her pulse hammering in her ears. She took a seat, straightened her gown, and exhaled slowly. She had done it. She had made it this far.

Charles leaned in and whispered, "You mustn't talk under any circumstance. Do you understand?"

"I do," she murmured.

He gave her a pointed look. "You just talked."

"Well, you asked me a question," she whispered back. "What would you have me do?"

"Pretend you are mute," Charles quipped.

Eugenie rolled her eyes, but she understood his cause for concern. The last thing she wanted was to cause trouble—not for Charles, not for the professor, and certainly not for herself.

The door to the hall swung shut, and Professor Addington strode towards the front, placing his satchel on the desk with practiced ease. He turned to address the students, his voice commanding.

"Good morning," he said. "I trust you are all eager to continue our discussion on the fall of the Roman Empire."

Eugenie's anticipation heightened as the lecture began. She leaned forward, attempting to absorb every word. Each time the professor paused for effect, she had the strangest urge to applaud. But, of course, that would immediately give her away.

So, for now, she remained silent.

But in her heart, she was celebrating.

Because, at last, she was exactly where she was meant to be.

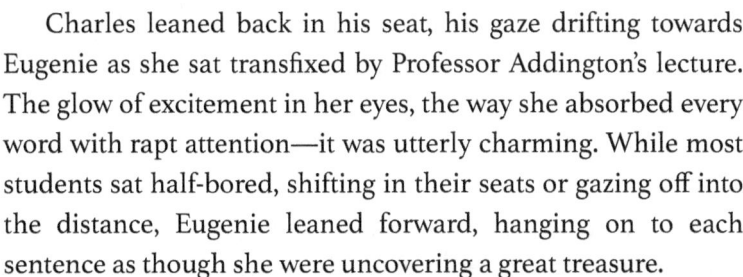

Charles leaned back in his seat, his gaze drifting towards Eugenie as she sat transfixed by Professor Addington's lecture. The glow of excitement in her eyes, the way she absorbed every word with rapt attention—it was utterly charming. While most students sat half-bored, shifting in their seats or gazing off into the distance, Eugenie leaned forward, hanging on to each sentence as though she were uncovering a great treasure.

His eyes traced the delicate features of her face. How her disguise had fooled anyone was beyond him. Even now, a stray wisp of blonde hair had escaped from beneath her ill-fitting wig and he had the strangest urge to reach out and tuck it back.

But that would draw attention. And he had already been looking at her for far too long.

The sound of polite clapping echoed through the lecture hall as the students began rising from their seats. Books snapped shut, chairs scraped against the floor, and conversations hummed in the background as the hall emptied.

Eugenie turned to him, her voice brimming with enthusiasm. "That was truly brilliant."

Charles smirked. "You must have misheard the lecture, then. It was merely on the rise and fall of the Roman Empire. Hardly the first time you've heard of such a thing."

"Yes, but Professor Addington has a way with his words," she countered, her expression alight with admiration.

"I'm truly glad you enjoyed it."

Before she could respond, Charles looked up to find Addington approaching, his leather satchel slung over his shoulder, and his sharp, assessing eyes fixed on Eugenie.

"Dare I ask how you enjoyed the lecture?" he inquired.

Eugenie sprang to her feet, beaming. "It was magnificent," she praised.

Addington puffed out his chest slightly, clearly pleased. "I daresay that is quite the compliment. Most of the time, I'm merely hoping the class doesn't fall asleep."

"I don't know how they could," Eugenie said. "I learned so many interesting things from your lecture. You are a truly gifted teacher."

Addington chuckled, his gaze flicking towards Charles. "I like this one."

Charles rose slowly from his chair, glancing around the nearly empty hall before saying, "Allow me to properly introduce you. This is Lady Eugenie, sister of Lord Westcott."

Addington's brows lifted in mild surprise. "I take it your brother doesn't know you're here?"

"You would be correct in your assumption," she replied.

Addington adjusted the strap of his satchel. "Your brother is a good man. I've heard he's been making quite an impact in the House of Lords."

"He is trying," Eugenie replied, holding his gaze steadily.

Charles narrowed his eyes slightly. He didn't particularly like the way Addington was looking at her. His interest in Eugenie was clear—too clear. Charles told himself it was merely an observation, nothing more. And yet, the way Addington's eyes lingered a fraction too long set him on edge.

"Well," Addington finally said, breaking the momentary pause. "I should be going. It was a pleasure having you in my class, Lady Eugenie."

"I truly appreciate you allowing me to attend," Eugenie said.

Addington flashed a smile. "You are always welcome as long as you wear your disguise. Though, I must say, your beauty still shines through."

Eugenie's cheeks tinged pink, and she ducked her head slightly. "You are kind to say so, sir."

"Professor," Addington corrected gently. "At Oxford, I am addressed as Professor."

Charles seized the opportunity to interject. "Addington is up for a fellowship."

Eugenie lifted her chin, her admiration apparent. "I can see why. You are a gifted scholar."

Addington's smile deepened. "You truly are a delight, my lady," he said. "I hope to see you at Lady Winter's ball this evening."

Charles half-expected Eugenie to make a face at the mention of a ball, but to his surprise, she merely nodded. "I will be there."

"Wonderful," Addington said, his voice turning slightly more intimate. "Perhaps you will even be gracious enough to save me a dance."

"I would greatly enjoy that," Eugenie replied.

Addington tipped his head. "Until tonight, my lady." His gaze lingered a moment longer than propriety allowed before he finally turned and strode towards the door.

Charles watched him go, an inexplicable irritation creeping up his spine. The moment Addington was out of earshot, he turned to Eugenie. "Dare I ask what that was about?"

A small crease formed between her brows. "I beg your pardon?"

"Were you flirting with Addington?"

Eugenie's eyes widened in clear disbelief. "Good heavens, why would you even ask such a thing?"

"It was fairly obvious," Charles replied, folding his arms.

Eugenie turned fully towards him, hands on her hips. "I was merely being gracious, considering he allowed me to sit in on his lecture."

Charles gave her a skeptical look. "Is that all it was?"

"It was," she insisted.

Charles knew he was being ridiculous, but he couldn't seem to stop himself. Why did it matter to him whom she flirted with? And why did the idea of her dancing with Addington at Lady Winter's ball send an uncomfortable twist through his chest?

He didn't have an answer.

And that troubled him more than anything.

"Regardless," Charles pressed, his tone still edged with irritation, "you should not be flirting with anyone when you are dressed like that."

Eugenie let out an exasperated sigh. "Again, I was not flirting with Professor Addington."

Charles studied her, searching for any flicker of insincerity. He wasn't entirely convinced, but pressing the issue further would likely get him nowhere. "Fine. I shall take you at your word," he muttered, though his voice came out much gruffer than intended. "Shall we depart?"

"I think that is wise."

Eugenie brushed past him, and as she did, a soft, familiar scent drifted in her wake. Lavender. The scent curled around him, light and fresh, yet entirely out of place amidst the old stone and parchment-filled halls of Oxford. Without thinking, the words tumbled from his lips.

"Why do you smell like that?"

Eugenie halted mid-step and slowly turned. "Pardon?"

"That scent. Why do you smell like lavender?"

Her brows furrowed. "And what, pray tell, is wrong with the way I smell?"

He hesitated. There was absolutely no way to answer that question without sounding like a fool. But since he had already made a mess of things, he pressed on. "You smell entirely too enticing."

Eugenie's mouth parted slightly in surprise. "Thank you?" she offered, though her tone made it clear she wasn't sure whether to take it as a compliment or an insult.

Charles shifted uncomfortably. "I only meant that men do not smell like lavender."

"And what do men smell like?"

He shrugged. "How should I know?" he asked. "I don't go around sniffing them."

Eugenie's lips twitched with barely contained laughter. "Just women, then?"

"I did not sniff you."

Her amusement only grew. "How else would you have noticed I smelled like lavender?"

Charles clenched his jaw. "You are impossible."

"And this entire conversation is utterly ludicrous," Eugenie countered with a wave of her hand. "Can we go now?"

He gestured towards the door. "After you."

As Eugenie stepped ahead, Charles mentally cursed himself. Their conversation had spiraled into sheer absurdity.

Why had he even commented on her scent in the first place? It wasn't as though men would get close enough to her to notice. At least, they had better not.

They walked down the corridor in silence, Charles quickening his pace to hold the door open for her. Once they stepped outside, Eugenie glanced up at him and said, "Thank you, Charles. Without you, today would not have been possible."

"I merely asked a friend to let you sit in on a lecture," he said, attempting to brush off the praise.

"It was more than that, and you know it." Her gaze was steady, unwavering. "You risked your reputation—and his. For me. And I cannot thank you enough for that."

Charles met her eyes, something unspoken passing between them. "You are welcome, Eugenie."

Her lips curled slightly. "I am surprised you called me by my given name and not Mr. Plunkett, given that we are still at Oxford."

"Would you prefer if I call you Mr. Plunkett?" he asked dryly.

She lifted a playful brow. "Could you not have thought of a better name for me?"

"What is wrong with Plunkett?"

"Nothing, but Anderson or Jones is a much more common surname," she teased.

He tilted his head slightly, as if considering. "But you are anything but common, my dear."

The words left his mouth before he could stop them.

Eugenie's smile faltered, her teasing expression fading into something unreadable. She quickly turned her gaze towards her waiting coach. "Thank you for escorting me," she said, her voice quieter than before.

Charles clenched his fists, resisting the urge to curse himself. Why had he called her that? *My dear?* What had possessed him? That was the problem—he hadn't been thinking.

A footman stepped forward and opened the carriage door. Eugenie moved to step in, but Charles instinctively reached out, his hand gently catching her arm.

"Eugenie..." he began, though he wasn't sure what he wanted to say—only that he needed to fix whatever tension had settled between them. "I shouldn't have called you that."

"It's all right," she murmured. "You need not trouble yourself over it."

But even as she stepped inside the coach and the door closed behind her, Charles found that he was troubled.

And he wasn't sure why.

D raped in a blue gown, Eugenie ascended the grand staircase. She was making her way to her bedchamber, hoping—though with little conviction—that she could steal a moment of rest. Sleep, however, felt impossible. Her mind was too preoccupied, her thoughts troubled.

My dear.

The words replayed in her mind, sending an unfamiliar flutter through her chest. Had Charles truly meant it? Or had it merely been a careless term of endearment, tossed out without thought? A part of her hoped it did mean something.

What was wrong with her? She was determined to remain a spinster, free from the expectations and constraints that came with marriage. And yet... Charles was unlike most of the gentlemen of the *ton*. He was different. Had he not just risked his reputation by sneaking her into Oxford so she could attend a lecture? How many men would have done such a thing for a woman?

And it certainly didn't help that he was devilishly handsome.

Eugenie exhaled sharply, resisting the urge to groan out

loud. This was foolishness. She needed to clear her mind, rest, and stop entertaining these thoughts. She strode down the dimly lit corridor, her hands tightening into fists at her sides as if to physically banish her traitorous emotions.

But any hope of respite vanished the moment she stepped into her bedchamber.

Sitting primly on the edge of her bed, arms crossed in a posture of quiet authority, was Elsbeth.

Eugenie's brow arched in curiosity as she met her sister-in-law's gaze. "Is everything all right?"

Elsbeth's expression remained unreadable. "Perhaps it might be best if you close the door," she said evenly. "There is something I wish to discuss with you."

A flicker of unease coiled in Eugenie's stomach. Something about Elsbeth's tone sent a shiver of apprehension down her spine. Silently, she pushed the door shut, the soft click sounding unnaturally loud in the quiet room.

"How was shopping?" Elsbeth asked, her voice innocent. Too innocent.

Eugenie mustered a smile. "It was wonderful."

"Did you make any purchases?"

A slight hesitation. "No, I did not."

"Interesting," Elsbeth murmured. "You didn't make any purchases last time either."

Eugenie waved a dismissive hand. "Nothing caught my eye, I'm afraid."

Elsbeth's eyes narrowed slightly. "It's just rather curious, isn't it? You go through the trouble of traveling all that way to shop on High Street twice and have yet to return with so much as a ribbon."

A trickle of unease slithered down Eugenie's spine. She forced a laugh. "It is merely a coincidence."

"Hmm." Elsbeth tilted her head, considering. "You know what else is on High Street? Oxford."

Eugenie's heart plummeted.

She knew.

Elsbeth uncrossed her arms and rose. "It makes me wonder," she mused, "if you have been spending time at Oxford."

Eugenie attempted a weak smile. "Women aren't allowed at Oxford," she countered, though even to her own ears, the excuse sounded feeble.

"True," Elsbeth acknowledged, "but it wouldn't surprise me if you found a way around that particular obstacle." Her gaze was piercing now. "Perhaps by disguising yourself as a man?"

Eugenie let out a hollow laugh, but her pulse was racing. "That is absurd."

"Is it?" Elsbeth lifted a brow. "You value learning more than anything, and I suspect you would go to great lengths to attend a lecture."

The game was up. Eugenie sighed and moved to sit beside her on the bed. "You aren't wrong." She studied Elsbeth's expression carefully. "Are you going to tell Niles?"

"That depends," Elsbeth replied. "Are you planning to continue attending lectures?"

"I don't know," she admitted. "I want to."

Elsbeth turned to face her fully, her sharp features softening slightly. "What if you're caught?" she asked. "You're risking your reputation—and this family's."

"I know," Eugenie whispered, "but it's a chance worth taking."

For a long moment, Elsbeth said nothing. Then, to Eugenie's surprise, she let out a soft sigh. "You and I are not so different, you know."

Eugenie frowned. "What do you mean?"

A playful smirk curled at Elsbeth's lips. "I have dressed in men's clothing before."

Eugenie blinked, certain she had misheard. "*You?*"

Elsbeth's smirk deepened. "Who do you think was the high-waywoman who terrorized the roads to Polperro?"

Eugenie's mouth fell open. "You were the highwaywoman?"

"I was," Elsbeth confirmed, amusement twinkling in her eyes. "I was trying to rob my stepfather's coach... but as luck would have it, I unintentionally robbed your coach instead. It was the first and only coach I robbed."

"Does Niles know?"

Elsbeth laughed lightly. "Oh, yes. He discovered the truth after I got shot."

"You were shot?"

"A minor wound, but enough to make me reconsider my... extracurricular activities," Elsbeth said. "It was too dangerous."

Eugenie stared at her, still trying to process this revelation. "Why were you trying to rob your stepfather's coach?"

A shadow passed over Elsbeth's face, her usually confident demeanor faltering. "I thought he was keeping secrets from me," she admitted. "I was convinced he wasn't the man my mother believed him to be. I wanted to prove it."

"And did you?"

A slow, rueful smile tugged at Elsbeth's lips. "I was wrong," she said simply. "He is a good man."

Eugenie sat back. They were, indeed, more alike than she had ever realized. And perhaps—just perhaps—she wasn't as alone in her unconventional choices as she had always thought.

Elsbeth continued. "I tell you this not to encourage you, but to make you understand that your actions have consequences. If you were to be discovered at Oxford, your reputation would be irreparably ruined. Society is not forgiving, especially to women who defy its rules."

"I am well aware of the risks, but Lord Bedford is helping me," she admitted. "He even secured permission from one of his friends, a professor at University College, to allow me to attend his lectures."

Elsbeth did not look pleased by her admission. "I shall have a word with my cousin."

"Do not be too hard on him. He was only trying to help me," Eugenie pleaded. "He is a good man. And if he hadn't assisted me, I would have found my own way into those lectures—with or without his help."

Elsbeth's brows knitted together. "I understand your thirst for knowledge, truly I do. But you must admit that this is reckless."

"Why is it reckless to seek an education? Why is it fair that women are denied the same opportunities as men?"

"It is not fair," Elsbeth conceded. "But it is the way of things —for now, at least." She turned slightly, studying Eugenie with concern. "And you have your future to think of."

Eugenie let out a dry, humorless laugh as she dropped onto the bed with an unceremonious thump. "Oh, yes, my *future*," she said wryly. "Niles wants me to marry, produce a horde of children, and settle into my role as a dutiful wife. But I want more out of life than just marriage and motherhood."

"Do you truly not wish to marry?"

Eugenie turned her eyes towards the window. "If I were to marry, I would be expected to fall in line," she murmured. "My husband would dictate what I can and cannot do. I would lose my freedom, my choices, my voice."

Elsbeth came to sit beside her on the bed. "Not every husband is a tyrant," she said. "Niles, for instance—he is the best of men."

Eugenie turned her head, searching Elsbeth's expression. There was an undeniable warmth in her tone, a quiet reverence when she spoke of her husband. It was true. Niles was not a cruel or controlling man. But he had chosen Elsbeth, a woman who fit into his world. Eugenie was different. She didn't think she could fit into anyone's world but her own.

"And if I cannot find a husband like Niles?" Eugenie ventured. "What then?"

"Then you must decide if the risk of being alone is worth more than the chance of finding someone who will let you be you."

Eugenie swallowed hard, her heart twisting. She had always been certain she would never marry. But lately—especially with Charles lingering in her thoughts—that certainty felt less like an unshakable truth and more like a desperate defense.

And she wasn't sure what to do about it.

Elsbeth placed a gentle hand on Eugenie's shoulder. "You are more than just my sister-in-law," she said. "You are my friend, as well. And I care about you deeply."

"I feel the same," she admitted.

"Good, because I am about to offer some more unsolicited advice," Elsbeth warned, lowering her hand to her side. "Do not be so quick to dismiss the idea of marriage. Life isn't a fairy tale or an effortless story. True love is built, not found. But I assure you that it is worth the wait."

After a moment of silence, Elsbeth arched a brow. "Do you need—or want—more advice? I can go on for hours, you know."

Eugenie laughed. "No, thank you. I think I have been sufficiently edified."

Satisfied with that response, Elsbeth turned towards the door, but not before tossing a final comment over her shoulder. "Then you had better hurry and get some rest before we have to start preparing for Lady Winter's ball."

Eugenie sighed, bracing herself for the long evening ahead. However, one lingering concern made her call out before Elsbeth could leave. "Are you going to tell Niles about what we discussed?"

Elsbeth stopped at the threshold, her hand resting lightly on the doorknob. Then she turned back. "I do not believe in keeping secrets, especially from one's husband," she admitted. "However, I will give you the opportunity to tell him first."

Eugenie groaned, already picturing her brother's reaction. "Niles will be furious. He might even send me off to a convent."

Elsbeth's lips twitched with amusement. "At least there will be books," she quipped. "Now, get some sleep."

With that, she departed, leaving Eugenie alone in her bedchamber. The moment the door clicked shut, she flopped onto her back, staring up at the embroidered canopy above her bed. How could she possibly sleep now?

Charles sat in the dimly lit coach as it rumbled through the darkened streets towards Lady Winter's townhouse. The steady clatter of hooves and the soft creak of the carriage did little to settle his restless mind. His thoughts were still entangled in the moment earlier—*my dear?* He had called Eugenie that term of endearment as naturally as breathing. Why? It was unlike him. And yet, disturbingly, it had felt... right.

A voice interrupted his musings. "You are awfully quiet this evening," his mother observed from across the carriage.

"I suppose I am," he responded, hoping a brief answer would deter further questioning.

She leaned forward slightly, her gloved hands neatly folded in her lap. "Anything you wish to talk about?"

"No," he replied, his tone clipped.

Before she could push further, the carriage rolled to a stop in front of a stately, whitewashed townhouse, its many windows aglow with warm candlelight. He wasted no time in exiting, reaching back only briefly to offer his mother his hand. Once on solid ground, she withdrew and smoothed the fabric of her maroon gown with practiced elegance.

"Do you intend to dance this evening?" she asked as he adjusted his cuffs.

"Perhaps," he said, keeping his answer deliberately vague.

She eyed him knowingly, but he ignored her scrutiny, his patience for conversation already wearing thin. As they ascended the front steps, the grand double doors swung open, revealing the elegant splendor within—chandeliers glittered above, gilded mirrors reflected the bustling crowd, and the distant sounds of an orchestra floated through the air.

Charles had barely stepped inside when his gaze landed on Viscount Alcott and his younger sister, Miss Charlotte Winslow, standing near one of the pillars.

"Excuse me," he murmured to his mother before striding towards his friend. He offered a polite smile. "Good evening."

Miss Winslow turned her bright, blue-eyed gaze on him and dipped into a low curtsy, the movement practiced and graceful. "My lord," she purred, a coy smile playing on her lips. "It is always a pleasure to see you."

Charles cleared his throat, forcing his eyes upward as he attempted to ignore the rather daring neckline of her gown. "Miss Winslow," he greeted, before shifting his attention to Alcott. "I'm surprised to see you here this evening."

Before Alcott could respond, his sister interjected with a playful bat of her lashes. "Oh, I forced him to come," she admitted. "I am hoping for an evening filled with dancing."

"I am sure you will have your wish," Charles said. It wasn't that Miss Winslow was unattractive—far from it. With her golden hair and fair complexion, she was quite lovely. But Charles had always regarded her as a younger sister, despite her frequent, and rather blatant, attempts to flirt with him.

Holding up her empty dance card, she pouted. "Would you believe I have yet to be asked for a single dance?" she lamented, tilting her head slightly.

Alcott huffed in exasperation. "Good. That might mean this godforsaken evening will end sooner rather than later."

Miss Winslow turned to him with mock horror. "You promised we would stay until the last dance," she reminded him before suddenly brightening. "Oh! They have champagne."

Alcott sighed. "You may have one glass."

"You are such a tyrant, Brother. What harm is there in having two glasses of champagne?"

"The harm," Alcott said dryly, "is when you start saying ridiculous things because you've had too much to drink."

Miss Winslow rolled her eyes and brushed past him towards the refreshment table. "You worry too much."

Alcott watched her go and exhaled heavily. "Do you want a sister?" he muttered. "She comes with a dowry."

Charles chuckled. "You seem to forget—I had a sister."

Alcott sobered instantly. "My apologies. I didn't mean to make light of it."

"You did no such thing," Charles reassured him. "I see that your sister hasn't changed much since I last saw her."

"If anything, she's grown more stubborn—" Alcott's words trailed off suddenly, and his expression turned grim. "Dear heavens, Charlotte is already on her second glass of champagne. Excuse me."

As Alcott hurried away, Charles continued into the ballroom, barely acknowledging the chalked dance floor. His gaze swept the crowd, searching—until it landed on the one person he had hoped to see.

Eugenie.

She stood near the rear of the ballroom, clad in an opulent gold gown that shimmered under the candlelight. Her blonde hair was arranged in an elegant chignon with two loose curls framing her delicate features.

Her gaze met his across the crowded dance floor and he realized that he had been caught staring. He should have looked away, but instead, he inclined his head in silent acknowledgment.

In response, she smiled. And for reasons he could not fully comprehend, it felt as if the entire room had grown a little brighter.

An unexpected and undeniable urge swept over him—the need to speak with her. To be near her.

As he crossed the ballroom, he searched his mind for something intelligent to say, something that might impress her with his wit or charm. But as he reached her, every clever thought abandoned him. Instead, the first thing that left his mouth was, "This is a *crush*."

"It is," she agreed.

Botheration. Why had he stated the obvious like a fool?

A familiar voice saved him from blabbering like a fool.

"Cousin," Elsbeth greeted, appearing beside Eugenie. "What a pleasant surprise. You normally avoid these social gatherings."

"I do not," he argued, though he knew it was a weak attempt.

Elsbeth smirked. "Yes, you do. You once told me that balls are nothing more than an opportunity for people to be seen in high Society."

Charles adjusted his sleeve with feigned interest. "I have since changed my mind."

"Does that mean you intend to dance?" Elsbeth asked, her tone suspiciously innocent. "Because Eugenie could use a partner for the first set."

"Is that so?" he asked, perhaps a touch too eagerly.

Eugenie's expression was unreadable as she folded her arms. "You need not concern yourself with me, my lord. I do not require a dance partner out of pity."

"I would like to dance with you," he said simply. And he meant it.

She still didn't look entirely convinced. "Very well, but it is out of protest and nothing more," she relented.

He extended his hand as the first set was announced. "Out of protest, then," he teased. "I have danced with young women for worse reasons."

That earned a small, reluctant smile from her. "I am sure young women flock to dance with you, seeing as you are an earl."

"Yes," he admitted wryly. "And that is precisely the problem. Those are the type of young women I have no desire to dance with."

"You poor earl," Eugenie quipped, amusement dancing in her eyes as she placed her gloved hand into his.

Charles straightened, puffing out his chest in mock grandeur. "Finally! Someone who recognizes the tragic burden I bear."

She laughed softly, but as he led her onto the dance floor, her demeanor shifted. Leaning in slightly, her voice lowered to a whisper. "Elsbeth has discovered our secret. She was waiting for me in my bedchamber earlier and somehow deduced that I have been visiting Oxford."

Charles stifled a groan. Of course Elsbeth had figured it out. She was many things, but a fool was not one of them. It was only a matter of time before she pieced everything together. "And what did you tell her?"

"The truth," Eugenie admitted. "And she informed me that she will be speaking to you about it shortly."

"Something to look forward to, then," he muttered.

The humor in her expression faded slightly. "It is not just Elsbeth I must worry about. I will have to tell Niles what I have been up to, and he will not be pleased."

"No, he certainly won't be," Charles agreed. "But there's always an alternative. We could elope to Gretna Green." He cast her a sideways glance, half-hoping, half-joking.

"Do be serious."

He grinned, undeterred. "You're right. I am an earl, after all. Quite the catch. You should be the one offering for me."

Her lips parted in mock disbelief. "And, pray tell, why would I ever offer for you?"

Placing a hand over his heart, he staggered back slightly as if she had just struck him. "You wound me, my lady! Am I not a man worth offering for?"

"I doubt I have wounded your pride."

Charles sighed dramatically. "You had your chance, Eugenie. Now you must live with regret. No need to beg."

She laughed, just as he had intended. "You are insufferable."

"And yet, you're still here," he pointed out as he led her to where the other young women were lining up.

Charles bowed slightly before he went to line up with the other men. It was only then that he realized he still had a smile on his lips.

9

Eugenie found that she rather liked dancing with Charles. Quite frankly, she enjoyed it far too much. There was something profoundly reassuring in the way he led her across the dance floor, their movements synchronized as though they had been dancing together for years. She felt safe. Comfortable.

But that would never do.

Charles was her friend. And she was certain her feelings were entirely unreciprocated, which was just as well. She would rather have Charles in her life as a friend than risk losing him altogether to foolish, unspoken affections.

As the final notes of the set echoed through the ballroom, Eugenie dropped into a practiced curtsy, lowering her gaze to steady herself. When she looked up, Charles was approaching with that easy, familiar smile of his—the one that never failed to make her feel as though the rest of the world faded away.

"You dance extraordinarily well, my lady," he praised, offering his arm.

She accepted it, arching a brow. "You sound surprised."

"It is not often that I encounter someone who can match my dancing prowess."

She laughed. "How very humble of you."

Charles puffed out his chest, feigning great pride. "The dancing master at Eton was abnormally attentive to me, I'll have you know. I do believe he once told me I wasn't the worst dancer he had ever come across."

"That is quite the high praise," she teased.

"Indeed," he replied before winking. "And it certainly helps that I had such a beautiful partner."

Eugenie felt a flicker of heat rush to her cheeks but refused to let him see how deeply his words affected her. She tilted her chin in mock skepticism. "Flattery, my lord?"

"Did it work?"

"No."

He tsked, shaking his head. "Pity. I shall have to try harder to win your favor."

"If you are truly intent on winning my favor, I do have a particular fondness for sweets."

"Duly noted."

As they strolled towards the edge of the dance floor, Eugenie's gaze drifted towards the rear of the ballroom, where Niles and Elsbeth stood in quiet conversation. It was then that she noticed the lingering stares of several young women—eyes trailing after Charles with thinly veiled interest. She wasn't surprised. He was, after all, one of the most eligible bachelors of the Season.

Charles suddenly muttered under his breath, drawing her attention back to him. "Oh, no," he sighed.

"Is something amiss?" Eugenie asked.

He gestured towards the refreshment table, where Miss Winslow stood sipping champagne, her cheeks flushed with drink.

"It appears Miss Winslow has been left unattended by her brother," Charles murmured. "And she is drinking another glass."

Eugenie frowned. "And that is a problem?"

"It is," he said, his brow furrowing.

Before she could press for further explanation, Charles released her arm and muttered, "Excuse me."

She watched him stride away before turning back towards her brother. "Why are you two not dancing?" she asked, addressing Niles and Elsbeth.

Niles shrugged. "Elsbeth is not particularly fond of dancing, and I have no complaints."

Elsbeth gave him an amused look. "I do not mind it, but we are here to chaperone you this evening. There is little time for dancing."

"You should dance the next set," Eugenie urged. "I promise to behave. I will not run off to Gretna Green with an eligible gentleman."

"I don't know..." Elsbeth hesitated.

Niles slipped an arm around his wife's waist. "It is only one dance, my love. And I have all the confidence in the world in Eugenie."

Elsbeth's face softened. "I would like to dance with you."

"Then it is settled," Niles said, turning back to Eugenie. "You will remain here."

Eugenie glanced towards the French doors. "I might step outside for some air, but I will stay on the veranda."

Niles gave a nod of approval.

The next set was announced, and Eugenie waved them off with a pointed look. "Go. Enjoy yourselves."

Without further hesitation, Niles led Elsbeth towards the dance floor, disappearing into the sea of elegantly dressed couples. Eugenie smiled as she watched them. They were so utterly content together, so in love. It was the kind of love match she had never truly believed in. A part of her had always dismissed the notion of marriage, assuming it was impossible to find such devotion. She was peculiar in her ways; she knew that much. Who could ever love her?

Her gaze wandered across the ballroom, searching for Charles. She scanned the refreshment table, but both he and Miss Winslow were gone.

A strange unease coiled in her stomach. Not that it was any of her concern. But curiosity got the better of her.

Slipping through the French doors, Eugenie stepped onto the veranda. Couples milled about, enjoying the crisp night air, but there was no sign of Charles. Then a burst of giggling caught her ear. It came from beyond the side of the townhouse.

A sudden, inexplicable urgency filled her as she descended the stairs, her slippers barely making a sound on the stone path. Rounding the corner, she came to an abrupt halt.

There, in the dim glow of the lantern light, stood Charles and Miss Winslow—locked in a scandalously intimate embrace.

Eugenie sucked in a breath, the sound betraying her before she could stop herself.

Charles's head snapped towards her, his eyes widening in horror. "Eugenie." He wrenched himself away from Miss Winslow, stepping forward as if to explain.

But she didn't wait to hear it.

Heart pounding, she turned on her heel and fled back towards the veranda.

How utterly mortifying. She had stumbled upon Charles in the middle of a romantic moment, and she had no right to feel so wounded by it.

She reminded herself, again and again, that it did not matter. Charles could be with whomever he wanted. They had no understanding. They were only friends. And yet, no matter how much she repeated it, the ache in her chest refused to fade.

"Eugenie! Wait!"

Charles's voice rang out behind her just as she was about to step back into the ballroom.

She froze as she debated about what she should do. Should she turn around and give him the chance to speak? But what right did she have to feel this way? He had done nothing wrong. Despite that, the image of him and Miss Winslow, pressed intimately together in the shadows of the gardens, was burned into her mind.

Before she could make a decision, Charles moved in front of her, effectively blocking her path. His breath was slightly uneven, as if he had hurried after her. "Eugenie... you must let me explain."

She lifted her chin. "There is no need, my lord—"

"Yes, there is," he interrupted, his voice firm. "What you saw back there was not what it seemed."

Her frown deepened. "It seemed as though Miss Winslow's chest was quite determinedly pressed against yours. Was I mistaken?"

Charles ran a hand through his neatly groomed hair, leaving it disheveled. "No... yes..." He groaned in frustration. "What you saw—what you think you saw—was entirely innocent."

A sharp pang of irritation shot through her. Did he think of her as a fool? That she had imagined the entire thing? "You do not need to explain yourself to me," she said curtly.

His hand lifted slightly as if to reach for her before he let it drop. His gaze flickered towards the lingering guests on the veranda before he lowered his voice. "Can we talk in private?"

Eugenie folded her arms, considering him. Charles was always composed, always unbothered. And yet now, he was anything but.

"I suppose," she said at last.

He gestured towards the far end of the veranda. "It will only take a moment. I promise."

She walked ahead, her posture stiff. As they reached the quieter, more secluded section, she turned to face him with an expectant look.

Charles looked deucedly out of sorts—his usual confident air was absent, replaced by something far more vulnerable. His hands curled into fists at his sides before he blew out a breath and met her gaze.

"Miss Winslow had too much to drink," he began. "I thought taking her for a short walk in the gardens might help clear her head. Unfortunately, she mistook my intentions and assumed I was trying to get her alone."

"Were you?"

"No! Heavens, no!" Charles exclaimed, his frustration evident. "I merely thought the cool air might sober her a little. I did not expect her to—" He paused, visibly uncomfortable, before finally admitting, "I did not expect her to try to kiss me."

"Regardless, it is none of my concern. You may kiss whomever you so desire."

Charles's expression grew even more frustrated. "But I had no intention of kissing her."

"It did not look that way."

Charles took a step closer, his voice lowering into something more urgent, more sincere. "You must believe me. I have no interest in Miss Winslow. I think of her as a younger sister—nothing more."

There was truth in his voice, a raw honesty she found rather convincing. And she wanted to believe him. Truly, she did.

But she could not erase the image from her mind.

Before she could respond, the sound of delicate footsteps approaching the veranda caught her attention.

Miss Winslow.

She glided up the steps with a satisfied smile curving her lips, her eyes bright with mischief. "Lord Bedford," she purred, tilting her head coyly. "I do hope you will save me a dance later."

Charles visibly tensed. "I think not."

"Oh, dear." Miss Winslow pouted, her eyes turning towards the ballroom. "My brother has finally found me."

A tall, dark-haired man strode up to them, his expression stormy. "Charlotte," he said in a low, controlled voice, "where have you been?"

Miss Winslow gave a little, careless laugh. "Lord Bedford and I took a stroll in the gardens."

Charles lifted a hand, interjecting, "I merely thought the cool air might help her inebriated state, Alcott."

Alcott's stern features darkened further. "That is all that I hope happened."

Miss Winslow giggled, unbothered. "Oh, Lord Bedford is far too stuffy for anything to have happened," she stated.

Stepping forward, Alcott took firm hold of his sister's arm. "You have had entirely too much to drink. It is time to go home."

Miss Winslow stomped her foot like a petulant child. "But I don't want to go home. I want to stay and dance with Lord Bedford."

Alcott's grip on her arm did not loosen. "Perhaps another time," he said, his voice brooking no argument. With that, he steered his sister down the veranda steps and towards the front of the townhouse. Only when they had disappeared into the night did Charles turn back to Eugenie, his eyes searching hers.

"Do you believe me now?"

She opened her mouth, intending to say something—what, she wasn't sure—but before she could utter a word, the sound of hurried footsteps met her ears.

Niles and Elsbeth broke through the lingering crowd at the

edge of the ballroom and approached them. "Eugenie... there you are," Elsbeth said.

Eugenie mustered a weak smile. "Here I am."

Niles's sharp gaze flickered between her and Charles before his jaw clenched. "And you were alone with Bedford. Wonderful," he muttered under his breath. "Shall we return to the ballroom before the next set is announced?"

"I think that would be wise," Eugenie agreed, eager to escape the weight of Charles's gaze and the unsettling flutter in her chest.

But Charles did not move. He remained rooted to the spot, his eyes steady on hers as he spoke. "Lady Eugenie, may I call upon you tomorrow?"

The question sent a ripple of unease through her. It was entirely unnecessary. "There is no need, my lord," she replied. "I believe you."

"Be that as it may," Charles remarked, his tone unwavering, "I would still like to call upon you."

After a long moment, she spoke. "Very well."

A flicker of something—relief, perhaps—passed over Charles's face, but before she could dwell on it, Niles placed a guiding hand on her elbow, leading her away from the veranda and back towards the golden glow of the ballroom.

Eugenie did not look back.

But she could feel Charles's eyes on her, watching, waiting.

———————

Charles sat slouched in the corner of White's, a half-full glass of brandy resting in his grip. The low hum of conversation filled the club, punctuated by occasional bursts of laughter from men who had clearly had far too much to drink. He, however, had no interest in jovial company tonight. It was late, but he found himself unwilling to go home.

He couldn't shake the image of Eugenie's face when she had stumbled upon him and Miss Winslow—the disbelief in her wide, blue eyes, the way her lips had parted in stunned silence before she had fled.

Botheration.

He had done nothing wrong. However, deep down, he knew better. He should never have allowed himself to be alone with Miss Winslow, not even for a moment. If someone else had come across them, if word had spread, he might have been forced into marriage with a woman he had no desire to wed.

The thought made his stomach twist. He would rather chew glass than be shackled to Miss Winslow. Somehow, that wasn't what truly unsettled him. What plagued him most was Eugenie. She had said she believed him but was it really that simple? The doubt lingering in her eyes suggested otherwise.

And why, above all else, did it matter so much to him?

There was no understanding between them. So why did he wish there was something between them?

That was the real problem.

With a sigh, he brought the glass to his lips, taking a slow sip as he stared blankly at the room. He had left the ball shortly after the disastrous encounter in the gardens, making his way here in the hopes of drowning his thoughts in liquor. It had not worked.

A familiar voice cut through his brooding. "Why do you look so blasted miserable?"

Charles didn't bother to look up. "Go away, Wilton."

His friend ignored him and slid into the chair across from him. He placed his own glass on the table and studied Charles with an amused expression. "You aren't drunk, which means this is a matter of wounded pride or a woman."

"How perceptive of you," he muttered.

Wilton smirked. "How much time do you need to wallow before you tell me what has you so upset?"

Charles tightened his grip on his glass. "Miss Winslow tried to kiss me."

Wilton raised an eyebrow. "Did she, now?" He leaned back in his chair. "And what did you do?"

"What could I do? She took me by surprise," Charles said, frustration lacing his voice.

Wilton's smirk widened. "Well, that depends. Did anyone witness this improper little encounter?"

Charles's jaw clenched. "Lady Eugenie."

Wilton let out a low whistle. "Ah. That explains the sulking."

Charles shot him a glare.

Wilton leaned forward, resting his elbows on the table. "Do you think she'll betray your confidence?"

"No," Charles said without hesitation. "She won't say a word."

"Then why are you brooding like a lovesick fool?" Wilton asked, taking a sip of his drink. "You aren't being forced into marriage, are you?"

"No, but—"

"Then what's the problem?" Wilton pressed.

Charles frowned. "I feel as if I've betrayed Eugenie."

"Why would you think that—" Wilton suddenly paused, his sharp gaze narrowing. "Wait. Are you pursuing Lady Eugenie?"

"No," Charles replied swiftly.

Wilton's eyes bored into him, skepticism clear. "You're making little sense, Bedford. Why would you feel as if you had betrayed Lady Eugenie if you didn't have some affection for her?"

"It is complicated."

"Then *un*complicate it," Wilton stated.

Charles didn't respond. Instead, he lifted his glass and took another sip, hoping the conversation would end there. It didn't.

Wilton gave him a knowing look. "You do care for her, don't you?"

Charles didn't confirm or deny it. He merely stared into his drink as if it held the answers to all his troubles.

Wilton shook his head. "Well, then. That does explain a lot since your silence is damning."

Deciding it was time for a change of subject, Charles leaned forward. "Were you drinking alone before you so rudely interrupted my brooding?"

Wilton gave him a look that suggested he saw right through the diversion but, mercifully, did not push the matter. Instead, he exhaled heavily. "I needed a moment to think."

"Do you not live in one of the largest townhouses in Town?" Charles quipped. "Surely you could have found privacy there."

Wilton sighed again, this time more heavily. "It is my sister."

"Olivia?" Charles asked, already dreading the answer. "What has she done this time?"

Wilton leaned forward, lowering his voice. "She eloped to Gretna Green last night."

Charles was taken aback. "She what?"

His friend shrugged, as though utterly defeated. "She's five-and-twenty. She doesn't need my permission to marry anymore."

"You could have stopped the anvil priest from performing the wedding."

Wilton let out a humorless chuckle. "Impossible. We didn't discover her letter until the morning. She had more than enough of a head start on us." He took a long sip of his drink before muttering, "My mother is beside herself."

"With good reason."

Wilton rubbed a hand down his face. "The worst part? We don't even know who she married."

"She didn't say in her letter?"

Wilton's mouth twisted in frustration. "She married a Mr. Smith. Do you know how many Mr. Smiths reside in London alone?" He huffed. "I suspect he's merely a fortune hunter. Olivia has a dowry of twenty thousand pounds."

Charles winced. "That's... unfortunate."

Wilton took a long, slow drink. "The gossiping hens will be clucking about this soon enough."

"No doubt."

"I do not like how headstrong Olivia is," Wilton muttered, swirling the amber liquid in his glass before setting it down with a dull clink. "She has always been stubborn, but this? Rushing into a marriage with a man we know nothing about? She will come to regret it, I have no doubt."

"How could she not?" Charles replied. "She snuck off in the dead of night to marry a man she dared not even introduce to her family. That alone speaks volumes."

Wilton rubbed his temple. "Perhaps she might have come to her senses before reaching Gretna Green. Called off the wedding on her own."

"Do you truly believe that?"

"No," Wilton admitted. "But one can hope, can they not?"

A dry chuckle escaped Charles. "If we had any sense, we would have married her off to Philip. It would have been a far better alternative than this mysterious Mr. Smith."

Wilton scoffed. "Philip and Olivia? That would have been a disaster. Can you imagine the arguments? They would have killed each other within a fortnight." He paused, then added, "Besides, I hear Philip has gotten himself into trouble yet again."

Charles looked heavenward. "He has," he confirmed. "He got a young woman pregnant and now has been challenged to a duel."

"That sounds about right. What are you going to do?"

"What can I do?" Charles asked. "If Philip is foolish enough to go through with this duel, then he deserves whatever comes of it."

Before Wilton could respond, a server approached their table, inclining his head politely. "May I get anyone another drink?"

Charles shoved his chair back, rising to his feet. "Not for me," he replied. "I should be going."

Wilton followed suit, stretching slightly as he stood. "I'll walk you out."

They made their way through the dimly lit hall, the low murmur of conversation and clinking glasses filling the air.

Once they stepped onto the pavement, the cool night air offering some reprieve from the stifling warmth of White's, Charles turned to his friend. "I would have gone with you to Gretna Green had you asked."

Wilton placed a hand on Charles's shoulder. "I know," he said simply. "That is why I tolerate you."

Charles's gaze flickered towards the row of waiting coaches lined along the street and he failed to spot Wilton's crest among them. "Where is your coach?"

"I sent it home," Wilton replied. "I figured a walk might do me some good."

"At this hour?" Charles asked.

Wilton merely smiled, his expression shadowed under the flickering glow of a street lamp. "I do not live too far off. Besides, I would welcome a fight from any miscreant foolish enough to try me this evening."

"Ever since you took up boxing, you've become insufferably cocky."

Wilton grinned. "You should join me in the morning. It might do you some good."

"I will pass, but thank you for the offer," Charles replied, stepping towards his own waiting carriage. "Are you sure you do not want a ride home?"

"I am." Wilton turned to leave, but something in the way he carried himself—his usual confidence undercut by a weariness that Charles rarely saw—compelled him to say one more thing.

"What Olivia did is not your fault."

Slowly, Wilton turned back around. "Then whose fault is it?" he demanded. "I have been so consumed with managing my estate, ensuring my tenants are provided for, my household is in order... that I failed to notice what was happening under my own roof. My own sister—" He exhaled sharply, shaking his head. "I should have seen it coming."

"If that is true, then I am just as guilty with Philip."

Wilton looked away, his gaze fixed on the darkened streets beyond. When he spoke again, his voice was quieter, heavier. "I never wanted this life, you know."

Charles didn't need to ask what he meant.

Wilton continued, his tone laced with resentment. "The responsibilities that come with being the Marquess of Wilton are staggering. Sometimes, it feels as if I am drowning under the weight of it all. Like no matter how hard I try, I will never be enough."

Charles understood that sentiment far too well. "Some would say we are ungrateful for not being content with our lot in life," he murmured.

"Perhaps we are. We both inherited our titles far too young."

"That we did."

For a moment, silence stretched between them, the city's distant noises the only sounds filling the space. Then Wilton exhaled, shoving his hands into his pockets as he took a step back.

"Well," he said, his usual lightness returning, though it didn't quite reach his eyes, "if you ever feel the need to hit something—or someone—meet me at the boxing ring tomorrow morning."

"As tempting as it is to hit you, I am otherwise occupied. I am calling upon Lady Eugenie."

Wilton studied him for a moment before his lips curled into a smile. "Now that," he mused, "will be far more interesting than a round in the ring."

Charles said nothing, merely stepping up into his coach. But as the carriage rolled away, he couldn't help but wonder if Wilton was right.

10

The following morning, Eugenie descended the grand staircase of her townhouse. Sunlight streamed in through the tall windows of the entry hall, illuminating the polished marble floors. She tipped her head at the butler, who stood at his usual post, ever composed.

"Good morning," she greeted.

"Good morning, my lady," Tanner responded with a slight bow. Then with a gesture towards a small side table near the entrance, he added, "A delivery arrived for you just moments ago."

Eugenie's gaze followed his gesture, landing on a magnificent bouquet of fresh flowers. It was customary for gentlemen to send flowers after a dance, but somehow, the sight of them still sent a flicker of excitement through her.

Stepping forward, she plucked the small ivory card nestled between the stems. With a growing sense of anticipation, she unfolded it and read the elegantly scrawled words:

. . .

THESE FLOWERS pale in comparison to your beauty...

EUGENIE BARELY STIFLED AN EYE ROLL. Was that truly the best line Charles could come up with? Dropping the card onto the table without bothering to read the rest, she turned on her heel and made her way towards the dining room.

As she walked, she couldn't shake the unsettled feeling that had been clinging to her since last night. It wasn't anger— not exactly. She had believed Charles when he assured her that nothing had happened with Miss Winslow, and yet... something still pricked at her, something she could not quite define.

Jealousy?

She scoffed at the ridiculousness of the thought. She had no claim over Charles, nor did she wish to. So why did the memory of Miss Winslow pressed against him still linger in the back of her mind?

Shaking the thought away, she entered the dining room.

Her brother was seated at the head of the long mahogany table, the newssheets spread open before him. The aroma of fresh bread, eggs, and chocolate filled the air, but he appeared far too engrossed in his reading to pay it any mind.

At the sound of her approaching footsteps, Niles looked up. His expression was unusually serious for such an early hour. "Good," he said, setting down the newssheets. "You're here."

Eugenie slid into her seat across from him, her brow furrowing. "Is something amiss?"

Without a word, Niles folded the newssheets and handed it to her. "Would you care to explain this?"

She accepted it, her gaze scanning the pages. "What am I supposed to be looking at?"

"The Society section," Niles said grimly. "Particularly the article titled *A Spinster's Guide to Scandal*."

Eugenie's breath caught. "They published it?" she whispered, barely believing her own words.

Niles leaned forward, his expression a mixture of exasperation and concern. "Apparently so," he replied. "Do you have any idea what could happen if someone were to discover that you wrote that article? Eugenie, you could be ruined."

She waved a dismissive hand, excitement still bubbling inside her. "I wrote it under a pseudonym." Her eyes skimmed over the article, her own words staring back at her in bold print. Pride swelled in her chest. She had done it!

But Niles was not sharing in her triumph. His expression remained uncertain as he lowered his voice. "You know how the servants like to gossip."

Eugenie gently set the newssheets on the table and met her brother's gaze with measured calm. "I will be careful," she said. "I am not reckless."

"Careful?" Niles scoffed. "You intend to continue writing, then?"

"Yes, for as long as they continue publishing my work."

Niles frowned, clearly displeased. "I do not think that is wise."

Eugenie knew that she needed to choose her next words carefully. "This is something I need to do."

Her brother studied her, his fingers drumming against the table's surface.

"You have never understood," she continued, her voice gaining quiet strength. "You are free to do as you please. To manage your estates, to make decisions that impact your future. But women? We are expected to do nothing but sit in drawing rooms and receive guests. Our lives are dictated by Society's rules. I refuse to accept that as my only fate."

Niles sighed heavily. "Women who defy convention are not looked kindly upon," he warned. "You might be opening Pandora's box with this article."

Eugenie held his gaze, unwavering. "Or perhaps," she countered, "I am opening a door to something wonderful."

Leaning back in his chair, Niles said, "I daresay you have been reading too many fairy tales," he muttered. "Not everyone gets a happy ending."

She smiled faintly, lifting her cup of chocolate to her lips. "No," she agreed. "But some of us are determined to try."

Before Niles could respond, Elsbeth stepped gracefully into the dining room, drawing their attention as she offered an apologetic smile. "I do hope I haven't kept you waiting. I apologize for being late to breakfast," she said as she approached the table.

Niles rose from his chair and pulled out a seat for her. "Nonsense, my love biscuit. You are right on time."

Eugenie wrinkled her nose. "Must you call her that?"

Niles smirked. "And miss the opportunity to see your reaction? Perish the thought."

Turning to Elsbeth with a raised brow, Eugenie asked, "Surely you do not enjoy being referred to as a 'love biscuit'?"

Elsbeth cast a sidelong glance at her husband. "I think it's rather sweet," she admitted with a soft smile.

Eugenie huffed and turned her attention to the plate of food that had just been placed in front of her. "You two are hopeless."

Elsbeth laughed as she lifted her fork. "Oh, that reminds me—will you be joining my sewing circle today?"

"Yes," Eugenie replied. "I find that I am actually looking forward to it."

"Wonderful. We have made great progress already, donating dozens of frocks to the young girls at the workhouse," Elsbeth shared. "But there is still much more to be done."

Curious, Eugenie studied her sister-in-law. "Were you close with Lady Jane before she gave you the cut direct?"

Elsbeth's smile faltered slightly. "We were as thick as thieves growing up. Our parents often attended the same house parties, and Jane and I would sneak into the ballroom, hiding under the tables so we could watch the dancing." A wistful look crossed her face. "We used to whisper about the gowns, the music, the couples waltzing across the floor, and we would pretend that one day, we, too, would be the belles of the ball."

"You never got caught?" Eugenie asked.

With an amused look, Elsbeth replied, "Oh, we got caught every time. Our nursemaids always managed to find us, giggling beneath the tablecloths."

Niles, who had been quietly listening, smiled fondly at his wife. "I can picture that perfectly."

Eugenie regarded Elsbeth with quiet sympathy. "It must have hurt when she turned her back on you."

Elsbeth's smile disappeared completely. "It did," she said. "When the scandal about my father broke, all my friends abandoned me. Every single one." Her voice softened, thick with the weight of old wounds. "It was a very lonely time."

Niles reached for her hand and gave it a reassuring squeeze. "Now the *ton* adores you again."

Elsbeth's lips curved into a wry smile. "I wouldn't say they adore me. They merely tolerate me because of the man I married."

Eugenie fell silent, stabbing absently at her breakfast. She had always admired Elsbeth's quiet resilience, but hearing the lingering pain in her voice made her chest tighten. The *ton* was a fickle beast, cruel and unforgiving when it chose to be.

Deciding to shift the subject, she reached for the newssheets, intending to peruse the Society pages as she sipped her chocolate. But the moment her eyes landed on a particular line, she gasped aloud.

Niles immediately looked up. "What is it?"

Eugenie didn't lift her gaze from the newssheets. "An article mentions me."

She finally looked up in time to catch Elsbeth exchanging a knowing glance with Niles before saying, "It is common for the Society pages to list whom a lady danced with at a ball."

Eugenie shook her head, her grip tightening on the newssheets. "No. That is not it." She inhaled deeply before reading aloud, "*Lady Eugenie was heard giggling on a path before reappearing on the veranda, with Lord Bedford following closely behind.*"

Elsbeth pressed her lips together. "Did that happen?"

"Yes... no..." Eugenie stumbled over her words before collecting her thoughts. "Last night, while you two were dancing, I heard giggling near the side of the townhouse. I went to investigate and found Miss Winslow..." she hesitated, glancing at Niles, "... pressed up against Lord Bedford."

Her brother's face held disapproval. "That was foolish of you. You should never have left the veranda."

"Well, I *did,* and there is no use arguing over it now," Eugenie responded. "When Lord Bedford saw me, he followed me back to the veranda and explained that Miss Winslow had tried to kiss him."

Niles crossed his arms. "And you believed him?"

Eugenie met his gaze without hesitation. "I did."

"Did the article say anything else about you?" Elsbeth asked.

"No," Eugenie admitted with a sigh. "But that was enough, was it not?"

Niles shoved back his chair, rising from his seat. He strode towards the window, peering out with an expression of deep contemplation. "I warned you, Eugenie. Your actions have consequences. And now, your name has been dragged into a scandal."

Eugenie gritted her teeth, knowing he was right, even if she loathed admitting it. "What am I to do?"

Elsbeth offered her a weak but reassuring smile. "We will weather this storm together," she said encouragingly. But then, after a brief pause, she added, "However... this does not bode well for you."

Eugenie's stomach twisted uncomfortably. "Am I ruined? Over a single article?"

Niles and Elsbeth exchanged a meaningful look, silent words passing between them. It was Elsbeth who finally spoke. "I can't say for certain—not yet."

Eugenie set the newssheets down with an unsteady hand. She had always understood the risks of defying Society's expectations, of daring to step outside the carefully constructed role set before her. But she had never truly feared the consequences.

Until now.

She had done nothing wrong. And yet, her reputation hung by a thread.

How was that fair?

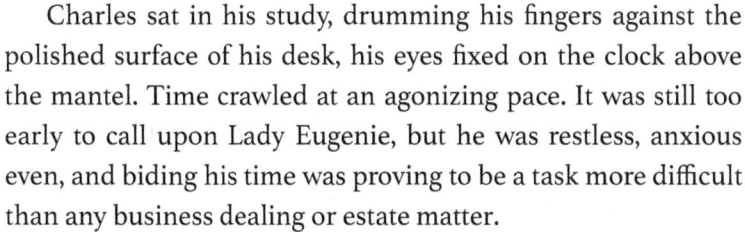

Charles sat in his study, drumming his fingers against the polished surface of his desk, his eyes fixed on the clock above the mantel. Time crawled at an agonizing pace. It was still too early to call upon Lady Eugenie, but he was restless, anxious even, and biding his time was proving to be a task more difficult than any business dealing or estate matter.

She had told him she believed him, yet something in her expression last night suggested it wasn't so simple. He needed to see her—to make sure she was truly all right.

But was that the only reason?

Somewhere along the way, without realizing it, he had developed feelings for Eugenie. Feelings that could no longer be brushed aside as mere fondness or friendship. He recognized that now.

And it was a problem.

Because Eugenie had made it clear, time and time again, that she was perfectly content remaining a spinster.

Would she welcome his pursuit? Or would she scoff at the idea, reminding him—yet again—that she had no interest in marriage?

The thought unsettled him more than he cared to admit.

His musings were interrupted when the door to his study swung open. His mother strode in, her usual composed demeanor offset by the firm grip she had on the newssheets in her hand. "Have you read this?" she demanded.

Charles sighed and closed the ledger in front of him, leaning back in his chair. "I have not yet taken my breakfast, much less read *The Morning Post*."

"Well, perhaps you should," she said, marching towards his desk and placing the newssheets before him with a pointed look. "You are mentioned in it."

Charles sat up straighter. A cold sense of dread settled in his gut. Had someone seen him with Miss Winslow in the gardens? His fingers tightened around the edges of the newssheets as he swiftly scanned the columns. His eyes landed on a particular passage, and his breath stilled.

Lady Eugenie. His name. An implication that they had shared a moment of... indiscretion.

It wasn't entirely untrue. But the way it was written— suggestive, salacious—painted an image of a romantic tryst. It didn't state outright that they had been alone together in the gardens, but the insinuation was clear.

His jaw clenched as he crushed the newssheets in his hands.

His mother folded her arms, her sharp eyes assessing him. "Well? Do you care to explain yourself?"

"No," he muttered, pressing his palm against his temple. "But I assure you, Eugenie is innocent in all of this."

His mother arched a brow. "The article suggests otherwise. It says you were seen together before reappearing on the veranda."

"Then the article is misleading," Charles snapped. "Lady Eugenie was not alone with me in the gardens. She happened upon Miss Winslow... attempting to kiss me."

His mother's expression did not soften. "So you were alone with Miss Winslow?"

"For a matter of moments," he admitted. "I took her outside for some air, thinking it might sober her up. Clearly, she mistook my intentions. But Eugenie—she merely stumbled upon the situation. She fled before I could explain, and I followed her to set the record straight."

His mother shook her head. "Well, that is not what was reported. And now Lady Eugenie finds herself ensnared in scandal."

Charles clenched his jaw. He should have been more careful. Should have known that even the hint of impropriety could be twisted into a full-blown scandal in a single day. He set the crumpled newssheets aside, inhaling deeply before declaring, "I will make this right. I will marry her."

His mother's posture shifted slightly, surprise flickering in her eyes. Slowly, she lowered herself onto the chair opposite his desk. "Do you even want to marry her?"

Charles met her gaze without hesitation. "I am not entirely opposed to it."

"*Not entirely opposed?*" she huffed.

He nodded. "Yes. And I hold Lady Eugenie in high regard. I believe a marriage between us would be... mutually beneficial."

His mother pursed her lips. "You are being quite practical about this, Charles. But love is anything but practical."

He lifted a hand. "I said nothing about love."

"No, you did not." His mother's voice took on a dry, knowing tone. "Lady Eugenie is a lucky lady, then."

Charles ignored her sarcasm.

She tilted her head, studying him as only a mother could. "Are you only offering for her to save her reputation?"

His mouth opened to reply, but the words didn't come immediately. Was he? It was a matter of honor—of course it was. But the moment he had told his mother of his intentions, the decision had settled deep within him, with a certainty he had not expected. A marriage between him and Eugenie would be more than a matter of honor. That much was sure.

His mother observed his silence and continued. "And do you believe Lady Eugenie will simply agree to this marriage of convenience?"

Charles hesitated. "I hope so," he admitted.

His mother rose from her chair with a sigh. "By all means, go and try to convince her. But I would be mindful to avoid insulting the poor girl."

Charles frowned. "How would I insult her?"

She gave him a pointed look. "I will let you determine that, Son."

Before he could respond, a knock came at the door, and Hagen entered. He inclined his head politely before speaking.

"I apologize for the interruption, my lord, but a Mr. Barton has requested a moment of your time," Hagen announced.

"Do I know a Mr. Barton? The name means nothing to me."

"He said he was a friend of Mr. Philip Ellsworth, my lord," Hagen responded.

His mother let out an exasperated sigh. "Good heavens. What sort of mess has Philip landed in this time?"

"Ah. That explains something, though not nearly enough,"

Charles said, addressing the butler. "Very well—send him in. I won't know what this is about until I've spoken with Mr. Barton... in private, if you don't mind."

"Of course, my lord." Hagen gave a small bow and withdrew.

His mother, already heading towards the door, paused only long enough to cast him a look of amusement. "I can take the hint. But I wish you luck with Lady Eugenie this morning. I fear that you need it."

"I do not need luck."

His mother merely sighed. "Now I am even more worried."

And with that unhelpful parting remark, she swept from the room, leaving Charles with far too much to consider.

A moment later, a short young man with rounded spectacles stepped into the room, his expression grim. "Thank you for agreeing to see me, my lord," he said with a polite bow.

Not bothering with pleasantries, Charles remarked, "I understand you are a friend of Philip's."

"I am. My name is Edward Barton, and I come bearing troubling news."

"I can only imagine."

"Philip refuses to apologize to Mr. Kingston," Mr. Barton continued, his tone serious. "Not that it would help the situation at this point. Kingston is out for blood—Philip's blood, to be exact."

Charles groaned. "My cousin is an idiot."

"That he is," Mr. Barton agreed as he stepped closer to the desk, lowering his voice. "Philip asked me to be his second. I have done everything in my power to mediate the situation, but Mr. Kingston will not be swayed. I fear he is not simply demanding an apology—he wants retribution."

"How do we know for certain? It is not uncommon for men of honor to fire into the sky, proving their point without spilling blood."

"Mr. Kingston has made it clear that this duel will not end until one of them is dead," Mr. Barton shared.

Charles sat upright, his brows shooting up in shock. "That is highly irregular. A duel is usually fought until first blood or until one of the participants is unable to continue."

Mr. Barton bobbed his head. "Kingston believes his family's honor has been grievously damaged. He refuses to accept anything short of Philip's death."

"Where and when is this duel set to take place?"

"At St. James' Park, before dawn, in four days' time."

Charles swore under his breath. "How did Philip react to this?"

"Delighted," Mr. Barton admitted with a wince. "He sees himself as a fine shot and is utterly convinced he will win. He isn't worried about the potential consequences—not to himself, nor to the reputation of your family. That is why I came to you. I was hoping you might talk some sense into him."

Charles rubbed a hand over his face, frustration simmering beneath his skin. "Believe me, I have tried. But I cannot simply stand by and do nothing while Philip marches to his death."

Mr. Barton met his gaze, sincerity etched into his features. "Philip is stubborn to a fault, but he does not deserve to die."

Charles pushed back from his desk, rising to his feet. "I will seek out Mr. Kingston after I tend to another pressing matter. In the meantime, keep me informed."

"As you wish, my lord."

As Mr. Barton turned to leave, Charles called after him, "Keep this matter discreet. I do not want the *ton* catching wind of it and turning the duel into a spectacle."

Mr. Barton paused at the door and inclined his head in acknowledgment. "You need not fear on that account. I understand the importance of discretion."

With that, Mr. Barton departed, and Charles dropped back onto his chair. Philip. His blasted cousin. Did the fool not care about anything beyond his own reckless impulses? How could he be so careless? So completely oblivious to the damage he was causing? He only hoped he had enough time to fix this before it was too late.

The door creaked open again, and this time, his mother stepped inside. "I couldn't help but overhear."

Charles arched a brow. "Are you in the habit of eavesdropping now, Mother?"

Ignoring his question, she asked one of her own. "Do you think speaking to Mr. Kingston will solve anything?"

He shrugged. "It is worth a try, is it not?"

Her lips pressed into a thin line. He could see the worry in her eyes and how she wrung her hands together as though trying to contain her rising anxiety. And he did not fault her for it. Philip was young, but surely, he understood the gravity of the situation.

"You are right," she conceded after a moment. "I only hope Mr. Kingston is feeling reasonable today."

Charles let out a humorless laugh. "Philip took liberties with his sister. If I were Mr. Kingston, I doubt I would be reasonable either."

His mother paled slightly, her hands twisting together more tightly. "I have seen Philip shoot," she murmured. "He is... not proficient."

That much was true.

Charles came around his desk, stopping in front of her. "Try not to worry. I will take care of this."

"And if you can't?"

Charles forced a confident smile. "Then I will pay Mr. Kingston off."

"With what money?"

He placed a reassuring hand on her arm. "I will sell some land if I must. There is always a way," he said. "Now, if you will excuse me, it is time I call upon Lady Eugenie."

"Ah, yes. Your grand plan to offer for Lady Eugenie."

Charles straightened his cuffs, preparing himself for the morning ahead. "Not offer—convince," he corrected. "There is a difference."

"Of course there is," his mother remarked. "But I would prefer a daughter-in-law who wasn't coerced into marriage."

And with that, Charles strode from the room, determined to mend one disaster before another had the chance to unfold.

11

E ugenie pulled the needle from the fabric with more force than necessary, her stitches uneven and haphazard as her mind drifted elsewhere. Around her, the soft hum of conversation filled the drawing room, but she paid little attention to it. Elsbeth was speaking to Phoebe, their voices lilting in pleasant discussion, but Eugenie wasn't in the mood for idle chatter.

Her thoughts remained fixated on the article in *The Morning Post*—the blatant falsehoods printed about her. She still couldn't fathom how someone had the audacity to suggest she had been alone with Charles in the gardens, much less giggling.

Who had written such an outrageous piece? She would find out. And once she did, she would demand a retraction. Would that even help, though? Once a rumor had taken hold, it was nearly impossible to dislodge.

Sometimes, it was truly wretched to be a lady.

The sharp sound of Elsbeth's voice broke through her musings. "Careful with the fabric, Eugenie," she advised.

Eugenie blinked, snapping back to the present. "Pardon?"

"You are attacking that poor cloth rather viciously," Elsbeth teased, her eyes twinkling with amusement. "If you're not careful, you'll either tear the fabric or prick yourself. Neither would be ideal."

Glancing down at the embroidery in her lap, Eugenie set it aside. "My apologies. I was woolgathering."

"No harm done," Elsbeth said with a small smile, returning to her own work.

Phoebe, who had been quietly stitching beside them, glanced up. "Dare I ask what has you so preoccupied?"

Eugenie let out an exasperated sigh. "I cannot stop thinking about that dreadful article in the newssheets. It was utterly unfair."

"Yes, it was," Phoebe agreed, frowning. "Unfair and insufferably nosy. But that is the nature of the Society pages."

Elsbeth placed her embroidery down and reached for the teapot. "What you need is a cup of tea," she said. "It will help calm your nerves."

"I need something stronger. Brandy, perhaps," Eugenie said, half-joking.

Elsbeth gave her a disapproving shake of her head. "A lady does not drink brandy."

Before Eugenie could argue the merits of her preferred solution, Tanner stepped into the room and met Elsbeth's gaze. "Lady Jane has arrived, my lady."

Elsbeth brightened. "Send her in."

A moment later, Lady Jane entered, her expression tight with concern. Her sharp gaze swept the room before landing on Eugenie. "How are you faring?" she asked, moving towards the settee where she sat.

"Terribly," Eugenie admitted.

Lady Jane hesitated before lowering herself onto the seat

beside her. "My father and brother would kill me if they discovered I was here, but I couldn't stay away."

Eugenie straightened slightly, a new thought forming. "Could you ask your uncle who wrote that article in *The Morning Post*?"

Lady Jane made a thoughtful noise. "I can try," she said, though her expression was doubtful. "But he is rather tight-lipped about his contributors."

"Please, Jane," Eugenie pressed. "I need to know who wrote it."

Lady Jane's frown deepened. "May I ask why?"

Eugenie sighed, her hands twisting in her lap. "Because the writer claimed I was alone with Lord Bedford, but I was not." She paused, unwilling to betray Charles's confidence, but knowing she needed to offer some sort of explanation. "I... I caught him in a compromising position with someone else."

Lady Jane's brows shot up, intrigue sparking in her eyes. "Compromising?"

Eugenie nodded her head quickly. "Yes, but it was all a misunderstanding. The point is, when Lord Bedford realized I had seen him, he followed me and explained to me what truly happened. That is all. But now the *ton* believes something far worse."

Lady Jane sighed. "Regardless of what truly happened, the *ton* believes you were alone with him. What are you going to do?"

Eugenie spread her hands helplessly. "What can I do?"

As if conjured by their very discussion, Charles entered the room, his blue eyes locking on Eugenie the moment he stepped inside.

Elsbeth looked up. "Cousin! What brings you by?"

Charles barely acknowledged her, his attention solely fixed on Eugenie. "I was hoping to speak with Lady Eugenie. *Privately,* if you don't mind."

Eugenie stiffened. "I do not believe there is anything we need to say to one another."

"I disagree." His voice was calm, but there was an edge to it —an unspoken plea. "Perhaps we might take a walk in your gardens?"

"No, I do not think that is wise," she replied.

Charles took another step closer. "Please, Eugenie. Just a moment of your time."

There it was again—the quiet urgency in his voice, the sincerity in his expression. It was that which made her heart lurch in an altogether inconvenient way.

"Very well," Eugenie responded. "I suppose I have a moment or two."

Something in Charles's posture relaxed ever so slightly. "Thank you," he said, stepping forward and offering his arm.

With a steadying breath, Eugenie placed her hand upon his offered arm, acutely aware of the warmth seeping through the fine fabric of his coat. She did not want to feel anything for this man—*should not* feel anything. And yet, heaven help her, she did.

They moved in silence towards the rear of the townhouse, their steps synchronized, though neither spoke. The footman stationed at the door gave a small bow before pulling it open, allowing them passage into the gardens.

Once they stepped onto the gravel path, Eugenie slipped her hand from his arm, clasping her hands together at her waist. She wasn't quite sure what to say—whether she should address the glaring reason for his visit or pretend, for just a moment longer, that she wasn't caught in the center of a scandal.

But Charles, it seemed, had no intention of pretending. "How are you faring, Eugenie?"

"I am well," she answered.

Charles didn't look convinced. His blue eyes studied her with unnerving scrutiny before he gestured towards a wrought-iron bench just off the path. "Would you care to sit for a moment?"

Eugenie went and lowered herself onto the bench, smoothing down the fabric of her pale green gown.

Charles took his seat beside her and turned slightly, his gaze unwavering. "We should get married."

Eugenie stared back at him, certain she had misheard. "I beg your pardon?"

Charles leaned forward, his voice steady. "It only makes sense. It is because of me that your name has been dragged into this mess. The only way to repair the damage is for me to offer for you."

Eugenie shot to her feet. "Have you lost your senses?"

Charles stood as well. "I know that, in time, you will see that this is the only logical solution."

She let out a sharp laugh, though there was no humor in it. "Logical? Charles, do you even want to marry me?"

He hesitated. It was just for a fraction of a second, but it was enough. "Of course, I do," he rushed out. "We get along well enough..."

"That is not an answer," she snapped, her hands curling into fists at her sides.

"My answer is yes," he amended quickly. "I do want to marry you."

Eugenie studied him, searching for sincerity beyond his frustrating sense of duty. "Because it is the honorable thing to do?"

He inclined his head. "It is the honorable thing to do. But I would also be a good husband to you." He took a measured breath, his voice turning softer. "If you are in agreement, I will have my solicitor draw up the marriage contract."

"I am not in agreement."

Charles exhaled sharply. "Eugenie—"

She took a step back, shaking her head. "I will not be forced into a marriage of convenience."

He frowned. "This is not forced—"

"Oh, it most certainly is," she interrupted. "You are asking me to wed you not out of affection or desire, but because you believe it is your duty. Well, I do not require a husband bound to me by duty alone."

Charles took a step closer, his gaze intense. "This is the only way. You will see that soon enough."

Eugenie lifted her chin. "I would rather be a spinster than enter a marriage where I am nothing more than an obligation."

"Be reasonable, Eugenie."

She huffed. "Me, reasonable? You come here, announce that we must marry, and expect me to accept it without question. And I suspect that you do not want this marriage any more than I do."

Charles ran a frustrated hand through his dark hair. "I am not entirely opposed to it."

"That is not the declaration of a man eager to wed."

"We are friends, are we not?" he pressed.

With a bob of her head, she replied, "And for the sake of our friendship, I propose we pretend this conversation never happened."

His jaw tightened. "But it did happen."

Eugenie rolled her eyes. "Try a little harder not to be a muttonhead."

"I am a muttonhead now?" he asked, his voice rising.

She crossed her arms over her chest. "If you think I will quietly accept this ridiculous proposal, then yes, you are a muttonhead."

"I know you think you want to be a spinster," he started,

"but it is a lonely life. I am offering you companionship. A chance to have a family."

Eugenie held her ground. "At what cost?" she asked. "What if we marry and discover we do not suit? What then? Would we grow to resent one another?"

His gaze softened slightly. "I could never resent you."

The vulnerability in his words caused her breath to hitch, but she forced herself to push past the momentary weakness. "You say that now, but do you not wish to marry for love?"

"Love?" Charles repeated. "I am far too pragmatic for such notions. I have always known I would need to marry a young woman with a hefty dowry."

"So I fit the bill?"

He leaned in slightly, his expression almost pleading. "I know I have bungled this proposal. But we would be good together, Eugenie. You know that."

Eugenie swallowed against the lump in her throat and placed her palm against his chest. "I am not afraid of being alone, Charles," she whispered.

And then she stepped back, severing the connection.

The space between them suddenly felt vast.

Charles opened his mouth, as if to say something—perhaps to argue, perhaps to plead. But no words came.

Eugenie offered him a small, sad smile before turning away, walking back towards the townhouse with slow, deliberate steps.

He did not stop her.

And that, she supposed, was answer enough.

———————◦———————

Charles had botched the proposal to Eugenie. He had spent the ride over to her townhouse preparing, crafting the perfect words, rehearsing the logical case for marriage, ensuring he had an argument so sound she could not refuse. However, the moment he had looked at her, his carefully prepared speech had vanished. Instead, he had blurted out that they should get married.

Like a muttonhead.

How could he have been so foolish? He knew Eugenie well enough to anticipate her reaction. Knew she valued her independence too much to simply accept marriage as a matter of duty. But Charles wasn't about to give up. This was a matter of honor. He would convince her.

But not today.

He had another pressing matter to deal with—one that, if handled poorly, could cost his cousin his life.

As the coach rattled to a stop in front of a narrow brick building in Bloomsbury Square, Charles forced thoughts of Eugenie aside. He straightened his coat, mentally preparing himself for the meeting ahead. Philip's recklessness had landed them all in a dangerous predicament, and now it fell upon Charles to undo the damage.

The footman opened the carriage door, and Charles stepped onto the pavement. The street was bustling with vendors calling out their wares, apprentices hurrying to their shops, and the ever-present scent of city life lingering in the air.

He approached the door of the modest townhouse and knocked firmly.

A long moment passed before it creaked open, revealing a middle-aged woman with a streak of white in her dark hair. She wore a clean, though well-worn, apron and eyed him with mild suspicion. "May I help you?"

Charles inclined his head. "I would like to speak with Mr. Kingston."

The woman's brows lifted. "And who may I say is calling?"

"Lord Bedford."

Her eyes widened slightly. "Do come in, my lord," she said quickly, stepping aside. "There's no need for you to be standing about in the street."

Charles entered the narrow entry hall, his gaze sweeping over the modest interior. The home bore the marks of genteel poverty—the furnishings were clean but threadbare, the paint along the walls flaking, the floorboards worn from years of foot traffic. It was evident that Mr. Kingston had fallen on hard times.

"Wait here," the woman instructed before disappearing down the corridor.

Charles clasped his hands behind his back, his mind already racing through the arguments he would present to Mr. Kingston.

Moments later, the woman reappeared. "Mr. Kingston and Miss Kingston will see you, my lord."

She led him into a small sitting room, where a man of average height, with slicked black hair and a rigid posture, stood beside a young woman. She was petite, clutching a piece of fabric in her hands as though it were a lifeline.

Mr. Kingston met his gaze with barely concealed hostility. "I am not surprised you have come, my lord," he said gruffly. "But you needn't have troubled yourself. This matter is between Mr. Ellsworth and me."

"I'm afraid it is far more complicated than that. Philip is my heir. I cannot simply stand by and allow him to participate in this duel," Charles responded.

"You have little choice," Mr. Kingston countered. "Mr. Ellsworth has already accepted my challenge."

"What is it you hope to achieve with this duel?"

Mr. Kingston's chest puffed slightly. "Mr. Ellsworth wronged my sister, and he shall pay for what he has done."

"With his life?"

Mr. Kingston did not flinch. "So be it. Mr. Ellsworth has stolen my sister's future."

Charles turned his gaze fully on Miss Kingston. She was far too young to be shouldering the weight of a ruined reputation.

He met Mr. Kingston's gaze once more. "And are you prepared to die, leaving your sister truly unprotected?"

Mr. Kingston scoffed. "I am an excellent shot. I am not worried."

Charles decided to test him. He let out a knowing hum and folded his arms. "I am not sure what you have heard, but Philip is an expert marksman." A complete fabrication, but Mr. Kingston didn't need to know that. "Why do you think he didn't hesitate to accept your challenge?"

Mr. Kingston's shoulders stiffened ever so slightly. "I hadn't realized," he admitted. "But it makes little difference now."

Charles saw an opening. "Call off the duel, and I will ensure that Philip does right by your sister."

Mr. Kingston's eyes narrowed. "This would all go away if he agreed to marry her. But Mr. Ellsworth refuses."

"Philip is only eighteen years old."

With a slight gesture towards his sister, Mr. Kingston countered, "And Ruth is only seventeen. They are young, yes, but they can grow together. It would be an advantageous marriage for Ruth, which is only fair, given the circumstances."

Charles studied Mr. Kingston closely. He believed this was the right solution. In his eyes, securing a marriage for his sister was the only way to salvage her future. But Philip was young. Selfish. He would never be an attentive husband, and Miss Kingston would suffer for it.

"I know you want what is best for your sister," Charles said carefully. "But marrying Philip is not it. He is reckless and careless. I worry he would not treat her kindly."

"But she would have the protection of his name," Mr. Kingston argued.

Charles turned to Miss Kingston. "Is that what you want?"

Miss Kingston's lips pressed into a thin line. "It is what I deserve."

Charles resisted the urge to sigh. The girl had resigned herself to this marriage, believing it the only path to security. But she had no idea what a disaster it would be.

Mr. Kingston squared his shoulders. "Is there anything else, my lord?"

Charles was running out of options. He grasped at straws. "What if I ensured that Philip acknowledged the child and provided for it?"

Mr. Kingston's expression hardened. "That is not good enough. My sister would still be ruined, left to raise a child alone."

"I understand that," Charles said, his patience wearing thin. "But surely you must see—"

"No, it is you who must see," Mr. Kingston cut him off. "Mr. Ellsworth made his bed, and now he must lie in it. If he does not agree to marry my sister, I will not call off the duel."

"That is incredibly foolish."

Mr. Kingston's lips curled in a humorless smile. "Duly noted, my lord. But you are wasting your breath. If you want someone to do the right thing, I suggest you speak with your cousin."

It was painfully evident that Mr. Kingston would not be swayed. This meeting had been a colossal waste of time. "Good day, Mr. Kingston. Miss Kingston."

Charles strode from the townhouse, his irritation mounting with every step. Once inside his coach, he let out a heavy sigh. There was only one person left to deal with now. Philip. The only person who could stop this. And yet, Charles had a sinking feeling that Philip would rather die than marry Miss Kingston.

A short time later, Charles's coach came to a halt in front

of Philip's townhouse, a modest yet respectable residence nestled within a quieter street of Mayfair. He barely waited for the footman to open the door before stepping out, his boots striking against the cobbled pavement with determined force.

Without hesitation, he strode up the front steps and knocked briskly. The door swung open, revealing Warnick, the household's long-suffering butler.

"Good morning, my lord," Warnick said, bowing slightly as he opened the door wider, granting him entry.

Charles wasted no time. "Is Mr. Ellsworth home?"

"He is, but he is still sleeping, my lord."

Charles's jaw clenched. It was nearly midday, and the fool was still in bed. "Wake him up," he ordered curtly. "Inform him that I must speak to him at once."

Warnick dipped his head in acknowledgment before disappearing down the corridor.

Before Charles could take another step, a familiar voice called out from the drawing room.

"Is this about the duel?"

Charles turned to see his Aunt Phoebe. Worry lined her face, and her hands twisted anxiously together as she studied him.

"It is," he confirmed. "I have come to talk him out of it."

"I doubt you will be successful. It is all Philip has spoken about these past couple of days, and I fear no amount of pleading will sway him."

"That seems to be a common theme with Philip," Charles muttered.

His aunt's face fell. "What are we to do?" she whispered, the fear in her voice evident.

Before he could respond, a drawling voice echoed from the staircase above. "Ah, the high and mighty Lord Bedford has descended from on high to grace our humble home."

Charles gritted his teeth before turning towards the source of the voice.

Philip stood at the top of the narrow stairs, his shirt untucked, and his dark hair mussed from sleep. "What is it this time?" he asked as he began descending the stairs, moving with the infuriating ease of a man who had not a single care in the world.

Rather than dignify Philip's mockery with a response, Charles said simply, "I have just come from Mr. Kingston's home."

Philip paused on the last step, brows lifting slightly. "Whyever would you do that?"

Charles held his cousin's gaze. "I was hoping to reach a resolution before you get yourself killed."

"Mr. Kingston won't kill me," Philip said confidently, a smirk playing on his lips. "He wants me to marry his sister, not put me in a coffin."

"You might be underestimating just how much Mr. Kingston despises you."

Philip's smirk only widened. "I promise you, Charles, I am not in any danger. Mr. Kingston may be angry, but he isn't a murderer." He crossed his arms, clearly dismissing the severity of the situation. "Is that why you came all this way? To scold me about my supposed impending doom?"

Charles exhaled slowly, forcing himself to remain calm. "Among other things."

"Go on, then. Lecture away."

"I have work that needs to be done at my estate," Charles stated. "And you have not been fulfilling your responsibilities. When was the last time you even stepped foot in my townhouse?"

Philip shrugged. "Why bother? I won't be your heir much longer, will I? I have heard that you've been sniffing around Lady Eugenie's skirts."

Something inside Charles snapped. He took a sharp step forward, his voice dropping to a dangerously low register. "I would tread very carefully when speaking of Lady Eugenie."

Philip blinked at the sudden shift in Charles's demeanor, but, infuriatingly, the amusement remained in his gaze. "Do you not constantly lecture me about honor?" he asked. "And you and Lady Eugenie were seen alone together—"

Charles closed the remaining distance in a few strides. Philip visibly tensed as Charles loomed over him, his fists curling at his sides. "Choose your next words wisely," he warned.

A flicker of uncertainty passed through Philip's expression, and for the first time since their conversation began, the younger man seemed to consider his words carefully. "I merely meant—"

"I know what you meant," Charles interjected. "And you are wrong to even dare utter Lady Eugenie's name in such a manner. She is innocent in all of this. She has done nothing wrong."

Philip shifted uncomfortably as he glanced away. "My apologies," he muttered.

Charles did not move. "See that it does not happen again," he said firmly. "Next time, I won't be so forgiving."

As he finally took a step back, his aunt—who had been watching the exchange with wide eyes—spoke up. "What about the duel?"

"Philip will meet me in my study later today, and we will discuss it then," Charles responded.

Philip tossed his hands up. "Fine. I suppose I can grace you with my presence, since you're so determined to play my keeper."

Charles turned on his heel, heading towards the door, determined to put as much space between himself and his insufferable cousin as possible before he did something truly regrettable. He stepped outside and the cool air did little to help his temper.

So far this entire day had been a waste of time. Philip would not take this duel seriously. Mr. Kingston would not be swayed. And Eugenie had made it clear where she stood. She would rather be a spinster than marry him.

Botheration.

Why would no one listen to him?

12

---

ugenie walked stiffly down the pavement, her gloved hands clasped tightly together as she focused on the rhythmic tapping of her boots against the stone. Gunter's Tea Shop loomed ahead, its cheerful striped awning at odds with the storm brewing in her heart.

She had no desire for lemon ice. No desire for polite conversation or idle distractions. But Elsbeth had insisted, claiming a walk would do her some good. Eugenie wasn't so sure fresh air would make a difference. She would much rather be curled up in bed, buried beneath her blankets, pretending the world did not exist—pretending her life was not falling apart.

And Charles...

What had he been thinking when he had offered for her? He had not spoken of love, not even of genuine regard. Only duty. *Honor.* How she was beginning to hate those words.

Elsbeth looped her arm through Eugenie's and squeezed gently. "All your troubles will be forgotten once you have some lemon ice."

"I highly doubt that," Eugenie muttered.

"No, it's true," Elsbeth insisted, her voice light, determined.

"My mother always said that lemon ice is the cure for all manner of ills."

Eugenie huffed. "It's just ice."

"True, but delicious ice," Elsbeth countered. "Besides, it's good for you to be out of that townhouse—away from your thoughts, away from your problems."

Eugenie adjusted the strings of her straw hat, her gaze fixed ahead. "I would rather be alone in my bed, drinking chocolate."

Elsbeth sighed, her eyes filling with quiet sympathy. "I know Charles bungled his proposal, but he meant well. He was trying to protect you by giving you the protection of his name."

Eugenie's lips pressed into a thin line. "If I am ever foolish enough to marry, it will be for love. Not duty."

"As well it should be," Elsbeth agreed.

Before Eugenie could reply, a ripple of movement in the crowded street caught her attention. A familiar figure stepped into their path. Miss Winslow. Good heavens. Could this day get any worse?

The young woman's face lit up in an eager smile as she approached. "Lady Eugenie, Lady Westcott! What a pleasant surprise."

Eugenie stiffened. "Is it?" she muttered under her breath, only to receive a quick nudge from Elsbeth's elbow.

Ignoring her, Elsbeth returned Miss Winslow's smile with a politeness Eugenie could not fathom. "Are you enjoying the shops today?"

Miss Winslow turned slightly, gesturing towards the maid standing behind her, whose arms were weighed down with neatly wrapped packages. "Indeed, I do so love shopping in Town. There is nothing quite like it."

Turning back to Eugenie, Miss Winslow's expression grew somewhat sincere. "I must say I am truly sorry for what was written in *The Morning Post* this morning. It was terribly unfair of them to print such a falsehood."

Eugenie hesitated, unsure how to respond. The words sounded kind, but the glint in Miss Winslow's eyes said otherwise. Still, she forced herself to nod. "Thank you."

A slow, knowing smile spread across Miss Winslow's lips. "Although," she added, "there are far worse things than marrying Lord Bedford."

Eugenie went rigid. "I am not marrying Lord Bedford."

Miss Winslow's brows lifted in mock surprise. "Oh? Do you have a choice?" she asked. "I only mean—who else would want you now?"

Eugenie's stomach twisted into knots. She opened her mouth—whether to retaliate or to flee, she wasn't sure—but Elsbeth was already stepping forward.

With a tight smile and a voice laced with unmistakable steel, Elsbeth said, "Thank you for your opinion, Miss Winslow, but we must be on our way."

And without waiting for a response, Elsbeth took Eugenie's arm and led her briskly down the pavement, leaving Miss Winslow standing there, blinking in mild shock.

"That young woman is insufferable," Elsbeth muttered under her breath. "Do try to ignore her and her opinions."

Eugenie swallowed hard. "She isn't wrong, though."

"Utter nonsense," Elsbeth snapped. "You are clever, witty, and an absolute delight to be around."

Eugenie forced a smile. "I daresay you are biased, being my sister-in-law."

"Biased or not, I am right."

But as they walked, Eugenie found herself unable to shake the weight of Miss Winslow's words. The looks from the men and women they passed felt sharper now, their eyes lingering just a moment too long, their whispers carrying just loud enough to sting.

Eugenie kept her chin lifted and her expression composed. But inside, her confidence wavered. Even she had her limits.

Elsbeth must have noticed, for she leaned in and murmured, "There are good days, and there are bad days. But the important thing is that you live each one."

Eugenie nodded, though she wasn't sure she truly believed Elsbeth's words. Would the passing of time truly make things easier? Would the stares and whispers from the *ton* ever fade? Would she ever feel like herself again—unburdened, free?

She wasn't certain.

As they arrived at Gunter's Tea Shop, the cheerful chatter of patrons and the scent of freshly baked pastries filled the air. The sight of the pristine white and gold façade, the delicate lettering etched onto the glass window, stirred a faint flicker of nostalgia within Eugenie. She hadn't been here in years. Not since her mother had passed.

The memory tugged at her, vivid and warm. How her mother had loved their little outings here. They would often indulge in lemon ice after an exhausting day of shopping, laughing over nothing. For a fleeting moment, she could almost hear it.

They placed their orders, and before long, two delicate glass bowls filled with lemon ice were set before them at a small table outside. The sun shone brightly, the warmth a contrast to the icy sweetness on her tongue as she took a bite.

Elsbeth sighed contentedly. "See? I told you. Lemon ice solves everything."

Eugenie let the tartness linger on her tongue, willing herself to enjoy it. Her mother had believed that, too. She blinked against the sudden sting of tears.

"Are you all right?" Elsbeth asked gently.

Eugenie set her spoon down. "I was merely thinking about my mother. I miss her."

Elsbeth reached across the table, squeezing Eugenie's hand. "From what Niles has told me, it sounds like she was a remarkable woman."

A soft, wistful smile played at Eugenie's lips. "She was. If I could be even half the woman she was, I would be content."

"I understand your parents loved each other deeply."

"They did," Eugenie murmured. "That's part of the reason why I hesitate to marry. What if I never find that kind of love? What if I marry someone out of obligation and spend my life trapped in a loveless union?"

Elsbeth squeezed Eugenie's hand again. "You will find love, Eugenie."

"How can you be so sure?"

A knowing smile curved on Elsbeth's lips. "Because when you find true love, you will feel seen, understood and valued. As if all of your complicated, imperfect pieces fit perfectly together. It is a wonderful feeling."

Eugenie swallowed hard. That was what she wanted more than anything.

She knew she was different than most women of the *ton*. She was brazen and opinionated, willing to take risks to be who she truly was. And she wanted someone who would embrace her for who she was—not who Society thought she was.

Not someone who merely tolerated her.

Not someone who married her out of duty.

Her mind wandered and, before she could stop herself, her thoughts drifted to Charles. She resisted the urge to groan. Why did her thoughts constantly return to him? She scooped another bite of lemon ice, letting its tartness distract her.

But it didn't help.

Charles was different. He asked her real questions, ones that made her think. He treated her as an equal, not as some fragile thing to be managed. And he had even arranged for her to attend a lecture at University College because he knew it would matter to her.

The realization settled into her chest, unwanted and undeniable. She was halfway in love with Charles. Her spoon clattered against the empty glass dish.

"Drat," she muttered under her breath.

Elsbeth raised a brow. "What is wrong?"

Eugenie quickly schooled her features. "Nothing."

"You were awfully quiet, and then you just cursed at your empty bowl," Elsbeth remarked with a smile. "We can get you more lemon ice if you like."

Eugenie shook her head, rising to her feet. "No, thank you. Shall we return home?"

Elsbeth studied her for a moment before standing, as well. "Very well," she said, linking arms with Eugenie. "But I am rather curious what you were thinking about."

They had only taken a few steps down the pavement when the sudden arrival of a sleek black coach interrupted their stride.

The door flung open.

A stout man leaped out and grabbed Eugenie by the arm, yanking her towards the coach with startling force. A gasp lodged in her throat as panic surged through her. Before she could struggle—before she could even process what was happening—the sharp, unmistakable sound of a pistol cocking sliced through the air.

The man froze.

"Unhand her."

Eugenie turned her head in shock. Elsbeth stood a few paces away, her reticule discarded at her feet, a pistol gripped steadily in her hands.

The man chuckled dryly, his grip on Eugenie tightening slightly. "You wouldn't dare shoot me."

Elsbeth's eyes did not waver. "Believe me," she said firmly, "I would. And I would be perfectly justified in doing so."

There was a tense silence. Then after a moment, the man released Eugenie's arm. Without another word, he scrambled back into the coach, slamming the door behind him. The driver snapped the reins, and the coach sped down the street at a reckless speed, vanishing into the bustling traffic.

Elsbeth remained still for a moment before slowly lowering the pistol. She turned towards Eugenie, her gaze scanning her sister-in-law's face. "Are you all right?"

Eugenie could only stare at Elsbeth, her body trembling. "What just happened?" she whispered. Her mind was still reeling, trying to comprehend that she had just nearly been abducted.

Elsbeth placed a steadying hand on her arm. "We need to get you home."

Eugenie nodded—at least, she thought she did. She wasn't certain. Everything felt numb.

She barely registered the walk back to their own carriage or the moment she stepped inside.

As she settled against the cushioned bench, her mind was still struggling to make sense of it all.

Across from her, Elsbeth said, "It is a good thing I always carry a pistol in my reticule."

"You would have shot him?"

To her surprise, Elsbeth laughed. "Heavens, no!" she admitted. "My pistol isn't even loaded. I'm just very glad he didn't call my bluff."

"You were bluffing?"

"It's dangerous to carry a loaded pistol in a reticule," Elsbeth said with a smile. "Can you imagine if I accidentally shot myself in the foot? What an unglamorous way to get hurt."

Eugenie's heart still pounded in her chest, her limbs trembling from the shock of nearly being dragged into a coach by an unknown man. "Thank you," she murmured, her voice softer now, more earnest. "For saving me."

Elsbeth's teasing expression faded into something gentler. "Always," she said simply.

Eugenie turned her gaze to the window as the question lingered in her mind, pressing down on her like a weight she could not shake.

Who would want to abduct her?

What reason could there be?

None of this made any sense.

───────⌇───────

Charles sat at his desk in the study of his townhouse as he tried to focus on the ledger before him, but his mind refused to cooperate. He needed to prepare himself before Philip arrived. A calm head was essential when dealing with that insufferable boy. Philip was aggravating beyond belief, yet Charles had no desire to see him dead.

How could he possibly convince Philip that dueling was a fool's errand? Even if he miraculously survived, how would he live with the knowledge that he had taken another man's life?

A gentle rustling of fabric signaled his mother's entrance before she spoke. "What did Eugenie say to your... uh... proposal? Or shall I say 'command'?"

Charles groaned, closing his eyes for a brief moment. This was the last conversation he wanted to have, but ignoring his mother was not an option. "It did not go well," he admitted, dragging his fingers through his dark hair.

His mother hummed knowingly, stepping farther into the room. "Interesting," she mused. "I can't imagine why. Can you?"

Charles snapped the ledger shut with a bit more force than necessary. "Is there something I can help you with, Mother?" he asked, attempting to redirect the conversation.

She raised a delicate hand. "Oh, nothing in particular. I was merely curious."

Leaning back in his chair, he regarded her with a tired

expression. "You were right," he confessed grudgingly. "Eugenie did not take kindly to my method of proposing. Are you satisfied?"

A triumphant smile curled at the corners of his mother's lips. "Did you just admit that you were wrong?"

Charles narrowed his gaze. "You will not be in my good graces much longer if you gloat."

"Oh, forgive me, dear child," she said with mock sincerity, her amusement only deepening. "It is just so unlike you to admit such a thing."

He reached for another ledger, flipping it open in a desperate bid to end the discussion. "Will that be all, Mother? I have work to attend to."

She gave a nonchalant wave of her hand. "Before I go, I should mention that I have accepted Elsbeth's invitation for dinner this evening."

Charles's head snapped up, his full attention now fixed on her. "I beg your pardon?"

His mother tilted her head ever so slightly, feigning innocence. "An invitation arrived earlier today, and I couldn't possibly refuse. Elsbeth would have been most insulted." Her eyes twinkled with mischief. "And surely you wouldn't wish to offend them, would you?"

His jaw tightened. Was he ready to face Eugenie so soon after his disastrous proposal? If he declined to attend, she might assume he was avoiding her. And he would not give her —or anyone else—that satisfaction.

Before he could respond, the door burst open, and Philip strode in, his expression already set in irritation. "I'm here," he announced. "The lecture can commence."

Charles's mother turned, offering a polite smile. "It is good to see you, Philip."

"At least someone is happy to see me," Philip muttered.

"Well, I shall leave you two to it," she said. "I have other matters to attend to." With that, she exited, closing the door behind her.

Charles gestured towards the chair opposite his desk. "Sit."

Philip sighed dramatically, dragging his feet as he crossed the room. "For what purpose? We both know what this is—an interrogation."

"Sit," Charles repeated, his tone brooking no argument.

Rolling his eyes, Philip flopped onto the chair with exaggerated movements. "Happy?"

Charles pinned him with a level stare. "You are my heir. But more importantly, you are my cousin. Whatever you may think, I do care for you and have your best interests at heart."

"Now you sound like my mother," Philip mumbled.

Charles ignored the remark. "What do you intend to do with your life if I marry and my wife bears me sons?"

Philip looked unbothered. "I haven't thought about it."

"You should. It ought to be your every waking thought," Charles said firmly. "You have a mother to provide for."

"My mother has a small jointure," Philip countered. "She will manage."

Charles looked heavenward. "So your grand plan is to live off your mother?"

"I never said that," Philip snapped as he leaned back lazily, crossing his arms. "Besides, I'm only eighteen. I have plenty of time to think about my future. Perhaps I'll marry an heiress."

Charles's lips pressed into a thin line. "So you aspire to be a fortune hunter, then?"

Philip shrugged. "There are worse things. I've grown rather accustomed to a certain lifestyle."

"You are a cad."

Philip smirked. "Did you summon me here merely to insult me?"

Charles pushed back his chair, stood, and walked to the window, clasping his hands behind his back as he gazed out into the gardens. "As my heir, I forbid you from engaging in this duel."

Philip shot upright in his chair. "You forbid me?"

"I do," Charles said, turning back to face him. "Which means you must make this situation right."

"No!" Philip exploded, jumping to his feet. "I won't marry that chit!"

"That 'chit' is the mother of your child," Charles stated plainly. "And you will treat her with the respect she deserves."

Philip's hands clenched at his sides. "You want me to throw away my future for some whore?"

Charles took a deep breath as he attempted to quell his growing irritation. "You chose to sleep with her, and actions have consequences. You need to rise up and be a man."

Philip let out a bitter laugh. "She is the daughter of gentry. How low have I fallen?"

Charles unclasped his hands and took a step towards him. "You will marry her, and I will see that you are both provided for."

Philip's lips curled in disdain. "For how long?" He arched a brow. "I only ask because of... Lady Eugenie."

"Lady Eugenie has nothing to do with this," he growled.

"This isn't a request. It's a command. And if I refuse, I suppose you'll threaten to cut me off," Philip said as he glared at him. "So this is how it's to be, then?"

Charles met his gaze with unyielding resolve. "This is how it must be."

A heavy silence settled between them, the weight of unspoken words pressing into the room. Philip was the first to break it with a cluck of his tongue. "So be it," he declared, his voice laced with defiance. "I would rather be cut off than marry that chit. It doesn't matter if she has an inheritance. She is still lowbred, and nothing will ever change that."

"Fine," Charles responded. "You've made your choice."

Philip turned sharply on his heel, striding towards the door. But before he reached it, he paused, one hand gripping the frame. "You think I need your money, but I don't. I can make my own way in the world."

Charles folded his arms across his chest. "With what skills?" he asked, his tone dripping with exasperation. "You were kicked out of Oxford, you have no trade, no title of your own, and, by all accounts, you are a dreadful gambler."

"I won ten pounds last night," Philip announced proudly.

Charles walked over to his desk, lifting the ledger with a pointed motion. "Ten pounds wouldn't even come close to covering your expenses for the month."

Philip waved a hand dismissively. "Yes, but if I win ten pounds every night, it most certainly would."

Charles let out a short, humorless laugh and gestured towards the door. "By all means, prove me wrong."

Philip tilted his chin upward. "I will. And when I do, you'll regret this."

"I very much doubt that," Charles replied as he returned to his seat, flipping open the ledger once more. "You may go now."

Philip hesitated for a moment before scoffing under his breath and striding out of the study, the door clicking shut behind him with a decisive finality.

A brief moment of silence followed before his mother entered the room. "Well," she said dryly, "that went well."

"Eavesdropping again, Mother?"

She did not look the least bit repentant. "I am entitled to listen to conversations that happen under my roof."

"Next time, I'll just invite you to stay."

His mother's laugh rang out. "Finally, we are in agreement on something."

He furrowed his brow. "How can you joke at a time like this?"

The humor in her expression softened, replaced by something more thoughtful. "I am sorry," she said, her tone gentler now. "I know you've been trying to mentor Philip, to shape him into a man who could one day take your place as earl. But, my dear, I fear it is a lost cause."

"I refuse to give up on him just yet."

"I know. And that is why you are my favorite son."

Charles shook his head. "I am your only son."

His mother pressed a hand to her chest in mock concern. "You are? Oh, dear. I think I may have misplaced one or two without realizing it."

Despite himself, Charles let out a reluctant chuckle, the tension in his shoulders easing ever so slightly. "Thank you. I do believe I needed a reason to laugh today."

His mother's lips curled in satisfaction. "Then my work here is done," she quipped as she settled into the chair across from him.

Charles exhaled, the brief moment of levity fading as his thoughts drifted back to Philip. "Do you think he will ever grow up and face his responsibilities?"

His mother studied him for a moment before speaking. "You have done everything in your power to help him— perhaps even to a fault—but in the end, Philip is his own person. You cannot force a man to change if he does not wish to."

Charles leaned back in his chair, his gaze drifting towards the ceiling as he contemplated her words. "I know Aunt Phoebe will be disappointed."

"In Philip, not you," his mother corrected. "She sees the effort you've put into guiding him. She knows how hard you have tried."

The rhythmic ticking of the clock filled the silence between them until the deep chime of the hour echoed through the room. His mother rose. "Come," she encouraged. "We should begin getting ready for supper. We wouldn't want to be late."

"And what, pray tell, shall I say to Eugenie?"

His mother briefly considered him before answering, "I would suggest using words when speaking to her. Preferably arranged in an order that forms a coherent sentence. Women tend to like that."

"Why do I even bother with you?"

A radiant smile spread across his mother's face as she moved towards the door. "Because you love me."

"That I do," Charles said.

13

Eugenie sat before her dressing table, staring at her reflection as she willed herself to believe that tonight wouldn't end in disaster. No matter how many times she told herself that this evening would be just another dinner, the anxiety twisting in her stomach would not relent.

Elsbeth had informed her that Charles would be dining with them, and the moment she heard his name, all she felt was dread.

What on earth would she say to him? Would he expect her to acknowledge his proposal? Should she bring it up herself, or let silence swallow it whole, pretending as though it hadn't occupied her thoughts all day?

And truly, she had far more pressing concerns than Charles. Someone had attempted to abduct her right outside of Gunter's Tea Shop. She had little doubt that a scandal was brewing, considering Elsbeth had saved her by retrieving her pistol.

What would Lady Jane's uncle think when whispers began to circulate? Would he dismiss her submissions the moment her name—her real name—was associated with such impropriety? She hoped not. Eugenie stood and adjusted the sleeves of her pale pink gown. She had taken extra care with her appearance tonight, but it certainly wasn't for Charles. At least, that was what she kept telling herself.

The clock on the mantel chimed. Time had run out. She could no longer delay the inevitable.

With a deep breath, she straightened her shoulders. She could do this. She *would* do this. It wasn't as if she could remain hidden away in her bedchamber. Besides, she had done nothing wrong. Rejecting Charles's proposal had been the right decision—no matter how much it weighed on her—because the truth remained unchanged. He did not love her.

Leaving her bedchamber, Eugenie stepped into the dimly lit corridor, her footsteps muted against the plush carpet. Each step forward felt heavier than the last, as though she were marching towards a battle she had no hope of winning.

A voice from behind startled her. "Dare I ask what you are doing?"

Eugenie turned to find her brother, Niles, leaning against the wall, arms crossed, one brow arched in amusement.

"Pardon?" she asked.

"You're moving slower than a zombie."

Eugenie narrowed her eyes. "And how exactly do you know how a zombie moves?"

Niles smirked. "Common knowledge, I imagine. They are stiff, lumbering creatures."

She tilted her head, feeling a need to goad him. "You sound quite certain. Have you encountered a zombie recently?"

"Not personally, no." His smirk widened. "But I am confident in my assessment."

"Then allow me to correct you. I am not walking like a zombie. I am gracefully making my way to the drawing room."

"If you say so." His voice was laced with mirth, but when she didn't respond, his expression softened. "You seem unsettled. Is something bothering you?"

She hesitated before admitting, "I suppose I'm a little on edge, especially after what happened earlier."

At once, the humor vanished from Niles's face, replaced by a hardened seriousness. "Your attempted abduction," he stated. "I should have been there. I should have protected you."

The guilt in his voice was unmistakable, and Eugenie felt an immediate need to reassure him. She stepped closer. "How could you have known what would happen?" she asked. "Besides, Elsbeth was with me, and she made sure I was safe."

Niles didn't look convinced. His fingers curled into fists at his sides before he exhaled sharply, placing a firm hand on her shoulder. "I don't know what I would do if something happened to you, Eugenie."

She met his gaze. "And I feel the same way about you."

His grip on her shoulder tightened briefly before he let his hand drop. "I would feel much better if you remained at the townhouse until I've arranged for a Bow Street Runner to investigate the matter properly."

Eugenie instinctively wanted to argue. But Niles had a point. Someone had attempted to snatch her in broad daylight —right outside Gunter's Tea Shop, no less. If the man had been bold enough to strike once, there was no guarantee he wouldn't try again. "I agree," she said at last.

Niles grinned. "I like this agreeable side of you."

"Don't get used to it," she replied dryly.

He chuckled, stepping back. "Shall we adjourn to the drawing room?"

"That sounds like a grand idea."

As they made their way down the corridor together, Niles glanced sideways at her. "Elsbeth told me about what happened with Bedford."

"I assumed as much."

His brow furrowed. "Would it be so awful for you to marry him?"

Eugenie came to an abrupt halt. "Surely you cannot be in earnest?"

"I am," Niles said, lifting a hand before she could protest. "But hear me out before you start yelling."

Niles started slowly, deliberately. "He is an earl, Eugenie. He could provide you with the protection of his name."

"And what of your name, dear brother? Or have you conveniently forgotten that you, too, are an earl?"

Niles rubbed the back of his neck. "No, I have not forgotten. But you know as well as I do that the *ton* will be far more forgiving if you marry Bedford, especially after your indiscretion."

Eugenie's mouth fell open. "There was no indiscretion."

"So you've insisted—repeatedly, I might add—but the *ton* believes otherwise. And their belief, unfair as it may be, will dictate your reputation."

Eugenie took a step towards her brother, her jaw set. "I am not going to marry Lord Bedford simply because the *ton* enjoys their gossip," she said. "And quite frankly, I am shocked that you would even suggest such a thing."

Niles's gaze filled with something dangerously close to pity. "I only want what is best for you."

Eugenie's fingers curled into her palms. "What is best for me," she countered, "is for you to mind your own business."

It was unkind, and she knew it. But she also knew she had no interest in discussing this further.

Niles studied her for a long moment before nodding slightly. "I understand that you're angry," he said. "But you cannot ignore this. And now, with news of your attempted abduction spreading, your name will be dragged through the mud even more. You need to consider—"

The distant chime of the dinner bell cut through the tense air, an almost welcome reprieve from the conversation.

Eugenie spoke over him. "We should go down to dinner."

A flicker of resignation passed over Niles's face. "Very well. But this conversation isn't over."

"Wonderful," she muttered under her breath.

They continued down the corridor, descending the grand staircase without another word. As they reached the drawing room, Eugenie instinctively schooled her expression into one of composure. But the moment she stepped through the threshold, her breath caught ever so slightly.

There, standing near the fireplace, was Charles. And he looked entirely too handsome for his own good. Did he realize the effect he had on her?

She forced herself to move forward, willing herself to remain indifferent. But as if sensing her presence, Charles turned his head, his blue eyes locking on to hers with an unreadable intensity.

His lips curved ever so slightly. And to her utter dismay, she found herself responding in kind. His reaction boded well for her. Perhaps he wasn't too upset with her for turning down his marriage proposal.

She watched as Charles closed the distance between them, stopping just before her. With a slight bow, he greeted, "Good evening, Eugenie."

She dipped into a curtsy. "Good evening, Charles."

His gaze swept over her, warm and appraising. "You are looking lovely this evening."

There was a spark in his eyes—one of approval, of admiration. And blast it all, she felt her traitorous heart respond in kind.

"Thank you," was all Eugenie could manage to say, her voice softer than she intended.

Charles's gaze lingered on her, searching. "Dare I ask how your day unfolded after I called upon you this morning?"

She waved a hand in front of her dismissively. "Well, it began pleasantly enough with a visit to Gunter's Tea Shop, but then someone attempted to abduct me."

"*What?*" Charles's voice rose sharply, drawing the attention of those nearby. His entire body tensed, taking a step closer. "Someone tried to abduct you?"

Eugenie blinked, slightly taken aback by his reaction. "I thought you knew."

"No, I haven't heard a word of this," Charles said, his tone clipped. His gaze swept over her, as if checking for injuries. "Are you all right?"

A reassuring smile played on her lips, though it did little to ease the worry etched across his face. "I am unharmed, I assure you. Elsbeth was with me, and she chased him off with her pistol."

At that, a muscle in Charles's cheek twitched as he turned sharply towards Niles, his fury barely contained. "And what say you, Westcott?" he asked. "What are you going to do about this injustice?"

Niles met Charles's stare with a solemn expression. "I have already sent word to Bow Street to request an investigation."

Charles didn't seem remotely appeased. His hands curled into fists at his sides. "And what of Lady Eugenie's safety? What precautions have you taken?"

Elsbeth, standing near Niles, chimed in. "She is perfectly safe here at our townhouse," she assured him. "No harm will come to her here."

But Charles still looked rattled, his brows furrowed deeply in frustration.

Eugenie reached out, her fingers resting lightly on his sleeve. "Do not trouble yourself," she said. "I am well. Truly. And I will take the necessary precautions."

His gaze dropped to where her hand lay on his jacket. "It's just..." His voice trailed off, his brows knitting together. "I cannot bear the thought of something happening to you."

The sincerity in his tone sent a strange warmth through her chest. "And nothing will happen to me," she insisted.

But Charles did not look entirely convinced. His blue eyes flickered with doubt before settling into something more resolute. "Do you know who it was?"

"No," Eugenie replied. "It was a strange man who leaped from a coach. I had never seen him before."

"Then I think it would be best if you forgo your visits to University College for the time being." His tone was firm, brooking no argument.

Niles snapped his attention towards her, his expression thunderous. "What visits to University College?"

Eugenie winced.

Drat.

She offered her brother a placating smile. "Well, I... may have taken a short trip to Oxford to attend a lecture," she admitted. "That's where I ran into Lord Bedford."

"Women are not permitted to attend lectures at Oxford," Niles remarked.

"That is true," she acknowledged, "but they are far more accommodating when one is dressed as a man."

Niles sucked in a sharp breath. "You dressed like a man?" His voice was a mix of horror and disbelief. "Are you mad?"

Eugenie shifted uncomfortably under his scrutiny. "Yes, but it was harmless."

Taking a step closer to her, Niles asked, "Did you even visit your friend or go shopping on High Street?"

Eugenie paused, knowing her brother would not be pleased with what she was about to admit. "No, I did not."

"So you lied to me?" Niles pressed.

"I did," she admitted, lowering her gaze. "However, no one else but Lord Bedford knew what I was about."

Charles interjected. "Professor Addington knew as well, but he allowed her to sit in on his lecture. He won't betray her confidences."

Niles turned his glare towards Charles. "And you let her do this?"

"She was quite determined, Westcott," Charles replied. "Had I not been there, she would have attended regardless."

Niles let out a sound of frustration, leveling them both with a hard stare. "Do you realize what would have happened if she had been discovered?"

Eugenie opened her mouth to argue. "But I wasn't—"

"How many times have you done this?" he asked, cutting her off.

She bit her lower lip before slowly lifting her hand, three fingers extended.

Niles's nostrils flared, his entire body going rigid. He pinched the bridge of his nose, clearly trying to rein in his temper. "We will discuss this later." His voice was tight with restraint. Then he turned to Charles. "But first, I would like a word with you. Alone."

Elsbeth placed a gentle hand on Niles's arm. "Can it not wait until after dinner, my love?"

"No." His reply was swift, absolute. "I want to speak to him now. In my study."

Without another word, Niles turned on his heel and strode out of the drawing room, leaving behind a tense silence in his wake.

Charles exchanged a wary glance with Elsbeth before asking, "Does Westcott keep any pistols in his study?"

"He won't shoot you." Elsbeth paused, then added, "At least, I hope not."

As Charles strode towards Westcott's study, uncertainty gnawed at him. He wasn't entirely sure what to expect from this conversation. He had been half-joking earlier about Westcott shooting him, but the possibility didn't seem all that far-fetched. It wasn't long ago that the two of them had been at odds, but they had set those differences aside for the sake of Elsbeth.

And now, Charles had given Westcott yet another reason to be furious with him. He had helped Eugenie sneak into Oxford, allowing her to disguise herself as a man and attend a lecture. It was a decision that had placed not only her reputation but his own at great risk. He had known it was dangerous, but it hadn't been enough to dissuade him. Because if he hadn't helped her, she would have done it alone.

Charles entered the study and saw Westcott standing by the drink cart, his back partially turned as he reached for the decanter. Without looking up, he lifted the crystal bottle. "Care for a drink?"

Charles lifted a hand in polite refusal. "No, thank you."

Westcott shrugged, pouring himself a generous measure of brandy. He swirled the amber liquid in his glass before finally glancing at Charles. "What you did with Eugenie was reckless," he said, his voice firm. "Foolish, even. If she had been caught, she would have been ruined."

"I'm aware of that," Charles admitted. "But she would have done it with or without my help."

Westcott studied him for a moment, then gave a slow nod. "I agree."

Charles blinked. He had been prepared for a verbal lashing, perhaps even a thinly veiled threat. Agreement, however, was not what he had expected.

Westcott took a sip of his drink before continuing. "Which is why I wanted to thank you for helping her."

Charles's brows shot up. "You're thanking me?"

"I am," Westcott confirmed, settling into one of the leather armchairs by the fireplace. He gestured for Charles to do the same. "Eugenie is stubborn, almost to a fault. She does as she pleases, consequences be damned." His lips twitched. "Much like you."

Charles let out a dry chuckle. "So now you're insulting me?"

Westcott smirked. "It's not an insult. Just an observation."

That sounded more like the Westcott he knew.

Westcott swirled the brandy in his glass, his expression growing more serious. "But we have a larger issue at hand. I assume you've seen the latest newssheets?"

"I have," Charles responded. "Which is why I offered for Eugenie, but she turned me down. She says she would rather be a spinster than marry me." He tried to keep the bitterness out of his voice, but the sting of rejection still lingered.

Westcott frowned, his fingers tapping idly against the arm of his chair. "Eugenie has always been fiercely independent. She has a rather misguided notion that marriage would stifle her. A makeshift prison, if you will."

Charles leaned forward, resting his elbows on his knees. "I wouldn't try to control her," he said. "If she agreed to be my wife, I would never—"

"I know that," Westcott interrupted. "And I do believe you would be good for Eugenie."

"You do?"

Westcott grinned, taking another sip of brandy. "Don't look so surprised. We may have been at odds in the past, but I've come to find you tolerable."

"That is a glowing endorsement," Charles joked.

Westcott grew solemn. He set his glass down on the table

beside him. "I am serious, Bedford. I ask you—no, I plead with you—not to give up on Eugenie."

"I have no intention of giving up on her," Charles admitted.

Westcott nodded approvingly. "Good. Because if she doesn't marry you, I do believe she'll make good on her ridiculous threat of remaining a spinster."

A wry smile tugged at Charles's lips. "Do you have any ideas on how I might persuade her otherwise?"

Westcott sighed, glancing down at his brandy. "I don't," he admitted. "But Elsbeth might. She's been playing matchmaker this entire time."

"I assumed as much, given the number of dinner invitations."

Westcott hesitated before speaking again. "I do believe my parents indulged Eugenie too much." His voice was quieter now, more thoughtful. "It wasn't always that way, but after her accident, everything changed."

Charles straightened. "Accident?"

Westcott placed his nearly full glass onto the table, his fingers tapping lightly against the rim. "A few years ago, she fell from her horse and hit her head," he explained. "She was unconscious for days. When she woke, she struggled to remember the events leading up to the fall." He shook his head. "To this day, she refuses to go riding. She's uneasy around horses, despite once loving them more than anything."

"I hadn't realized."

Westcott's gaze grew distant. "When she was younger, we couldn't keep her off her horse. She spent more time in the saddle than anywhere else. I daresay she would have slept in the stables if our parents had allowed it."

A small, fond smile touched Charles's lips. "I can picture that."

"I had hoped that time would help," Westcott admitted. "That eventually, she'd find her way back to riding. But even now, after all these years, she still refuses to get back into the saddle or even go to the stables."

Charles sat back, digesting this new piece of information. Eugenie's stubbornness, her insistence on independence—it had always been a part of her nature. But this? This was something else entirely. This was fear. And fear was far more difficult to reason with than mere pride.

Westcott rose from his chair, adjusting the cuffs of his coat. "Shall we return to the ladies?"

Charles followed suit. "That would be wise."

As they made their way back towards the drawing room, Westcott cast a sidelong glance at him. "I know about the kiss."

Charles came to an abrupt halt. "Pardon?"

Westcott turned to fully face him, his arms crossing over his chest. "Eugenie told me that you kissed her at Lady Britton's ball."

A slow breath left Charles's lips. So she had confessed it to her brother. He wasn't entirely surprised, but he would have preferred to learn this in a less confrontational manner.

Westcott's gaze sharpened. "I do hope you don't intend to engage in such behaviors again until you are properly wed."

This was a conversation he had no desire to have with Westcott, particularly when he had been looking forward to kissing Eugenie again. Assuming she would let him. "I can't promise I won't kiss her once we're engaged," he said.

Westcott stared at him for a long moment before conceding. "One kiss. That is all, but only after she accepts your proposal."

Satisfied that the conversation had concluded, Charles resumed walking, feeling an odd mixture of relief and amusement. He would never have imagined a day when Westcott would grant him permission to kiss his sister.

When they reached the drawing room, he saw the ladies were seated upon the settees, engaged in animated conversation.

Elsbeth glanced up at their entrance, her eyes flicking between them before she let out an exaggerated sigh of relief. "I was certain one of you wouldn't make it out of that study alive."

Westcott chuckled, moving to stand beside her. "Bedford and I have come to an understanding. Haven't we?"

Charles inclined his head. "We have."

Elsbeth's eyes sparkled with mischief. "Excellent. Now, shall we adjourn to dinner? I would hate for the meal to grow cold."

Charles stepped forward to offer his hand to his mother, assisting her with care as she rose. "I am rather famished," he admitted.

"That is because you skipped your midday meal," his mother lightly chided. "You must take better care of yourself, Charles. You need nourishment."

Charles turned his head towards Eugenie, extending his hand. "May I?"

Eugenie hesitated briefly before slipping her gloved fingers into his. The contact sent a jolt of awareness up his arm, a sensation that left his skin tingling. Did she feel it, too?

"Thank you," she murmured.

As they exited the drawing room, Charles fell into step beside Eugenie. "Dare I ask what you ladies were discussing when we walked in?"

A teasing smile curved Eugenie's lips and he knew he was in trouble. "Your mother was sharing stories about you as a child," she revealed.

Charles groaned. "Should I be worried?"

Her grin widened. "You should be."

"Dare I ask what embarrassing tales she shared?"

"Well," Eugenie mused, tilting her head, "I now understand that you had a habit of sneaking frogs into the nursery."

"In my defense, I thought frogs deserved to sleep in a nice, warm bed. It was a flawless plan until my nursemaid stepped on one in the middle of the night." He winced. "Her screams woke the entire household."

"Frogs, truly?" Eugenie asked with a giggle.

"I was eight," Charles admitted with a small shrug. "I had a fascination with reptiles. I even begged for a pet snake, but my parents refused."

His mother, walking just ahead, cast him a knowing glance. "For good reason," she said. "The last thing we wanted was a snake slithering loose in our home."

"My parents were no fun," he said with mock solemnity.

"Do not get me started on the snails," his mother said.

Eugenie cast him a curious look. "Snails?"

"When I was five, I developed a deep fondness for snails," Charles shared. "I had an entire collection. Unfortunately, one managed to escape and found its way into my mother's slipper."

Eugenie covered her mouth, stifling her laughter.

His mother sighed dramatically. "I discovered it only when I put my foot in the slipper." She gave Charles a pointed look. "Crushing the poor thing in the process."

"After that," Charles said, "snails were banned from our home."

Eugenie's laughter spilled over. "I have to side with your mother on this one," she said. "Snails are not meant to be pets."

Charles placed a hand over his heart. "You wound me."

"You know what would make a good pet?" Eugenie asked.

He arched a brow. "Enlighten me."

"A dog."

"I did have a dog, actually. His name was Boots."

"Boots?" Eugenie repeated, incredulous. "That is a terrible name for a dog. Was Slipper already taken?"

Charles feigned offense. "My dog had a particular fondness for eating my boots, hence the name. It was either Boots or Muskrat. In my defense, the dog did resemble a wet rodent."

They arrived at the dining room, the warm glow of candlelight illuminating the richly adorned table. Charles moved ahead, pulling out a chair for Eugenie.

Elsbeth, settling into her seat at one end of the table, interjected. "I must agree with Charles. Boots did look like a rodent."

His mother bobbed her head. "Boots was a rather unfortunate-looking dog, I'll admit. Tufts of hair sticking out in every direction, and a face that looked permanently pushed in. But he was the only dog we could find on such short notice."

Eugenie turned to Charles, amusement flickering in her eyes. "Your poor dog."

"He was a beloved companion," Charles admitted with a fond smile, "even if he wasn't the brightest of dogs."

"No, he most certainly was not," his mother agreed.

"What was it that made him so dimwitted?" Eugenie asked.

Charles grew thoughtful. "Well, for starters, he had an unfortunate habit of running headfirst into furniture. Repeatedly. No matter how many times we tried to guide him away, he would charge straight into table legs, chair arms—he even knocked himself unconscious twice after misjudging the doorway."

"Oh, poor thing!" Eugenie exclaimed.

"My father once joked that Boots had precisely two thoughts in his head at any given time—food and mischief," Charles continued, shaking his head. "Though I daresay thinking was a rather generous term for what went on in that skull of his."

Elsbeth interjected with mirth in her voice. "I do recall a certain incident with the Christmas pudding."

"Oh, that was unforgettable," his mother chimed in. "Boots somehow managed to sneak into the kitchen and steal an entire pudding off the counter. He dragged it under the dining table and devoured the whole thing before the cook even realized it was missing."

"Needless to say," Charles added, "he had a rather difficult night afterward."

"I think I rather like the sound of Boots. He had character," Eugenie said.

Charles felt unexpectedly lighthearted. After the day's events, it felt good to laugh, to indulge in these small, silly recollections of the past. With Eugenie. Everything always seemed better with her there.

14

E ugenie lay still in her bed as the morning sun streamed through the tall windows. She squeezed her eyes shut, as if doing so could banish the one thought that had consumed her since waking.

Charles.

No matter how hard she tried to push him from her mind, he kept creeping back in.

She thought of last night, of the way his deep laughter had filled the room as they played card games, his sharp wit making even the most mundane of moments entertaining. Charles had a rare talent—he could always make her laugh, no matter the circumstance. And that was precisely the problem.

A sharp knock at the door interrupted her thoughts. Before she could respond, Alice stepped inside. "Good morning, my lady," she greeted.

Eugenie groaned dramatically and grabbed a pillow, covering her face. "I am sleeping."

"That is unfortunate because Lord Bedford has arrived and is waiting for you at the stables."

The pillow was yanked away in an instant. Eugenie sat up, blinking at Alice in confusion. "Why is he at the stables?"

Alice shrugged. "He didn't say."

Curiosity stirred in Eugenie's chest. It had been years since she had set foot in the stables. Not since her accident. Her fingers drifted to the back of her head, the place where she had struck the ground so violently that day. The scar had long since healed, but the memory of waking in a haze, unable to recall how she had fallen, still haunted her.

Alice's expression softened. "Perhaps it is time, my lady. You used to love visiting the stables."

"That was before I almost died, Alice. It feels like a lifetime ago."

Alice stepped closer, offering her a kind smile. "It was a long time ago. But going to the stables doesn't mean you have to ride."

Eugenie hesitated. The idea of returning to the stables sent a nervous flutter through her chest. "I suppose there's no harm in a visit," she murmured. "But I won't ride."

"I don't think Lord Bedford would push you into anything you aren't ready for," Alice assured her as she moved towards the wardrobe, pulling out a gown of soft blue. "But you don't want to keep him waiting too long."

Eugenie rose from the bed, making her way to the dressing table. She reached for the brush and pulled it through her long blonde hair.

Alice approached and held out a hand. "Allow me, my lady."

Eugenie relinquished the brush and let Alice take over, watching her reflection as her maid worked the strands into an elegant chignon.

"What do you think of Lord Bedford?" Eugenie asked.

Alice gave her a knowing look in the looking glass. "From what you've told me, he sounds like an honorable gentleman."

"He is. Which is the only reason he offered for me."

Alice pinned the final strand of hair in place. "Would you have accepted his offer under different circumstances?"

"No," she said firmly. "I am content with my life."

"And you don't think there is room for Lord Bedford in it?"

Eugenie fell silent. Charles had already found a way into her heart. But that isn't what scared her the most. She didn't want to feel anything for him, but he made her feel everything. When had her life become so complicated?

Alice stepped back and studied her handiwork. "Do you like your hair, my lady?"

Eugenie turned her head slightly, admiring the intricate coiffure. "You've outdone yourself."

"Then let's get you dressed," Alice said as she went to retrieve the gown.

Eugenie slipped out of her dressing gown and into the morning gown, standing patiently as Alice fastened the buttons at her back.

As Alice secured the last one, Eugenie found herself asking, "Do you think I was too quick to dismiss Lord Bedford's marriage offer?"

Alice's hands stilled. "It doesn't matter what I think," she said. "Do you think you made a mistake?"

Eugenie's lips parted, but no words came. She had to admit that the thought of marriage to Charles did hold some appeal.

Alice stepped back. "I do believe that you have your answer," she said. "But I will support you, no matter what you do."

Eugenie swallowed the lump forming in her throat. "Thank you." She turned towards the door before she could second-guess herself.

She hurried down the corridors until she arrived at the back door. The morning air was refreshing as Eugenie made her way across the grounds. The path to the stables was familiar but strangely foreign after so many years.

When she reached the stables, Charles was already there, standing near the entrance. He caught sight of her and lifted his hand in greeting. "Good morning, my lady."

Eugenie stopped in front of him. "Good morning, my lord." She eyed him suspiciously. "Dare I ask why you are waiting for me at the stables?"

Charles's easy smile dimmed slightly. "Your brother told me about your accident. And how you no longer ride, despite your love for horses."

Eugenie's stomach tightened. She had known someone would tell him eventually, but hearing him say it aloud felt like a reopened wound. "It's true," she admitted, catching the familiar scent of hay drifting from the stable doors. Once, it had been a comforting scent. Now, it only served as a reminder of what she had lost.

Charles took a step closer, though he was careful to maintain a proper distance. "I want to help you get back in the saddle."

She shook her head. "That is kind of you, but my riding days are over."

His blue eyes searched hers. "Are you saying that because you want them to be over?" He let the question hang between them before adding, "Or because of fear?"

Eugenie bristled at his words. "I almost died, Charles," she responded firmly. "I don't think I will ever be ready to sit atop a horse again."

Charles studied her, his expression giving nothing away. "So you've given up," he said finally. "Letting fear win?"

She drew in a sharp breath, her hands clenching at her sides. "I am not giving up," she said through gritted teeth.

"Then prove it."

Eugenie narrowed her eyes. "And how do you suggest I do that?"

His smile returned. "Take a walk with me through the stables." He gestured towards the open doors. "Just that. Nothing more."

Eugenie glanced towards the shadowed interior, her heart pounding. It was just a walk. She could do that, couldn't she?

After a long pause, she squared her shoulders. "Very well, my lord," she said. "Lead the way."

Charles extended his arm to her, and she placed her gloved hand atop his. As they stepped inside, the scent of leather, hay, and horses enveloped her, stirring old memories. And, for the first time in years, Eugenie wondered if maybe—just maybe—she wasn't as ready to close this chapter of her life as she had once believed.

"I must admit, I have a surprise for you," Charles said. His voice held a quiet excitement, as if he had been anticipating this moment for some time. He gestured towards the row of stalls lining the stables. "It's in the first stall."

Eugenie didn't dare to guess what the surprise could be, but Charles's expression was enough to send a thrill of curiosity through her. Without hesitation, she hurried to the first stall, her boots clicking against the wooden floor.

As she peered inside, her breath caught. Standing there, nestled in a bed of fresh straw, was the smallest foal she had ever laid eyes on. Its coat was a rich, warm brown, speckled with delicate white spots, as if someone had scattered flecks of snow across its fur. Its dark eyes, round and filled with innocence, gazed up at her.

Charles came to stand next to her. "I thought a miniature horse might help ease you back into your love of horses," he said.

Eugenie quickly unlatched the stall door and slipped inside, moving cautiously so as not to startle the young creature. Extending her hand, she let it hover in the space between them, allowing the foal to approach on its own terms.

To her delight, the foal showed no hesitation. It took a bold step forward, its velvety muzzle brushing against her fingertips. A smile spread across her face as she ran her hand down the foal's neck, feeling the fine, silky hair beneath her palm.

"I love it," she murmured, her voice thick with emotion. She turned towards Charles. "Thank you. Truly."

"I'm glad," he said simply.

Eugenie felt an overwhelming sense of gratitude. This wasn't just a gift. It was a gesture of understanding, of care. "This is the most thoughtful gift anyone has ever given me. How can I ever repay you?"

Charles held her gaze. "All I want is for you to be happy, Eugenie."

"I am happy."

He grinned. "Then my work here is done."

But she wasn't ready for him to step away just yet. A boldness she hadn't expected surged through her, and she took a step closer, placing a hand against his chest. "I do think a kiss is in order," she murmured, tilting her head up to meet his gaze.

"I have no objections."

She leaned in and could feel the warmth of his breath against her lips. Her heart pounded so loudly she feared he might hear it, but she didn't pull away. Just a few inches more...

When their lips met, it was like everything stilled. It wasn't their first kiss, but it was the kiss that made her realize she didn't want to kiss anyone else.

Then the sudden creak of the stable door jolted them apart. Charles immediately took a step back, his posture straightening as though preparing for the interruption.

A moment later, Elsbeth appeared, her eyes flicking between the two of them with thinly veiled amusement. "I do hope I'm not interrupting anything," she said with a knowing look.

Eugenie, still slightly breathless, gestured towards the foal. "Look what Charles gave me."

Elsbeth's eyes widened with delight as she stepped closer. "What an adorable foal!" she gushed.

"It is, isn't it?" Eugenie agreed, crouching down and wrapping her arms around the tiny creature's neck. The foal let out a soft neigh, nudging her affectionately.

"Have you decided what to name him?" Elsbeth asked.

Eugenie grew thoughtful. "I think I shall call him Sir Spotticus."

Charles let out a short laugh. "A fine name," he said approvingly.

Eugenie nodded, pleased with her choice. Rising to her feet, she gave the foal an encouraging pat. "Come along, Sir Spotticus," she ordered. "There's a whole world outside the stables, and I've much to show you."

The colt flicked his ears forward and, with an eager little step, followed at her heels as she led him out of the stall.

She glanced at Charles, and he winked at her. It was such a simple gesture, yet it made her heart race. Perhaps marriage to him wouldn't be as dreadful as she had once believed.

Charles watched as Eugenie strode out of the stables with Sir Spotticus trotting eagerly at her heels. A bemused smile played at his lips. He still couldn't quite believe that she had kissed him. That fleeting moment, her lips soft against his, had taken him entirely by surprise. If he had known that a mere foal would inspire such a reaction, he would have gifted her one much sooner.

His thoughts were interrupted by Elsbeth's voice. "When are you going to tell her?"

He turned to her with a perplexed frown. "Tell her what?"

"That you love her." She gave him a pointed look, her arms crossing in front of her as if daring him to deny it.

He scoffed, shaking his head. "I do not love Eugenie."

Elsbeth raised a skeptical brow but simply lifted a hand in surrender. "All I'm saying is that you appear quite taken with her."

"That is different from being in love," he countered swiftly. "Besides, I think I would know if I were in love with her."

Her lips twitched. "My apologies. I should never have brought it up."

"No, you shouldn't have," he agreed, brushing past the topic as if it hadn't lodged itself stubbornly in his mind. "I should depart. I am meeting Addington and Alcott at White's for a drink."

"At this hour?"

He shrugged. "It's the only time we could arrange to meet."

As they stepped out of the stables together, Elsbeth glanced around with a small frown. "I don't see Eugenie. Do you think she took Sir Spotticus into the townhouse?"

Charles chuckled. "I wouldn't put it past her."

Elsbeth sighed. "Niles will be livid if he finds a miniature horse inside. He already despises Eugenie's cat."

"He may as well get used to it," Charles said. "Eugenie does as she pleases, regardless of her brother's wrath."

"She always does," Elsbeth agreed before giving him a sidelong glance. "Now, how are we going to get you two married?"

"I am trying."

She bobbed her head. "I know, and I do believe it's working. However, we need to convince Eugenie that you are the man she cannot live without."

Charles shot her a dry look. "And how do you propose we do that?"

Her face lit up with excitement. "We host a ball! A grand affair with dancing, music—perhaps even fireworks. The perfect opportunity for you to propose again. Who could possibly refuse a proposal under a sky full of fireworks?"

"Did you forget that your family's name is currently shrouded in scandal? It may not be the best time to throw a ball."

Elsbeth's enthusiasm dimmed. "You make a valid point." She pursed her lips. "Very well, I shall keep thinking on it."

They reached the back door of the townhouse and a footman stepped forward, opening it for them. As soon as they entered the corridor, Westcott's head appeared from the doorway of his study.

"There you are, Charles," he said, his voice clipped. "A word, please."

Elsbeth smiled. "Good luck, Cousin," she murmured before disappearing down the hall.

Charles stepped inside the study, and his gaze immediately fell on the tall, brawny man standing beside Westcott. The stranger looked stern, and a deep, jagged scar marked his right cheek. His steel-gray eyes met Charles's with a level, assessing gaze.

Westcott gestured towards the man. "Allow me to introduce Stevens, the man I asked to investigate Eugenie's attempted abduction."

Charles tipped his head in greeting. "It's a pleasure to meet you."

Stevens, however, did not offer pleasantries. His sharp gaze remained fixed on Charles as he spoke. "What was your coach doing in the rookeries a few days ago?"

Charles blinked, caught off guard. "I... what?" He frowned. "I'm not sure what you're referring to."

Stevens folded his arms. "Your coach was seen in the rookeries around the same time a meeting took place at the Plucky Squirrel pub."

Charles pressed his lips together, his mind racing. "I haven't been to the rookeries in ages."

Stevens gave a short, unimpressed huff. "Just your coach, then?"

"I have no idea why my coach was in the rookeries," Charles said, his tone growing with frustration. "But I can assure you, I have never set foot in that pub."

"Then who else has access to your coaches?" Stevens pressed.

Charles turned to Westcott, irritation flaring. "What is this about?"

Westcott exchanged a glance with Stevens before answering. "Stevens tracked down the two individuals who attempted to abduct Eugenie."

"That's excellent news," Charles responded. "Are they in Newgate?"

Stevens didn't share in his relief. "Not yet, but they will be soon enough. I believe they were hired by someone."

Realization struck Charles like a blow to the chest. "You think I hired them?" he demanded, his voice rising with disbelief. "Are you mad?"

Stevens leveled a hard gaze at Charles. "Did you?"

Charles's temper flared. "Good gads, no!" he exclaimed, his voice ringing through the study. "Why in the blazes would I attempt to abduct Eugenie? I am trying to convince her to marry me, not terrify her!"

Stevens remained unmoved, his expression cool and assessing. "I've seen this kind of scheme before," he said, his tone laced with suspicion. "A man arranges for a woman to be taken, only to miraculously save her, ensuring she falls right into his arms."

Charles took a step forward, meeting Stevens's gaze with determination. "I would never resort to such deceitful means. I care for Eugenie far too much to ever risk her safety, let alone orchestrate something so vile."

Westcott, who had remained silent until now, turned to Stevens. "Are you satisfied?" he asked. "I told you Bedford had nothing to do with this."

The tension in Stevens's stance eased slightly. "I believe you," he admitted. "But that still doesn't explain how Lord Bedford's coach ended up in the rookeries."

Charles set his jaw. "I can't explain that, but I fully intend to find out."

Stevens gave a curt nod. "Do that. I'll be in touch." Without another word, he turned and strode out of the study, leaving a heavy silence in his wake.

Turning towards Westcott, Charles demanded, "Would you care to explain what that was about?"

Westcott sighed, rubbing his temples before sinking into the chair behind his desk. "Stevens insisted on questioning you himself, despite my repeated assurances that you were not involved."

"And just how competent is this Bow Street Runner?"

Westcott leaned back, steepling his fingers. "One of the best," he admitted. "Which is precisely why I hired him."

Charles dropped into the chair opposite Westcott. "Then let's focus on what's important. I suppose someone could have borrowed my coach."

"Who has access to it?"

Charles thought for a moment. "My mother... Philip—" He stopped abruptly, shaking his head. "No, not Philip. He has no reason to harm Eugenie."

"Then who else?"

Charles pushed himself to his feet and began pacing the study. "Philip is many things, but he wouldn't do something this despicable. He knows how much I care for Eugenie—he's even commented on it."

"Does he normally borrow your coach?"

"On occasion," Charles replied. "I take no issue with it, considering he is my heir."

Westcott gave him a measured look. "Regardless, I would suggest speaking to your coachmen first. You don't want to reveal too much before you know the truth."

A thought crept into his mind. "I did cut Philip off recently. Do you think he might have done this out of spite?"

"I don't know. But for now, Eugenie is safest here. I've already hired additional guards—disguised as footmen—to ensure her protection."

"That was wise," Charles admitted, though the unease in his chest did not dissipate.

Westcott pushed back from his desk. "Why don't you join us for breakfast?"

Charles pulled his pocket watch from his waistcoat and flicked it open. "I suppose I have time before meeting my friends at White's."

Westcott led the way towards the dining room. "Elsbeth and Eugenie should already be there."

As they walked down the corridor, a sudden, high-pitched neigh echoed through the house. Both men stopped in their tracks.

Westcott frowned. "Did you hear that?"

Charles suppressed a knowing grin. "I did."

Westcott continued walking. "It almost sounded like a horse..." His voice trailed off as they reached the dining room and stepped inside.

The scene before them was almost too absurd to believe. Eugenie sat at the elegantly set breakfast table, her posture utterly serene as she cut a piece of fruit and held it out to the small foal standing beside her. Sir Spotticus, completely unbothered by his surroundings, eagerly accepted the offering, chewing with contentment.

Westcott's face turned a dangerous shade of red. "*What in the blazes?!*" he roared. "What is that horse doing in my dining room?"

Unbothered, Eugenie reached up and placed her hands gently over Sir Spotticus's ears. "Not so loud," she chided. "Sir Spotticus doesn't like yelling."

Westcott turned a disbelieving stare towards his wife, who sat calmly at the other end of the table, flipping through the morning newssheets. "You allowed this?"

Elsbeth didn't even look up as she turned a page. "I didn't think it was my place to tell Eugenie no."

Westcott's nostrils flared. "A horse does not belong in a grand townhouse," he thundered. "Where did you even get that midget horse?"

Eugenie's smile was radiant as she patted Sir Spotticus's neck. "It is a *miniature* horse and Charles gave him to me."

Westcott's head swiveled slowly towards Charles, his expression thunderous. "And you thought this was a good idea?"

Charles, fighting the urge to laugh, merely clasped his hands behind his back and met Westcott's furious gaze. "It seemed like an excellent idea at the time."

"Do not fuss over this, Brother," Eugenie said airily as she stroked Sir Spotticus's neck. "He and I are to be the best of friends."

Westcott moved to sit at the head of the table. "Once breakfast is over, you will return that animal to the stables where it belongs."

Eugenie, unperturbed, cut another piece of fruit and offered it to Sir Spotticus. "Or..." she said thoughtfully, "Sir Spotticus can accompany me to the drawing room while I read us a book."

"Horses do not care about books," Westcott bristled.

Eugenie tsked at him, running a hand down the foal's spotted neck. "This horse does. He will be well-read and properly educated. I daresay he will have better manners than some people in this room."

Charles, who had been quietly observing the exchange, hid his smirk behind his hand. He knew well enough that Eugenie did not take orders kindly, and Westcott was walking directly into a battle he was bound to lose.

"Eugenie..." Westcott's voice took on a sharper edge, his patience clearly wearing thin. "I forbid that horse from being in here. Just think of the mess he will make. Be sensible in this."

Eugenie's back straightened, and a familiar defiant glint sparked in her eyes. "You, dear brother, do not get to dictate my actions. This is my home as well."

"That may be," Westcott countered, "but I am the lord of this manor, and I have the final say."

Eugenie feigned deep contemplation, tapping a finger against her chin. Then, as if struck by a marvelous idea, she smiled. "Well then, if Sir Spotticus is to remain in the stables, I shall move in with him."

Westcott's fork clattered against his plate as he stared at her in disbelief. "You cannot reside in the stables."

Eugenie lifted her cup of tea with an air of serenity. "Whyever not? There is ample space, fresh air, and delightful company." She looked to Charles as though seeking his agreement. "I do think my bed would look rather lovely in the corner of the stables, don't you?"

Charles coughed into his fist as he fought the urge to laugh outright. He had no doubt that Eugenie was perfectly serious, and he almost wished to see how far she would take this absurd battle of wills.

Westcott pinched the bridge of his nose, muttering something under his breath that sounded very much like a plea for divine patience. "Eugenie," he said, voice dangerously low, "you are not moving into the stables."

"Well," she said with a careless shrug, reaching for another piece of fruit, "then I suppose Sir Spotticus shall remain right here."

Charles leaned back in his chair, thoroughly enjoying the spectacle. This, he thought, was why life was never dull with Eugenie.

15

E ugenie sat in the drawing room, one hand holding a book while the other idly stroked Sir Spotticus's soft mane as he lay curled at her feet. Sunlight streamed through the tall windows, casting a golden glow over the room's elegant furnishings. She read aloud, her voice lilting as she brought the words on the page to life, though the deep, rhythmic breathing of the foal at her feet indicated he cared little for the literature being recited. Still, she continued, undeterred. If her brother happened to pass by and see her engaging in such an "improper" activity—reading aloud to a miniature horse in a drawing room—his irritation would be worth every word.

She had just reached a rather dramatic passage when Tanner stepped into the room and cleared his throat. "Lady Jane is here to call upon you, my lady."

At the unexpected intrusion, Sir Spotticus lifted his head, ears twitching, his large, dark eyes peering curiously towards the doorway.

Eugenie smiled, giving the foal a reassuring pat. "Please send her in."

A moment later, Jane swept into the room, her muslin skirts rustling as she came to an abrupt halt just past the threshold. Her gaze dropped instantly to the floor, her eyes widening with astonishment. "Is that a miniature horse?" she gasped.

Eugenie, as if this were the most normal thing in the world, simply nodded. "It is."

Jane let out a delighted squeal and hurried over, dropping gracefully to her knees beside Sir Spotticus. "I simply adore miniature horses! I have wanted one for years, but my brother insists they are pointless animals."

"My brother shares your brother's sentiment, but as you can see, I care little for his opinion on the matter."

Jane stroked Sir Spotticus's coat, her expression wistful. "How do you manage such defiance?" she asked. "Does your brother not control your pin money?"

"Mostly, yes. But I have a small inheritance from my grandmother that is entirely my own."

Jane sighed, continuing to pet the foal. "My brother won't even allow me to have a dog. He insists my time would be better spent pursuing womanly accomplishments."

Eugenie wrinkled her nose. "I don't believe I would get along very well with your brother."

Jane hesitated, her hand stilling for the briefest moment before she murmured, "For the most part, he is kind to me."

Eugenie studied her carefully, detecting something unspoken in those words. "I'm sorry," she said, unsure of what else to say.

Jane straightened, brushing invisible dust from her skirts before moving to the settee opposite Eugenie. "Sometimes," she admitted, "I feel more like an afterthought than anything else."

"That must be difficult."

"It is," Jane admitted with a small, weary smile. "But what can I do about it? I am merely a young woman in a man's world."

The quiet resignation in her voice made Eugenie's heart ache for Jane. She had been fortunate, raised in a family that—despite their exasperation with her—had never truly tried to suppress her spirit. To feel insignificant within one's own home was a burden she could not imagine bearing.

Jane quickly shook off her melancholy and brightened. "But enough about that. I didn't come here to be such a naysayer."

"You don't need a reason to call upon me," Eugenie reassured her.

A mischievous smile flickered across Jane's lips. "In that case, I have rather interesting news." She leaned in conspiratorially. "I discovered who wrote that article about you and Lord Bedford."

Eugenie sat up straighter. "You did? How were you able to manage that?"

Jane's grin widened. "I called upon my uncle and asked him outright."

"And he told you?" she asked. "Just like that?"

"Oh, absolutely not," Jane said, tossing her head back with a laugh. "But when he refused, I simply waited until he left his study, then searched his desk."

Eugenie's mouth parted in shock. "You searched his desk?"

"I did," Jane said proudly, lifting her chin. "And I must say, the author of the article may surprise you."

Eugenie leaned forward. "Who is it?"

Jane folded her hands neatly in her lap before saying, matter-of-factly, "Miss Winslow."

"Miss Winslow?" she repeated, taken aback. "Why would she write such a thing? She was there that night. She was the reason I left the veranda in the first place."

Jane's brow furrowed. "Miss Winslow was there? With you and Lord Bedford?"

"No," Eugenie said, knowing it was time to trust Jane with

her secret. "I was alone on the veranda when I heard giggling. I went to investigate and saw Miss Winslow attempting to kiss Lord Bedford. When I made my presence known, he followed me back to explain what had happened."

Jane frowned. "Then why would she report that you were alone with Lord Bedford?"

"Precisely," Eugenie said, frustration creeping into her tone. "It doesn't make any sense."

Jane bit her lower lip, deep in thought. "Do you think she fabricated the article purely for the sake of gossip?"

"But why target me? I hardly know her."

Jane considered this before offering, "What if you convinced her to print a retraction? If she did, the *ton* would move on to some other piece of gossip soon enough."

Eugenie leaned back against the cushions, tapping a finger against her knee. "And what if she denies writing the article? I have no tangible proof, and I wouldn't dare reveal how I discovered this information."

Jane pressed her lips together. "That is a conundrum."

Eugenie nodded grimly, her mind already turning over possibilities. If Miss Winslow had orchestrated this scandal, then she had to have a reason. But what did she have to gain from this?

The door swung open with a soft creak, and Elsbeth stepped into the drawing room. A warm smile spread across her face the moment her eyes landed on Lady Jane. "Jane, what a pleasant surprise," she said as she crossed the room.

Jane returned her smile with equal warmth. "Good afternoon, Elsbeth. I would have arrived much earlier had I known Eugenie keeps a miniature horse as a pet."

Elsbeth let out a soft laugh. "Ah," she said with amusement glinting in her eyes. "That is rather a sore subject in this household, I'm afraid. My husband insists Sir Spotticus should reside in the stables with the other horses."

"But he is not like most horses," Eugenie interjected. "He is far too tiny, far too delicate. He needs our attention."

Elsbeth gracefully lowered herself into a chair opposite them. "As you can see, we are at an impasse," she said with an air of playful resignation. "And I am wisely choosing to stay out of this particular battle."

Jane laughed. "A smart woman, indeed."

Eugenie shifted to face Elsbeth and addressed her. "What do you know about Miss Winslow?"

Elsbeth's brows knitted together in mild confusion. "Miss Winslow?" she repeated. "I know very little about her, truth be told. She is a few years younger than me. May I ask why you're inquiring?"

Eugenie hesitated for only a moment before exchanging a glance with Jane, who gave her a subtle nod of approval. Turning back to Elsbeth, Eugenie revealed, "She is the one who wrote the article about me."

Elsbeth's eyes widened slightly. "Whatever for?"

Eugenie shrugged. "That is precisely what I intend to find out."

"And how, may I ask, do you plan on doing that?" Elsbeth inquired.

"That is an excellent question," Eugenie mused, tapping her fingers against her knee. "One for which I shall ponder and hopefully devise an answer in due time."

Elsbeth shifted in her seat, considering for a moment before offering, "I have heard that Miss Winslow is rather... shallow. She is exceedingly eager to find a match this Season."

Eugenie let out a small scoff. "What young woman in the *ton* isn't?"

"A fair point," Elsbeth conceded. Then, after a brief pause, she added, "May I ask how you discovered that Miss Winslow was the one behind the article?"

Jane spoke up. "I found proof when I searched my uncle's

desk. Apparently, Miss Winslow has been writing under the pseudonym of Mr. Fairchild for over a year now."

Elsbeth's eyebrows shot up in surprise. "Miss Winslow? Writing for the newssheets? I wouldn't have thought her clever enough for such a venture."

"I daresay there is more than meets the eye when it comes to Miss Winslow," Eugenie remarked.

Before anyone could respond, Niles strode in with a purposeful stride. His gaze immediately fell to the miniature horse at Eugenie's feet, and his expression darkened with exasperation.

"Why," he asked in a tone of long-suffering patience, "is that midget horse in the drawing room?"

"I was reading to him," Eugenie replied, knowing that revelation would irritate her brother to no end.

Niles pressed two fingers to his temple, as though warding off an impending headache. "Are you actively trying to give me a heart attack?"

Elsbeth quickly rose from her seat. "Perhaps we could take a turn around the gardens," she suggested, stepping towards her husband.

Niles's tense expression eased ever so slightly, the corners of his mouth twitching in reluctant affection. "I would like that," he admitted. Then, turning back towards Eugenie, his eyes narrowed once more. "And when I return, that horse will be gone."

Eugenie lifted her chin defiantly. "I can't promise that," she said. "Sir Spotticus goes wherever I go."

Elsbeth slipped her arm through Niles's, gently tugging him towards the door. "Shall we, my love?"

For a moment, it seemed Niles would press the matter further, his lips parting as if to launch one final argument. But then with a resigned sigh, he relented. "Very well," he muttered. "I could use some fresh air."

As the couple departed, their murmured conversation fading into the hallway, Jane let out a wistful sigh. "I find that I am rather envious of Elsbeth," she admitted, her gaze lingering on the doorway. "Despite all odds, she found love."

Eugenie let out an amused scoff. "You should try riding in a carriage with them," she quipped. "They are so utterly bewitched by one another that they hardly notice anyone else exists."

Jane's lips curled into a soft smile. "That is sweet."

"Perhaps I said it wrong, then," Eugenie said with a mock shudder.

Jane's laughter was brief but genuine, though it faded almost as quickly as it had come. "I do not even dare to dream of marrying for love," she confessed. "My father has made it abundantly clear that he will be the one choosing my husband."

"And you're simply going to accept that?"

"What choice do I have?" Jane asked, a trace of bitterness creeping into her tone. "Without my father's approval, I have nothing. No home, no security. The only thing I truly possess is a substantial dowry, and that, too, will belong to my husband the moment I marry."

Eugenie fixed her with a pointed stare. "So you're going to let him dictate your entire life?"

Jane held Eugenie's gaze for a long moment before offering a weak smile. "Not everyone is as fortunate as you, Eugenie."

The words hit Eugenie harder than she expected. She was indeed fortunate—perhaps more than she had ever truly considered. She had a brother who loved her unconditionally, who defended her even when she was at her most impossible. She had the freedom to speak her mind, to make choices for herself, and to live a life that many young women of the *ton* could only dream of.

But what was she doing with her life?

An image of Charles came to her mind. And a realization struck her. Every day, he was the first thing she was grateful for. That thought should have comforted her, but instead, it terrified her. For he wasn't just a part of her life; he was the best part of it.

Charles settled into the plush leather armchair at White's, his fingers loosely curled around a glass of brandy that had long since lost his attention. The rich scent of tobacco and the low murmur of conversation filled the gentlemen's club, but his mind was elsewhere. The news from his coachman still rang in his ears—Philip had indeed used his coach to travel into the rookeries. What was his cousin thinking? Could he truly be entangled in the attempted abduction of Lady Eugenie? The notion seemed absurd, yet the evidence was mounting.

His brooding was interrupted when a man took the seat across from him. Dark-haired, well-groomed, and dressed as a gentleman, the newcomer's transformation was striking. The fitted blue jacket and buff trousers were a stark contrast to the rough, clandestine figure Charles had encountered before. But the scar on his right cheek was unmistakable.

Stevens.

Charles's gaze narrowed. "What are you doing here?" he asked in a low voice.

Stevens smirked, an expression that didn't quite reach his calculating eyes. "I do not know why you look so surprised. I am a member of this club."

"You are a member of White's?" he repeated back in disbelief.

"I daresay that you know very little about me," Stevens

responded smoothly. "Besides, I am merely doing my friend, Westcott, a favor."

Charles leaned back, studying him. The man was an enigma, and he disliked puzzles he could not solve.

Stevens's expression turned serious. "Did you speak to your coachman?"

"I did," Charles confirmed. "Philip, my cousin, used my coach to travel to the rookeries."

Stevens nodded as if he had expected this.

Charles lifted a hand. "But that doesn't mean my cousin attended a meeting with the alleged abductors," he argued. "There is a notorious gambling hell near the pub. He may have gone there instead."

Stevens's brows lifted. "Did your coachman say how long Mr. Ellsworth was gone?"

"About an hour."

Stevens exchanged a knowing look with him. "I daresay your cousin usually spends a considerably longer amount of time in gambling hells."

Charles's grip tightened around his glass. "How would you know that?"

Stevens's smirk returned. "Consider it a lucky guess. But let's assume for a moment that Mr. Ellsworth did meet with the men who attempted the abduction. Do you have any reason as to why?"

"I don't. It wouldn't benefit Philip at all if Lady Eugenie were abducted."

"There must be a reason."

Before Charles could respond, a familiar voice interrupted them.

"Warwicke," Alcott greeted, coming to stand beside their table. "I hadn't realized you had returned to Town."

Charles's head snapped towards Alcott, his brows furrowing

in surprise. "Warwicke? As in Baron Warwicke? The war hero that came back from the dead?"

Alcott bobbed his head. "The one and the same," he confirmed. "This man fought right alongside Wellington."

Warwicke—Stevens—rose abruptly. "I am no war hero," he said gruffly, excusing himself before either of them could press further.

Alcott watched him go, his gaze thoughtful. "From what I have heard, he does not talk about what happened to him in the war."

Charles was left with more questions than answers. If Warwicke was a baron, why was he working as a Bow Street Runner?

Alcott took the vacant seat. "I was not aware that you were acquainted with Warwicke."

"I'm not, really," Charles admitted. "I only met the man earlier today at Westcott's townhouse."

"I fought alongside Warwicke for a short time," Alcott mused. "I do not think I have met a finer soldier."

Addington approached, taking a seat beside them. "I do apologize for arriving late."

"Well, you are here now," Charles said.

With a curious look, Addington remarked, "I have not seen your 'friend' at Oxford since the last lecture you both attended."

"Which friend is that?" Alcott asked, glancing between them.

Charles shrugged. "Someone you do not know."

Alcott arched an eyebrow. "Do you have more friends than us?" he teased. "I scarcely believe that."

"It is true," Charles said before taking a sip of his drink. "I hope to bring my 'friend' to one of your lectures in the near future."

"Now I am even more curious," Alcott said. "Would I at least know of him?"

Charles leaned forward and placed his glass onto the table. "I would prefer if we discussed something else."

"We could discuss how I am a Fellow now," Addington announced proudly. "It was confirmed this morning."

"Well done!" Charles praised.

Alcott shifted to face Addington. "You are rather young to be a Fellow, are you not?"

In response, he puffed out his chest. "I am."

"Have you told your father yet?" Alcott asked.

Addington's pleased expression dimmed. "I have not, but I doubt he will care. He thinks a profession in academia is pointless."

"Well, what you have done is rather impressive," Charles said, raising his glass. "You worked hard, and you are reaping the rewards."

"Thank you, Bedford," Addington said.

Charles lowered his glass. "Fellow Addington. That has a nice ring to it."

A short, balding server approached with a tray. "May I get you gentlemen something to drink?"

"We have cause for celebration," Alcott declared. "Bring three glasses of your finest brandy."

The server nodded and disappeared to fulfill the order.

Alcott settled back in his chair. "Perhaps we have two causes for celebration," he said, meeting Charles's gaze. "Are you engaged to Lady Eugenie?"

"Not yet, but not for lack of trying," Charles admitted, seeing no reason to deny it.

"I assumed as much since I read about your... situation in the newssheets," Alcott said.

Charles crossed his arms over his chest as his irritation

flared. "The only reason why there was a 'situation' was because you got distracted by a political debate."

Alcott gave him a baffled look. "What does that mean?"

"I took your sister outside because she was rather drunk and then she tried to kiss me," Charles explained. "Lady Eugenie happened upon us, and I followed her to the veranda to try to explain what happened."

"My sister tried to kiss you?" Alcott asked in disbelief.

Addington grinned. "Interesting," he muttered.

Alcott ignored him and pressed forward. "I hadn't realized. She said nothing of this when she returned to the ballroom. So why was it reported that you were alone with Lady Eugenie?"

Charles tossed his hands up in frustration. "I cannot say. But a Mr. Fairchild wrote the article for the Society page."

Addington leaned in and whispered, "Some people say that Mr. Fairchild is actually a lady writing under a pseudonym."

"I wouldn't be surprised," Alcott said, shaking his head with a knowing smirk. He leaned back in his chair. "Women do love their gossip."

"Regardless, Mr. Fairchild was utterly mistaken about Lady Eugenie and me, yet no one will believe it. The damage is done," Charles said as he clenched his jaw.

Addington merely shrugged. "There are worse women to marry."

Alcott grew somber. "Thank you for what you did for my sister. I am truly sorry to have gotten you into this predicament."

Before Charles could reply, the server stepped forward and set their glasses down. "Will there be anything else, gentlemen?"

"No, thank you," Charles said, barely sparing him a glance.

Alcott picked up his drink, swirling the amber liquid idly before taking a sip. "I must admit that I have no desire to fall prey to the parson's mousetrap. Marriage is the least of my concerns when I can barely manage my sister as it is."

Addington lowered his voice, glancing around as if ensuring they weren't overheard. "Did you read the newssheets this morning?"

"I did," Alcott replied grimly. "Poor Wilton. The *ton* has finally caught wind of his sister running off to Gretna Green to elope."

Charles shook his head. "That is most unfortunate."

"But what's worse is that it was reported Lady Olivia has returned home... without a husband," Addington added.

Alcott's brows shot up. "Where did the husband go?"

"No one knows," Addington said, his voice taking on a conspiratorial edge. "The rumor is he abandoned her the moment he claimed her dowry."

"That man is despicable," Charles said, his tone sharp with disapproval.

Addington leaned back in his seat. "I won't argue with you there."

Charles tossed back the rest of his drink in one swift motion and placed the empty glass onto the table with a dull thud. "If you will excuse me, I have matters to attend to."

"Would those 'matters' have anything to do with the duel?" Alcott asked with a knowing gleam in his eyes.

Charles let out a heavy sigh. "So, you've heard."

Alcott let out a dry chuckle. "Everyone has heard. Your cousin can't seem to keep his mouth shut about it."

"Wonderful," Charles muttered under his breath.

"If it's any consolation, getting shot might humble Philip," Alcott offered up.

Charles pushed back his chair and rose. "I'm more concerned about him getting killed."

The humor vanished from Alcott's expression. "There's always that risk when it comes to a duel," he said, his voice quieter now, edged with something that could have been concern or resignation.

"I am hoping to keep my cousin alive long enough for him to figure out what he actually wants out of life," Charles said. His tone was laced with exasperation, though beneath it, a sliver of worry remained. Philip had always been reckless, but this was pushing the limits of foolishness.

"I wish you luck with that," Addington said. "You'll need it."

Charles didn't reply. Instead, he strode towards the door. His frustration with Philip simmered beneath the surface, growing with every step. He had neither the time nor the patience for this sort of nonsense.

There were more pressing matters at hand—his estate, for one, which required constant attention. And then there was Eugenie. Convincing her to marry him was proving to be a far greater challenge than he had anticipated.

He tightened his jaw, shoving aside his irritation. He would handle Philip. He would handle the estate. And somehow, he would convince Lady Eugenie that marrying him was the right choice.

One way or another, he had no intention of losing.

16

A lone candle glowed on the writing desk as Eugenie sat in the library trying to think of something to write for her next article. What topic would capture the interest of her readers? And if she bared her soul upon the page, would it be enough?

As she tapped the feathered tip of the quill against her lips, Charles entered the room, looking far too handsome for his own good. She schooled her expression into an air of indifference. "Dare I ask why you are here?"

"To see you, of course," Charles replied, a devilish smile curving his lips.

She arched an eyebrow. "The truth, if you please."

Charles's smile merely grew. "Elsbeth extended an invitation for dinner, and I found it unwise to refuse. However," he added, stepping farther into the room, "I was not entirely dishonest. I did, indeed, come to see you."

"Well, you saw me. You can leave now," Eugenie said.

He moved to stand beside her, his gaze drifting towards the paper in front of her. "Did I interrupt something of importance?"

Eugenie placed the quill down, knowing she could trust Charles with her secret. "I was working on what to write for my next article in the Society page."

Charles's brow shot up. "You are writing articles for the newssheets?"

"I am," she affirmed.

Leaning in slightly, he asked in a low voice, "Are you Mr. James Fairchild?"

She shook her head. "No, I wrote the article titled *A Spinster's Guide to Scandal*." She hesitated before revealing, "But I know who is writing under Mr. Fairchild's name."

Curiosity flashed across his face. "Who?"

She took a deep breath before answering. "Miss Winslow."

His expression shifted to one of disbelief. "Are you quite certain?"

"I am," she confirmed. "But I cannot disclose how I came by this knowledge. Suffice it to say, my source is trustworthy."

He ran a hand through his hair, clearly unsettled. "But why would she write such fabrications? She was there. She knows the truth."

"I do not know," Eugenie admitted, determination settling in her chest. "But I intend to call upon her tomorrow and demand answers."

Charles frowned. "Your brother will never allow you to leave the townhouse, not after the recent attempt to abduct you."

Eugenie's lips pressed together in frustration. "I feared as much, but it changes nothing. I must go."

"Then I shall take you," he declared.

She lifted her gaze to his. "And risk my brother's wrath?"

Charles's lips twitched. "It would not be the first time I have endured his ire for your sake, nor will it be the last, I suspect. We shall go under the guise of a simple carriage ride."

Warmth spread through her chest. In that moment, she

thought she could not care for him more than she already did. "Thank you," she murmured.

Charles reached for the paper she had been toiling over, scanning its contents. "This is good," he acknowledged.

"You approve?" she asked.

His gaze softened as he set the paper down. "I support you in all that you do, Eugenie. No matter what. I only ask that you remain true to yourself."

She had been mistaken.

She did not merely care for Charles.

She loved him.

For how could she not? He saw her, truly saw her—the woman she kept hidden from the rest of the world.

Charles cleared his throat, drawing back her attention. "Elsbeth sent me to retrieve you. The dinner bell should sound soon."

Eugenie rose to her feet, the shift bringing her mere inches from him. Her heart pounded against her ribcage as she found herself caught in his gaze. "We should go," she managed.

"Yes," he murmured, leaning closer. "We should."

But she didn't want to go. Not now. Her eyes dropped to his lips and she hoped that he would kiss her again. She could feel his warm breath against her lips and she closed her eyes in anticipation.

"Eugenie..." His voice was hoarse.

She opened her eyes, finding his filled with raw intensity.

"If I kiss you, I won't let you go," he confessed, his fingers trailing up to cup her right cheek. "Is that what you want?"

Yes.

But the word lodged in her throat, held captive by uncertainty.

He continued. "I want you. I want us. I want it all. With you. Now and forever," he said. "I want to be the man at your side, your greatest supporter. I want to be your husband."

"Charles..." she whispered, her thoughts a tumult of emotions.

"Marry me, Eugenie," he said fervently. "I promise to be the man that you need."

It would be so easy to say yes, but something held her back. Charles said nothing about love. And that is what she wanted more than anything else.

With great reluctance, she took a step back. "I'm sorry, Charles, but I cannot accept."

His face fell, pain flashing across his features. "Whyever not?" he asked. "I care for you, and I suspect that you care for me as well."

She looked away. "I do, but I want more. I want love."

Charles reached for her hand, squeezing it gently. "I want that, too," he asserted. "I do believe I am already halfway there."

Eugenie's voice was barely above a whisper. "As am I... but I am scared."

"What are you scared of?"

She took a steadying breath. "My grandparents loved each other deeply, but when my grandfather died, a part of my grandmother died that day. She would sit in her armchair by the fireplace, day in and day out, and stare at the portrait of her husband. There was no consoling her. She longed for death because it meant she no longer had to endure another day without her true love," she shared. "When she died, the doctor said she had a smile on her face."

Charles's lips curved slightly. "That sounds beautiful."

"It terrifies me. I can't risk losing myself like that."

His grip on her hand tightened. "You don't know what the future holds. You should live and love every day like it is your last. Because one day, it will be. You must take chances and live your life."

"Yes, but it is safer not to risk one's heart."

He nodded. "Yes, it is safer," he agreed. "But love is not

something you search for. Love finds you, and when it does, whether you are ready or not, it will be the best thing to ever happen to you."

Eugenie searched his eyes. "And if you are wrong?"

"I am rarely wrong," he replied with a smirk.

Despite herself, a slight laugh escaped her lips. "You are being rather cocky."

"It is only when I know what I want, and I won't stop at anything to get it," Charles said. "And I am convinced the rest of my life looks like you."

"You aren't making this easy on me, are you?" Eugenie asked.

Charles's finger traced her cheek. "You know how I feel, but I won't force you," he said. "I care about you too much to do such a thing."

A loud clearing of a throat from the doorway shattered the moment, causing both Eugenie and Charles to jump apart. Eugenie's head snapped towards the source of the interruption, only to find Elsbeth standing there, arms crossed, a look of disapproval etched on her face.

"I do hope I am interrupting something," her sister-in-law remarked, her voice laced with dry humor.

Charles offered his cousin a wry smile. "I was merely attempting to convince Eugenie to marry me."

Elsbeth's gaze flickered between them, a knowing glint in her eyes. "Well, it seemed to be going rather well, but the dinner bell rang a few moments ago. Shall we adjourn to the dining room before the food turns cold?"

"Yes, I believe that is a splendid idea," Charles said, turning towards Eugenie and offering his arm.

Eugenie placed her hand on his sleeve. Together, they followed Elsbeth out of the library and into the dimly lit corridor, the silence between them filled with unspoken thoughts and emotions still lingering from their conversation.

It was Elsbeth who finally broke the quiet. "I am rather surprised I did not find Sir Spotticus curled up in the library with you."

Eugenie laughed. "I thought it best to return him to the stables for now. I found that horses, even miniature ones, are rather messy."

"Niles will be thrilled, no doubt, to hear that," Elsbeth said.

Eugenie turned her gaze towards Charles. "Have I properly thanked you for Sir Spotticus?"

"You have," he assured her. "And I am glad you have taken to him so well. Perhaps he will help you rediscover your love for horses."

She let out a small sigh. "I do love horses, Charles, but riding one is an entirely different matter. I am not certain I will ever be brave enough to get in the saddle again."

Charles reached over and gave her hand a reassuring pat. "Whether you do or not, you will always have my support."

As they stepped into the grand entry hall, she saw Niles standing in casual conversation with Charles's mother. His sharp gaze lifted to meet theirs, and his lips quirked in mild exasperation. "It is about time," he commented, his tone teasing but edged with impatience.

Elsbeth moved to stand beside him, giving him a playful nudge. "Leave them be," she said lightly. "They were engaged in a discussion of utmost importance."

"And what, pray tell, was so important?" Niles asked.

Elsbeth's expression remained composed. "It is none of our concern."

Niles looked as though he would press the matter further, his mouth opening slightly as if forming another protest. But after a moment, he exhaled a long, knowing sigh. "Very well. I suppose I should simply be grateful that the midget horse isn't with Eugenie."

"Again, it is a *miniature* horse, dear brother," Eugenie

corrected. "And if you continue to be unkind, I shall fetch him from the stables."

"The stables are precisely where that horse belongs," Niles grumbled.

Elsbeth, ever the peacemaker—or perhaps just eager to move things along—looped her arm through Niles's and began leading him towards the dining room. "We can continue this utterly fascinating debate over supper."

"Oh, wonderful," Niles muttered, though he allowed himself to be pulled along.

Charles's mother, who had remained an amused spectator thus far, finally spoke. "Now I find myself quite intrigued by this famed horse. When might I have the pleasure of meeting him?"

"I shall take you to the stables after supper," Eugenie promised eagerly. "You will adore Sir Spotticus, I have no doubt. Charles was the one who gifted him to me."

"Interesting," was all she said, though her eyes twinkled with unspoken speculation.

Charles merely offered a nonchalant shrug. "He suits her."

Eugenie glanced up at him, her heart giving an involuntary flutter at the quiet sentiment behind those simple words. The miniature horse had been a gift, yes, but Charles had known precisely what it would mean to her—how it would remind her of a time before fear had taken hold.

And that, more than anything, made Sir Spotticus all the more special.

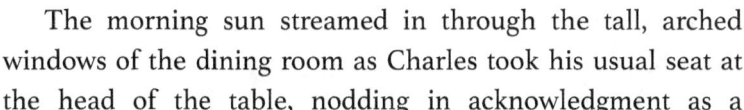

The morning sun streamed in through the tall, arched windows of the dining room as Charles took his usual seat at the head of the table, nodding in acknowledgment as a footman promptly stepped forward and placed a plate of freshly prepared food before him.

Before he could take his first bite, his mother entered the room, the newssheets clutched in her hand like a weapon of truth. She sat beside him and asked, "Have you read the newssheets yet?"

"No," Charles replied simply, slicing into his food with deliberate movements.

His mother exhaled dramatically. "I'm afraid you and Eugenie have been mentioned once more in an article by Mr. Fairchild."

Charles knew he would regret asking, but curiosity got the better of him. "What does it say?"

She lifted the newssheets and read aloud: "*Despite Lord Bedford visiting Lady Eugenie on numerous occasions, I have it on good authority that no engagement is forthcoming. One must wonder what they are discussing during these clandestine meetings...*" She glanced up from the page. "Shall I continue?"

"Please stop," Charles said, reaching for his glass. "I have no need to listen to such drivel."

His mother set the newssheets down with a pointed look. "It isn't nonsense, Dear. You and Eugenie are in a precarious situation, and the only way to silence these rumors is to convince her to marry you."

Charles clenched his jaw. "I am trying."

"I know, but you must try harder," she asserted.

With a shake of his head, he replied, "Eugenie wants love."

"And you can't give her that?"

Charles hesitated. "Yes... perhaps in time. But it is far too soon to speak of love and whatnot."

His mother folded the newssheets and placed them onto the table, her expression softening. "I loved your father from the moment I met him."

Charles scoffed. "That was infatuation, Mother. No one can fall in love that quickly."

"No, it wasn't," she insisted. "He took my heart by surprise, and I never wanted it back. It was wholly his, and I never regretted that choice."

Leaning back in his chair, Charles said, "Love is not that simple."

"It can be," she countered. "But people tend to overthink these matters. I believe your feelings for Eugenie run deeper than you allow yourself to admit."

"And why do you think that?"

His mother smiled knowingly. "Because I see the way your eyes linger on her whenever she is in the room."

Charles let out a huff. "That does not mean I love Eugenie. It only confirms that I find her beautiful. I don't deny that I have feelings for her, but love..." He shook his head. "Love comes much later in a relationship—if it comes at all."

She lifted her hands in mock surrender. "All right. You win. You clearly do not love Eugenie, and I was wrong to suggest you did."

"Thank you," he said, relieved to have finally gotten through to her.

A footman placed a cup of chocolate before his mother. She took a delicate sip before asking, "Since you do not love Lady Eugenie, I assume you wouldn't take issue with her marrying another?"

Charles nearly choked on his food. He straightened in his seat, his entire body tensing. "Absolutely not!"

His mother calmly set her cup back on the saucer. "If Eugenie desires love and you are unable to give it to her, shouldn't you let her find it elsewhere?"

"I never said I couldn't love her."

A knowing gleam entered her eyes. "Perhaps your feelings are muddled by the fact that you have kissed her."

"Pardon?" How in the blazes did his mother know about that?

His mother gave a dismissive wave of her hand. "Elsbeth and I do talk, Dear. She mentioned that she has caught you twice now in rather scandalous situations."

He sighed, running a hand through his hair. "It is true, but only because I have been trying to convince Eugenie to marry me."

"Do you even want to marry her?"

"Yes."

"Why?" she asked, her voice calm but probing. "Why is it so important that you marry Eugenie?"

Charles frowned. "It is my fault that her name has been tainted by scandal. It is the only honorable thing to do."

His mother nodded thoughtfully. "So you only wish to marry Eugenie for honor's sake?"

"Yes... no," he admitted, frustration creeping into his voice. "I also care for her."

"You keep saying as much. But I believe you are lying to yourself."

Charles's frown deepened. "This conversation is going nowhere. Can we please eat our breakfast in silence?"

"Yes, under one condition."

His gaze flickered warily to hers. "Which is?"

She leaned forward slightly. "Where do you see yourself in five years?"

"I don't know. In England."

She laughed. "Yes, but who do you see by your side? Do you wish for a family?"

"Of course, I want a family. I need an heir."

"If that is the case, any young woman would do," his mother pointed out. "Why go through the trouble of convincing Eugenie to marry you? There are plenty of young women who would leap at the chance to become your wife."

Charles set his fork down, his thoughts tangling in frustration. He knew precisely what his mother was doing. But he didn't want just any woman. He wanted Eugenie. But it wasn't because he loved her. No. He cared for her deeply. There was a difference. With Eugenie, he never had to pretend. She saw him, flaws and all, and never looked away. He showed her his imperfections, his fears, his burdens—and she, in turn, gave him her raw truth. Together, their broken pieces fit perfectly.

Fortunately, before Charles had the chance to formulate a response, Hagen entered the room, offering a timely and welcome distraction. He met Charles's gaze and announced, "Baron Warwicke has requested a moment of your time, my lord."

At this, his mother's eyes widened with curiosity. "I have heard that man survived being shot and stabbed—multiple times."

Charles let out a weary sigh. "Do not believe everything you read, Mother." Pushing back his chair, he rose to his feet and turned his attention to the butler. "Please show him into the study."

"As you wish, my lord," Hagen replied with a slight bow before departing to fulfill the order.

His mother tilted her head, still watching him with keen interest. "I was not aware that you were acquainted with Lord Warwicke."

"I only recently made his acquaintance," Charles answered, keeping his tone vague. The last thing he wanted was for his mother to pry into this particular matter. "If you will excuse me..." His voice trailed off as he made his way towards the door.

Just as he reached the doorway, his mother called after him, "Do you intend to call upon Eugenie today?"

He paused, glancing over his shoulder. "I do," he admitted. "I am taking her on a carriage ride this morning."

A bright, triumphant smile spread across his mother's face. "What wonderful news."

Rather than indulge her any further, Charles simply inclined his head and stepped out of the dining room, making his way towards the rear of the townhouse. His mother meant well, but her interference in his personal affairs was becoming tiresome. He had far more pressing concerns at the moment.

Upon arriving at the study, he found Baron Warwicke already present, standing beside the mantel. The man's expression was as stoic as ever, his presence commanding without effort.

"Good morning," Charles greeted, stepping farther into the room.

Warwicke wasted no time on pleasantries. "I followed your cousin to Mr. Kingston's home, where he remained for over an hour." His tone was direct, devoid of embellishment.

"That makes little sense," Charles responded. "Kingston despises Philip, and they are set to duel soon—unless I can put an end to this madness."

Warwicke's gaze remained sharp. "Mr. Ellsworth has accumulated a fair amount of gambling debt."

"I am aware, though it is still somewhat manageable. I had intended to settle the matter, but Philip's reckless behavior has tested my patience."

Picking up a small porcelain vase from the mantel, Warwicke studied it with casual disinterest. "The two men who attempted to abduct Lady Eugenie remain in Newgate. Thus far, they have remained tight-lipped about who hired them, but I have my suspicions."

"You still believe Philip is responsible?"

"That is a possibility," Warwicke admitted. "Mr. Ellsworth is reckless and seems to think only of himself."

Charles struggled to reconcile the image of his cousin with such treachery. "What would he possibly gain from it?"

Warwicke returned the vase to its place and turned to face him. "That is what I intend to find out. Until I do, I have instructed Westcott to keep his sister at their townhouse, where she will be safest."

Charles studied the man before him, his mind turning over the implications of everything Warwicke had just said. There was something about the baron—his calculated movements, his unwavering confidence—that made it difficult to gauge his true motivations.

After a pause, Charles decided to ask, "May I ask a question?"

"That depends on what it is."

Charles crossed his arms over his chest. "Why are you doing this? You are a baron, yet you seem oddly invested in these affairs."

Warwicke regarded him for a moment before saying, "As I told you, I am doing this as a favor to Westcott. Nothing more."

But something in his tone made Charles wonder if that was the entire truth. "Regardless, I thank you for what you are doing to keep Lady Eugenie safe."

Warwicke inclined his head slightly. "I will be in touch. Until then, be wary of Mr. Ellsworth. He is not someone to be trusted."

"My cousin is many things, but I do not believe he had anything to do with Lady Eugenie's abduction," Charles said firmly. "Philip wouldn't do such a thing."

The baron's sharp gaze didn't waver. "Did you not recently cut off his allowance?"

"I did, but—"

Warwicke cut him off. "That alone could serve as motive. Do not be deceived by his youth. I have seen men much younger than he commit unspeakable acts in desperation."

With reluctance in his tone, Charles replied, "I won't."

"Good," Warwicke said, his expression unreadable. "Good day."

With that, the baron strode from the study, leaving Charles standing motionless, his mind turning over every word exchanged.

Philip. At Mr. Kingston's home. For over an hour.

What had he been doing there? Was he attempting to negotiate terms, to put an end to the duel? Or was there something more sinister at play?

None of it made sense. And the more Charles thought about it, the more uneasy he became.

———————

17

Eugenie sat at the writing desk in the drawing room, a sheet of paper before her and a quill resting idly between her fingers. Sir Spotticus lay curled at her feet, his spotted coat rising and falling with each steady breath. Every so often, he flicked an ear or shifted his hooves, but for the most part, he dozed peacefully, unaware of her inner turmoil.

Eugenie sighed, her gaze drifting away from her half-written article and towards the long clock in the corner. Any moment now, Charles would arrive.

Not that she should be waiting for him. Not that she should care.

But she did.

Terribly.

Since coming to the realization that she was in love with Charles, everything had changed. The way she looked at him. The way she anticipated his visits. The way her heart insisted on quickening at the mere thought of his name. It would be so easy to accept his marriage proposal, to give in to the warmth and security he offered. And yet, the very idea sent a shiver of uncertainty through her. Marriage, after all, meant giving up the independence she had fought so hard to maintain.

Then again, Charles had never sought to stifle her. If anything, he had always encouraged her, always seen her for who she truly was rather than who Society expected her to be.

The soft creak of the door interrupted her thoughts, and she turned just as Tanner stepped into the drawing room. His expression was carefully composed, though she could have sworn there was the faintest twitch of amusement at the corner of his lips.

"My lady," he announced, bowing slightly. "Lord Bedford has come to call."

Eugenie immediately straightened in her chair as she tried to settle the flurry of emotions stirring within her.

"Please show him in," she said, pleased that her voice did not betray her excitement.

Tanner nodded. "Yes, my lady."

A moment later, Charles stepped into the room, dressed impeccably in a deep blue jacket, buff trousers, and a cream-colored waistcoat. The sight of him—so composed, so effort-lessly charming—made something tighten in her chest. He smiled, and in that instant, it felt as though the rest of the world had faded away, leaving only the two of them.

He bowed. "Lady Eugenie."

She inclined her head. "Lord Bedford."

"I hope I have not called upon you too early," he said, his blue eyes studying her.

"Not at all," she replied, though in truth, she had been waiting for him all morning.

His gaze flickered downward, and his expression turned amused. "I see Sir Spotticus is living his best life."

Eugenie followed his gaze to the miniature horse, who had now cracked one eye open, as if sensing that he had become the topic of conversation.

"He is," she said with a small laugh, reaching for a slice of apple from the dish beside her. She held it out, and Sir Spotticus eagerly accepted the treat, munching contentedly. "Though I suspect he only loves me because I feed him."

Charles stepped closer and crouched down beside the horse. "Whatever it takes." He ran a hand along the creature's coat. "I must say, I'm pleased he has such a pleasant disposition."

"Oh, he does," Eugenie agreed, "though he did nip at Niles once. I think he knows my brother disapproves of him."

"Horses are rather intelligent creatures."

She grinned. "Sir Spotticus is the most intelligent of them all. I read to him constantly."

"And does he ever answer back?" he teased.

"No," Eugenie mused, "but I am quite convinced that he listens. Even when he pretends to be asleep."

Charles laughed and then extended his hand towards her. "Shall we call upon Miss Winslow now?"

Eugenie hesitated only a moment before allowing him to assist her to her feet. His touch, though fleeting, sent warmth up her arm. "I think that is a grand idea," she said, "especially since my brother is occupied with a meeting with his solicitor."

"And where is Elsbeth?"

"She is at the dressmaker's."

Charles smiled. "Then we have perfect timing." He led her towards the entry hall, his hand resting lightly at the small of her back.

As they reached the main door, Eugenie turned to the butler. "I am going on a carriage ride with Lord Bedford."

Tanner's lips pressed into a thin line. "Are you certain that is wise, my lady?" he asked. "Lord Westcott has instructed you to remain home."

Eugenie lifted her chin. "I won't be long."

He still looked unconvinced. "Very well. But if you insist, I shall send additional footmen along for the ride."

Eugenie cast a glance at Charles. "I do not think that will be a problem," she said. "Do you, my lord?"

"Not at all," Charles replied.

Satisfied, Eugenie accepted the straw hat offered by the butler, securing it over her neatly pinned curls. "Will you ensure that Sir Spotticus returns to the stables?"

"I will, my lady," Tanner said.

With that, she stepped outside into the bright morning, making her way towards the open carriage waiting by the drive.

Charles extended his hand once more, steadying her as she climbed inside. As he took his seat beside her, she clasped her hands in her lap and willed herself to appear unaffected by his close proximity.

The carriage lurched forward, setting them on their way.

Eugenie inhaled deeply, attempting to quell her nerves. "It is a fine day we are having, is it not?" she blurted, then immediately regretted it. Drat. Of all the things she could have said, she had to settle on the weather.

Charles, however, seemed unbothered. "It is," he agreed, the corners of his lips twitching.

She bit her lower lip, racking her brain for something more interesting to say. Before she could, however, Charles spoke again. "How is your article coming along?"

"It is going well," she lied, shifting uncomfortably. In truth, she had barely written a word—her thoughts had been far too preoccupied with him. It was maddening.

"I am pleased to hear that," he said.

Finding herself curious, she turned towards him and asked, "Why are you so supportive of me?"

He stared back at her with a baffled expression, seemingly caught off guard. "Why wouldn't I be?"

"It is... surprising, to be honest," she admitted. "Most

gentlemen of the *ton* would not approve of a lady writing for the Society page."

"I think it is brilliant," Charles said without hesitation. "Women have a unique perspective on life, and it is refreshing to see it put into words."

Eugenie narrowed her eyes playfully and gave his arm a small poke.

He frowned. "What was that for?"

"I am merely ensuring you are real," she teased.

Charles chuckled. "I assure you, my lady, I am quite real."

The coach lurched unexpectedly as one of the wheels dipped into a rut, causing Eugenie to grasp the edge of her seat to steady herself. "I suppose we should discuss what we plan to say when we speak with Miss Winslow," she suggested, tilting her head towards him.

Charles leaned back slightly, one arm draped casually over the side of the carriage. "I figured we would start with the most obvious question—why she wrote the article."

Eugenie nodded. "And if she denies being Mr. Fairchild?"

A slow, mischievous smile crept across Charles's face as he waggled his eyebrows. "I can be quite persuasive when I need to be."

She laughed at that. "Oh? I suppose I have yet to witness such legendary persuasion."

With exaggerated offense, Charles placed a hand over his heart, his expression one of mock devastation. "You wound me, my lady. Truly."

Eugenie nudged his shoulder with her own in a playful manner. "I highly doubt that."

"You are the only person who refuses to take me seriously. Which is rather strange, considering how wise I am."

She shot him a knowing look. "And unbearably cocky."

He shrugged, entirely unbothered. "You have to be a little cocky to be an earl. It's practically a requirement."

"Oh? I hadn't realized," she teased, enjoying the easy rhythm of their banter.

"It's true."

Eugenie smiled to herself, settling back against the seat as the carriage continued its steady course down the road.

He glanced over at her. "You are smiling."

"I am," she admitted.

His gaze lingered on her, the usual lightheartedness in his eyes giving way to something more uncertain, more vulnerable. "Dare I hope that you are happy... with me?" His voice was quieter now, as though the answer truly mattered to him.

She turned fully towards him, meeting his gaze. There was no teasing in her tone when she admitted, "I am happy with you, Charles."

"Good," he replied. "Because I want to know everything about you. The good, the bad, and even the parts you stubbornly try to keep hidden."

"That could take quite some time," she teased, though her heart was hammering in her chest. No one had ever taken such an interest in her before.

He reached for her gloved hand. "I will make the time," he promised, his voice rich with sincerity. "Because you, my dear, are beautiful, valued, worthwhile."

Eugenie felt a warmth unfurling deep within her. For a moment, she feared she wouldn't be able to hide how much his declaration had affected her. But years of practice kept her expression schooled. She forced a lightness into her tone as she said, "I am beginning to understand your powers of persuasion."

Charles's lips twitched in amusement. "Then my work here is done," he quipped, leaning back against the plush seat of the carriage. And yet, despite his relaxed posture, he didn't let go of her hand.

Eugenie's gaze flickered towards their entwined hands. It

was such a simple gesture, yet it carried a weight that she wasn't sure she was ready to acknowledge. Would it always be like this with Charles? Would he always hold on to her so effortlessly, as if it were the most natural thing in the world?

The thought was both comforting and terrifying.

Because when she looked at him, really looked at him—into those blue eyes filled with humor and something deeper, something unspoken—she saw more than just the man sitting beside her. She saw her future. A life spent in his presence, filled with laughter, with adventure, with love.

And she knew that nothing in this world could ever change the way she felt about him. So why wasn't she strong enough to admit it? To say the words aloud and risk surrendering her heart completely?

Eugenie swallowed hard, pushing the thoughts away, locking them deep within the corners of her mind. For now, she would let him hold her hand.

The coach rolled to a stop before a stately three-story townhouse, its whitewashed brick façade gleaming in the midmorning light. The wrought-iron railings bordering the short front steps were freshly polished, and crisp white curtains framed the tall windows.

Charles stepped down from the carriage first and turned, offering his hand to Eugenie. He held on to her just a fraction longer than necessary before tucking her hand neatly into the crook of his arm.

As they made their way towards the entrance, Charles couldn't help but notice the way Eugenie squared her shoulders. He nearly laughed. It almost suggested she was bracing herself for battle.

But this was hardly a war.

They were simply calling upon Miss Winslow, an entitled young woman who used her charms to get her way.

Reaching the front door, he lifted the brass knocker and let it fall with a decisive thud. A few moments later, the heavy door swung open, revealing a tall, gaunt butler whose sharp gaze flicked between them with polite disinterest.

"May I help you, sir?" he asked.

Charles inclined his head. "Please inform Miss Winslow that Lord Bedford and Lady Eugenie request a moment of her time."

The butler stepped aside, widening the door. "If you would kindly wait here, my lord, I shall inform Miss Winslow of your presence." Without another word, he disappeared through a side door, leaving them alone in the grand entry hall.

Charles turned to Eugenie, studying her face. "Are you nervous?"

She hesitated before saying, "I am."

"Don't be," he said softly, offering her hand a gentle squeeze. "I am here with you."

Before she could respond, the butler returned. "Miss Winslow will see you now." He gestured towards a nearby open doorway.

As they walked together, Charles leaned in slightly. "We should think of a word to use if either of us feels uncomfortable during this conversation."

Eugenie furrowed her brow. "A word?"

"Something discreet. A signal of sorts."

She considered him for a moment before saying, "I could ask about the weather."

Charles chuckled. "That would work rather well, considering you bring up the weather whenever there's a lull in conversation."

Her mouth dropped open in mock indignation. "I do not."

"You do," he countered. "And it is merely one of the many things I've noticed about you."

She glanced at him, curiosity dancing in her eyes. "Oh? And what else have you noticed?"

He leaned closer, lowering his voice into something dangerously intimate. "I'm afraid the list is far too long to recite at this moment, my dear."

An adorable blush bloomed across her cheeks at his endearment, and Charles took immense satisfaction in knowing that she was not as immune to his charms as she often pretended to be.

As they stepped into the drawing room, Miss Winslow rose from a floral settee, her needlework still clutched in her hands. She was a vision of carefully curated elegance, her rose-colored gown perfectly tailored, and her golden curls artfully arranged. Her lips curved into a wide, too-eager smile as she set the embroidery aside.

"What a pleasant surprise!" she greeted, her voice bubbling with energy—perhaps a bit too much. "Come, sit, and have a cup of tea."

Charles exchanged a glance with Eugenie before turning back to Miss Winslow. His voice remained polite but firm. "I'm afraid we are here on a rather delicate matter."

Miss Winslow's expression shifted, a faint crease forming between her brows. "Well, do not keep me in suspense," she said, the cheer in her voice dimming. "What is it?"

Charles met her gaze evenly. "We know who you are."

She tilted her head slightly. "And I know who you are, my lord," she responded. "Is this a game? If so, I must say it's a rather dull one."

Eugenie released Charles's arm and stepped forward. "I have it on good authority that you write for *The Morning Post* under the name Mr. Fairchild."

Miss Winslow's lips parted slightly before pressing together in a thoughtful line. "Interesting," she murmured. "And, pray tell, who told you such a thing?"

"That is not important," Eugenie replied. "What is important is that we are here to request a retraction. We both know the events described in your article did not transpire the way you claimed."

Miss Winslow studied them both, her gaze sharp and assessing. And then, with a delicate sigh, she simply said, "No."

"I beg your pardon?" Eugenie asked.

Miss Winslow's smile did not falter. "Even if you are correct in assuming that I am Mr. Fairchild—which, of course, I have not confirmed—why would I print a retraction?" She leaned forward slightly. "I do believe it's best if we allow the stories to unfold on their own."

Eugenie pursed her lips. "My reputation has been besmirched by your article. Why would you print such faradiddles?" she asked, her voice rising.

Miss Winslow glanced towards the open doorway, then, with a graceful step, walked over and quietly closed the door. Her voice dropped to a hushed whisper when she turned back to them. "It is best if no one overhears this conversation. No one in my household knows I write for *The Morning Post*."

Charles folded his arms across his chest. "So you admit it?"

Miss Winslow's expression remained unbothered. "I write for the newssheets, just as Lady Eugenie does," she said. "I think we would all benefit from a bit of discretion."

Charles narrowed his eyes. "Then tell me this—why fabricate a story about us?"

Miss Winslow plucked at the sleeve of her gown, as if the matter was of little concern to her. "I may have enhanced certain aspects of the evening in question, but I did so for your benefit."

Eugenie's mouth fell open in disbelief. "Our benefit?"

Miss Winslow's lips curved into a knowing smile. "You two

needed a push to get married. And I gave you one," she said. "You are most welcome."

Charles let out a stunned laugh. "You expect us to believe that you fabricated an entire scandal simply to play matchmaker?"

Miss Winslow's gaze was unrepentant. "Certainly. You were already well on your way. I merely... hastened the inevitable."

"Surely you did not go to such great lengths just for us to marry," Eugenie remarked.

Miss Winslow settled back onto the settee with a graceful ease, lifting her teacup once more. She took a slow sip before finally responding, "Didn't I?" Her voice was light, almost teasing, as if she had done them a great favor rather than entangled them in a scandal.

She gestured towards the porcelain teapot resting on the table between them and continued. "You must try some of this tea. It's a delightful blend—imported, of course."

Eugenie, still bristling, folded her arms. "I do not want tea."

Miss Winslow let out a soft sigh, setting her cup and saucer down with a delicate clink. "That is a shame," she mused. "Well, if you're not here for tea, is there something else I can offer you?"

Charles stepped forward. "Miss Winslow, you must understand the precarious situation you have placed us in because of your article."

"Oh, I do understand," Miss Winslow responded. "And I did not write that article on a whim. Just as I imagine Lady Eugenie takes care with her own writings."

Eugenie stiffened. "But I only write the truth."

Miss Winslow lifted her cup once more, her lips curving as she took a deliberate sip. When she lowered it again, her gaze was sharp. "And what, pray tell, is truth, if not one's own version of it?"

Charles ran a hand along the back of his neck. "You implied

in your article that Eugenie and I were alone in the gardens. But we both know that was you and you tried to kiss me."

"Do we?" Miss Winslow asked, feigning innocence. "There were no other witnesses to say otherwise."

Charles's jaw tightened. "I tried to do the honorable thing when I saw that you had overindulged in champagne."

Miss Winslow waved a hand dismissively, as if the matter were trivial. "Oh, I was never truly drunk."

"You certainly seemed to be," Eugenie remarked.

Miss Winslow let out a soft, amused laugh. "Truth be told, I can't stand the taste of champagne."

"But you had three glasses," Charles countered.

"Did I?" Miss Winslow's smile turned impish. "If you had been watching more carefully, you would have noticed that the plant behind the refreshment table enjoyed the champagne far more than I did."

"You poured it into the plant?" Eugenie asked. "For what purpose?"

Miss Winslow lifted a single shoulder in a delicate shrug. "I needed people to believe I was bottle-weary."

"So it was all an act?" Charles inquired.

Miss Winslow's expression turned amused. "Of course. You'd be amazed by the things people whisper when they think a lady is too drunk to remember. It is quite enlightening, really."

With a shake of his head, Charles asked, "You orchestrated the entire scene so you could be alone with me?"

"Now, my lord, you mustn't be so arrogant," Miss Winslow said before setting the cup down. "It was never my intention to compromise you. I was merely... observing."

"Observing what, exactly?" Eugenie asked in a terse voice.

Miss Winslow sighed as if they were being terribly slow to catch on. "You two, of course. And my suspicions were correct —you needed a push. And I simply provided it."

Eugenie's hands curled into fists at her sides. "You manipulated an entire evening—our reputations—all so you could meddle in our lives?"

Miss Winslow appeared completely unrepentant. "Meddle? No, I prefer to think of it as encouragement." She leaned forward slightly, resting her elbow on the arm of the settee. "And if I am not mistaken... it worked. You two have been spending an abundant amount of time together."

Charles forced himself to rein in the anger that surged through him like a rolling tide. He was no stranger to manipulation, nor to the games that members of the *ton* played to secure their ambitions. But Miss Winslow had gone too far.

He leveled her with a hard stare. "Perhaps I should pay a visit to your brother," he said, his voice low and edged with warning. "I'm certain he would be most interested in learning how you occupy your time."

The amusement that had danced so freely in Miss Winslow's eyes vanished in an instant. A flicker of something—uncertainty, perhaps—passed over her features before she recovered. "You wouldn't do something so foolish," she said.

"And why is that?" Charles asked.

Miss Winslow's expression grew unreadable. "Because we both know that the pen is mightier than the sword," she stated. "And I wield mine with precision."

She paused just long enough for the weight of her words to settle. Then, with a pointed glance in Eugenie's direction, she added, "You wouldn't want Lady Eugenie's secret to come to light, now would you?"

Charles felt the air in the room tighten. A slow, simmering rage burned beneath his skin, but he forced himself to remain composed. Miss Winslow was no fool—she had seen through his threat, knowing he could not—*would not*—risk Eugenie's reputation.

Before he could reply, the door opened and Alcott stepped

into the room. "I thought I heard your voice," he said, addressing Charles.

Charles turned to face Alcott. "Good morning," he said before gesturing towards Eugenie. "Allow me the privilege of introducing you to Lady Eugenie."

Alcott's gaze shifted to her, and in that brief moment, Charles watched as his friend's expression changed. There was no mistaking the flicker of interest in his eyes as they traced the elegant line of Eugenie's figure, taking in the graceful tilt of her chin and the composed way she met his scrutiny.

"The pleasure is mine, my lady," Alcott said with a slight bow.

Eugenie dipped into a polite curtsy. "My lord," she murmured.

Charles felt an irrational spike of irritation at the exchange. He knew the look Alcott was giving her—that subtle, assessing gaze filled with quiet approval.

With deliberate intent, Charles stepped closer, positioning himself firmly beside her. "We should be going," he said, his tone leaving no room for argument.

"Why the rush?" Alcott's gaze flicked back to Eugenie, lingering. "We've only just been introduced."

Charles didn't like the way Alcott was looking at Eugenie. Not one bit. "Yes, but it is time I returned Lady Eugenie home. You understand, don't you?" he asked, offering his arm to her.

As they walked out of the drawing room, Alcott followed them to the main door and asked in a hushed voice, "What did my sister do, now?"

"Nothing," Charles lied, though the word lacked conviction. "We were merely calling upon her to discuss..." He faltered, his mind scrambling for a plausible excuse.

"The weather," Eugenie interjected.

Charles bobbed his head. "Yes, the weather."

Alcott's sharp gaze flickered between them. "Very well," he

said slowly. "If you do not wish to tell me, that is your prerogative. But do not insult my intelligence by claiming you were discussing the weather."

"Fair enough," Charles responded before he took Eugenie's arm and guided her down the stone steps towards the waiting carriage, leaving Alcott standing in the doorway, watching them with an expression that said he was far from fooled.

18

E ugenie adjusted her straw hat, ensuring it sat at the correct angle as she settled into the plush seat beside Charles in the carriage. The visit to Miss Winslow had gone far from planned, leaving her with an uneasy feeling in her chest. She only hoped no one had noticed her absence at the townhouse—though she knew that was wishful thinking.

The rhythmic clip-clop of the horses echoed against the cobblestone streets, lulling them into silence until, at last, the carriage came to a smooth stop in front of her townhouse. Before the footman could even move, Charles swiftly stepped out, the gravel crunching under his boots. He turned, extending his gloved hand towards her. Eugenie placed her fingers in his and allowed him to help her down, but the moment her feet touched the ground, she withdrew her hand.

Charles's sharp gaze studied her. "Is everything all right?"

She hesitated, glancing away as she tried to form the right response. "I suppose it is," she finally said, though her tone lacked conviction. "But I wish Miss Winslow had been more... accommodating."

"Indeed. It was rather odd, wasn't it? Her sudden interest in playing matchmaker between us." His expression grew thoughtful as he continued. "It begs the question—why us?"

Eugenie sighed. "I don't rightly know."

Charles rocked back slightly on his heels, his hands clasped behind his back as if weighing his next words carefully. "What if we did marry? Would it be so terrible?"

No.

The word formed instantly in her mind. But that wasn't the issue. Charles didn't love her. And Eugenie could not bring herself to marry someone who didn't feel as deeply for her as she did for him.

She placed a hand on his sleeve. "You are a good man, Charles. Perhaps the best I have ever known. But we both deserve more than a marriage of convenience."

"Is that what you think I'm offering?"

"Isn't it?" she countered.

A smile tugged at the corners of his lips. "I am offering you the chance to marry me. An earl. A handsome earl, I might add."

Despite herself, Eugenie let out a small laugh. "Well, now that you remind me of your title, I suppose I might reconsider my answer."

The humor left Charles's expression as he said, "We would be good together, you and I."

Before she could respond, the front door of the townhouse swung open, revealing Niles standing in the entryway. His nostrils flared as his sharp gaze landed on her.

"Eugenie," he growled. "Will you kindly come inside at once?"

Eugenie let out a slow breath, dropping her hand from Charles's sleeve. "It would appear my absence was, in fact, noticed."

Niles's glare shifted towards Charles. "I wish to speak with both of you. Now."

Charles extended his arm towards the door. "After you, my lady."

Holding her head high, Eugenie ascended the stone steps, stepping past Niles into the entry hall. The door closed with a decisive thud behind them.

Niles turned towards her. "Eugenie, are you mad?"

Feeling rather bold, she quipped, "No, but I haven't been tested."

His jaw tightened. "You think this is humorous?"

"I think you are overreacting."

Niles took a measured step closer. "You left the townhouse without my permission. We discussed this. You were nearly abducted a few days ago. Do you not have any care for your own safety?"

"I was perfectly safe," she insisted. "We only went to call upon Miss Winslow, and we had plenty of footmen accompanying us."

Niles turned his heated glare towards Charles. "And what do you have to say for yourself?"

Charles raised a placating hand. "I assure you, Eugenie was properly guarded the entire time."

"What was so urgent that you had to speak to Miss Winslow this very moment?" Niles demanded.

Eugenie pressed her lips together before replying softly, "We can't say."

Niles's brows shot up. "I beg your pardon?"

She lifted her chin. "We can't say," she repeated, her voice firmer this time.

Niles let out a frustrated sigh. "What am I to do with you, Eugenie? You have no regard for your well-being."

"Nothing happened to me," she countered. "No harm done."

Before Niles could retort, another voice interrupted from the doorway. "Dear me, what is all this shouting about?"

They all turned to see Elsbeth standing there, her gaze flicking between them with mild concern.

"Eugenie snuck out with Charles to visit Miss Winslow," Niles informed his wife.

"I did not sneak out," Eugenie corrected indignantly. "I used the main door and I told Tanner that I was leaving. That is the opposite of sneaking out."

Elsbeth gave her a look of disapproval. "That was unwise. What if someone attempted to abduct you again?"

Charles interjected. "The two men who attempted to abduct Eugenie are in Newgate."

"And how do you know that?" Niles asked.

"Warwicke told me," Charles replied.

Something in Niles's expression shifted. "I see he has finally revealed his true identity to you. That must mean he trusts you."

Eugenie glanced between them. "Who is Warwicke?"

Niles's tone had an unmistakable edge to it. "He is a man doing me a favor. You need not concern yourself with him."

Realization dawned in Eugenie's mind. "Are you speaking of Baron Warwicke?"

Niles paused, then nodded. "I am."

Curious, she asked, "And what sort of favor is he doing for you?"

"He agreed to investigate your attempted abduction," her brother revealed.

"But he's a baron," Eugenie said.

"He is now," Niles corrected. "Only recently. The king bestowed him that title for his service on the battlefield. Before that, he was a Bow Street Runner."

"A Bow Street Runner turned baron," Eugenie mused. "What a remarkable turn of events for him. One doesn't often hear of such drastic changes in fortune."

Niles met her gaze with the same unwavering intensity he

always carried when he was displeased. "I am still quite upset with you, Eugenie."

She offered him a small, appeasing smile. "I know," she admitted. "But can you continue chastising me over our midday meal? I am positively famished." She pressed a hand against her stomach for emphasis, as if to illustrate her desperate hunger.

Charles cleared his throat. "If you will excuse me, I believe it is time I take my leave."

"You would be correct," Niles said bluntly, his sharp gaze flicking towards him in clear dismissal.

Eugenie ignored her brother's brusqueness and turned to Charles. "Thank you for escorting me to Miss Winslow's townhouse."

"You are most kindly welcome," Charles replied, though his usual air of confidence was tinged with something else— something more uncertain. "And, if you should happen to change your mind about what we discussed..." His voice trailed off for a fraction of a second before he recovered, offering her a hopeful smile. "I would be more than grateful."

"I don't think I will," Eugenie responded.

A flicker of disappointment crossed Charles's face, so fleeting that, had she not been looking directly at him, she might have missed it. "Very well," he said simply. "I shall take my leave, then."

Eugenie watched as Charles strode out the main door, her eyes lingering long after he was gone.

Niles's voice cut through the silence. "What, exactly, have you discussed with Bedford?"

"He offered for me... again," she replied, seeing no reason to deny it.

"And you turned him down?" Niles asked.

She bit her lower lip before replying. "He offered me a

marriage of convenience," she said. "I would rather remain a spinster than marry a man who doesn't love me."

Niles studied her carefully, his silence stretching long enough to make her shift under his gaze. When he finally spoke, his voice was surprisingly gentle. "But you love him." It wasn't a question—it was a statement, spoken with certainty.

"I don't know what I feel," she lied, though even she could hear the lack of conviction in her own voice. "But it matters not. Now, about that food..." She made a show of rubbing her stomach again, hoping to shift the conversation.

But Niles wasn't so easily swayed. "There is nothing wrong with being in love with Bedford."

She swallowed, feeling the weight of those words settle deep in her chest. No, there was nothing wrong with it. But that didn't make it any less complicated.

"I am not going to pine after a man that does not love me," Eugenie remarked.

Elsbeth took a step closer to Eugenie. "How do you know what he feels for you?"

The question struck deeper than Eugenie anticipated, and for a brief moment, she felt utterly exposed. She stiffened, taking a quick step back as if physical distance could shield her from the conversation. "I can't have this discussion right now," she said, forcing a lightness into her tone. "I need sustenance, or I might simply perish where I stand."

It was a weak attempt at humor, and she knew it. A deflection. A coward's way out. But she wasn't ready for this conversation. She couldn't be.

If she admitted the truth—if she laid bare the depth of her feelings for Charles—she knew exactly what would follow. Concern. Gentle reassurances. Soft, pitying glances from those who would see her love as unrequited.

And she could not bear their pity.

She had not fallen in love with Charles because she was

lonely or bored. She fell in love with him after she got to know him, and she realized she wanted him in her life. Forever.

But he didn't feel the same.

Spinning on her heel, Eugenie headed towards the dining room, hoping to be alone. She needed space. A moment. Just one fleeting moment to herself where she could lower the carefully constructed walls and allow her thoughts to unravel.

Charles sat at his desk, fingers poised over the ledger, but his eyes remained unfocused on the neatly written columns of numbers. No matter how many times he willed himself to concentrate, his mind strayed—again and again—to Eugenie.

It was always Eugenie.

Botheration.

When would this torture end?

His jaw tightened as he rubbed a hand across his face, as if he could physically scrub away the thoughts of her. The accounts needed balancing, his estate required his full attention, and yet he could not string together a single productive thought.

A sharp knock at the door drew him from his reverie. He straightened as Hagen stepped into the room and announced, "Lord Alcott has requested a moment of your time, my lord."

Charles found himself grateful for the interruption. "Send him in."

A moment later, Alcott entered, his posture rigid. He did not bother with pleasantries. Instead, he strode forward and asked, "Do you want to explain why you truly visited my sister?"

Charles leaned back in his chair, feigning nonchalance. "It was of little consequence."

Alcott's eyes narrowed as he sank into the chair opposite the desk. "Do you expect me to believe that?"

"No," Charles admitted. "But I cannot reveal the true reason without betraying Lady Eugenie's confidences."

That seemed to settle Alcott—somewhat. He ran a hand through his dark hair, mussing it in frustration. "Life was much simpler on the battlefield," he muttered. "At least there, I knew my enemies. Here, I am forced to navigate my sister's whims, and it is exhausting."

"I think your sister may surprise you."

Alcott shot him a skeptical look. "She is always writing, yet she refuses to say for what purpose."

Charles knew precisely why Miss Winslow was writing, but he could not say. If he revealed the truth, she might follow through on her threat to expose Eugenie's identity to the *ton*, and that was a risk he could not take.

Alcott rose and strode towards the drink cart in the corner of the study. "Do you mind?"

"Not at all," Charles replied, watching as his friend poured a generous amount of brandy into a glass.

Alcott took a slow sip, his eyes distant. "It might be easier if I didn't feel like I was thrust into this life."

"Not many would complain about inheriting a viscountcy."

"I know," Alcott sighed, sinking back into his chair. "And I must sound terribly ungrateful, but I miss my life in the Royal Army. I left home for a reason."

Charles studied him for a moment before asking, "Why did you leave?"

Alcott lowered his glass. "I was at odds with my father. Again. I couldn't stand living under his rule, so I bought a commission and never looked back."

"How did your father take it?"

A wry smile came to Alcott's lips. "He was furious, of course. I was his heir and was supposed to focus on our estate. He tried to force me to return home, but I had already tasted freedom. There was no going back."

"Your father died while you were away. Do you regret not being there?"

The smile faded. "My father was not a good man," Alcott said simply. "I had to get away from him."

"What about your sister?"

Alcott let out a humorless huff. "According to my father, Charlotte was merely a useless female. He left her to the care of nursemaids and later a governess, barely acknowledging her existence."

Charles did not know what to say to that. After a pause, he murmured, "I'm sorry."

Alcott waved a dismissive hand. "Do not feel pity for me. We all have our lots in life. At least I am spared the trouble of a wife for now."

"A wife wouldn't be the worst thing."

Alcott's smile returned. "You are only saying that because of Lady Eugenie. But if I recall correctly, you had no intention of marrying until you were older and more established."

Charles sighed. "That is true. But everything changed when I met Eugenie."

Alcott's expression softened slightly. "I am happy for you."

Charles let out a short, humorless laugh. "Don't be. I cannot convince her to marry me, even though her name is marred with scandal. She would rather remain a spinster than be with me." He tried to keep the bitterness from his voice, but he knew it bled through.

Amusement flickered in Alcott's eyes. "Then convince her."

"Don't you think I have been trying just that?"

"You were one of the best debaters at Eton. Surely you can convince a young woman to marry you," Alcott teased. "What did you say when you told her that you loved her?"

Charles stiffened. "I didn't. Because I don't love her."

"You are either lying to me or to yourself. Which one is it?"

"It is the truth," Charles insisted.

Alcott smirked. "Ah. You don't see it, do you?"

Charles frowned. "See what?"

Alcott set his glass down on the desk, his expression turning contemplative. "You are undoubtedly in love with Lady Eugenie."

He tried to keep the annoyance out of his voice as he asked, "And you conclude that how?"

Alcott's gaze turned distant, as if recalling something from long ago. "Because I was in love once. And it ended poorly. But I remember how it made me feel—like I could do anything, be anything. It may have been short-lived, but it changed me."

Charles hesitated before speaking. "I care deeply for Eugenie, but love? How do I know?"

"Let's start at the beginning, shall we?" Alcott asked. "Why do you want to marry her?"

"It is the honorable thing to do."

Alcott lifted a brow. "What else?"

Charles grew silent as his thoughts spun in his mind, unraveling every interaction, every stolen glance, every moment where Eugenie had challenged him, comforted him, and made him feel alive in ways he never had before. The truth was that he needed Eugenie to say yes to his offer of marriage. He had cared for her since that first kiss. But she didn't feel the same. There were only so many ways a man's heart could break, and he had a feeling his couldn't survive another rejection.

A sudden realization struck him like a physical blow. He wanted to marry Eugenie. Not because it was the honorable thing to do. But because he loved her.

Alcott's smug voice broke through his thoughts. "You figured it out, didn't you?"

Charles met his friend's gaze. "I love her," he said, the words feeling both terrifying and inevitable.

"I don't know why you are telling me," Alcott said. "You should be telling Lady Eugenie."

"And what if I confess my feelings," Charles started, his voice edged with uncertainty, "and she still refuses my offer of marriage?"

Alcott rose from his chair with an air of finality, straightening his coat. "Then you must have said it wrong."

Charles opened his mouth to retort, but before he could form a response, the door swung open with sudden urgency. His aunt swept into the room, her brows drawn together in a tight furrow.

Sensing something amiss, Charles immediately rose from his seat. "What is wrong, Phoebe?"

Her sharp blue eyes flicked towards Alcott before returning to Charles. "May I speak with you privately?"

Charles nodded. "Of course."

"Mrs. Ellsworth," Alcott greeted with a respectful bow. "I shall leave you to it."

As soon as the door closed behind Alcott, Charles moved around his desk, his eyes scanning his aunt's face for answers. "Is this about Philip?"

Phoebe bobbed her head, worry creasing her features. "The duel has been pushed forward. It's happening at dusk."

A sharp bolt of frustration ran through Charles. "How do you know this?"

Phoebe's hands clenched at her sides. "I caught him cleaning his pistol and confronted him about it. I tried to talk him out of it—I pleaded with him—but he wouldn't listen."

Charles inhaled deeply, steadying his rising temper. "Did Philip mention where this duel is to take place?"

"St. James's Park," she replied without hesitation.

His gaze flickered towards the window. The late afternoon sun streamed through the glass and dusk was fast approaching.

If he wanted to prevent this madness, he had to act now. And he couldn't do it alone.

Bringing his eyes back to Phoebe's, he placed a reassuring hand on her sleeve. "Go to Lord Westcott. Tell him what you just told me and ask him to inform Warwicke."

Phoebe's brows knitted tighter. "Whatever for?"

"Just trust me," Charles said firmly. His voice held conviction, but beneath it, there was an edge of desperation. "I will bring Philip home... alive."

Phoebe searched his face as if looking for reassurance she wasn't certain she'd find. After a moment, she relented. "Very well. But you must hurry if you intend to talk him out of this madness."

Charles forced a confident smile. "Try not to worry. It will be all right." He hoped, with everything in him, that he wasn't making an empty promise.

"I am a mother, Charles. I will always worry," Phoebe replied, her voice laced with an unmistakable strain of fear.

Charles squeezed her hand briefly before stepping back. "Then let me give you one less reason to."

He turned sharply on his heel, his boots echoing against the polished floors as he strode towards the main door. Phoebe fell into step beside him, her skirts swishing with each hurried step.

As they moved through the grand hallway, Charles still couldn't quite believe it had come to this. A duel. Over what? Honor? Stubborn pride?

Philip was a fool.

Charles had seen men gamble with money, their reputations, even their livelihoods—but gambling with one's life was another matter entirely. And Philip was doing just that.

Charles came to an abrupt stop in the entry hall, his gaze locking on to the butler, who stood poised near the door. "Have my horse prepared—and quickly," he commanded, his voice clipped with urgency.

"At once, my lord." Hagen turned and hurried towards the servants' quarters to see the order carried out.

Charles turned towards his aunt, his expression taut with determination. "We must move quickly. Take your carriage to Lord Westcott and deliver my message. Do not delay."

Phoebe's lips pressed together in worry, but she understood the gravity of the situation. Without another word, she swept out of the townhouse, disappearing into the growing shadows of the afternoon.

Now alone, Charles exhaled sharply, his fingers instinctively reaching for his pocket watch. He flipped it open and glanced at the time, but instead of providing clarity, the ticking hands only mocked him.

Each passing second felt excruciatingly slow.

Would he reach Philip in time?

He shoved the watch back into his waistcoat pocket and started pacing. Every moment that slipped by was another moment closer to disaster.

19

E ugenie had just finished the last line of her article, setting down her quill with a satisfied sigh, when a sudden, frantic pounding on the main door shattered the quiet. She stiffened, her pulse quickening at the urgency in the sound.

Curious, she rose from her writing desk, running her ink-stained fingers against her skirts as she hurried out into the entry hall. She arrived just as the butler swung open the door, revealing Phoebe standing on the threshold.

Phoebe was out of breath, her brows knitted together and her normally composed demeanor entirely absent. Strands of brown hair had come loose from her bonnet, her gloved hands clenching at her shawl.

Eugenie rushed forward, alarmed. "What is wrong?"

Phoebe's eyes were unfocused for a moment before they landed sharply on her. "Where is your brother, Lord Westcott?"

"In his study," Eugenie replied without hesitation. "May I ask why?"

"It is imperative that I speak with him at once," Phoebe said breathlessly, striding forward without waiting for permission.

A knot of dread tightened in Eugenie's stomach. Something was wrong—terribly wrong. And she had a sinking feeling that it had to do with Charles. Without a second thought, she followed closely behind.

Phoebe pushed open the study doors without a preamble and announced, "I need your help."

Niles looked up from behind his desk, his brows drawing together as he quickly stood. "Mrs. Ellsworth, do come in." He gestured towards a chair. "What can I do for you?"

Phoebe remained standing. "It's Philip," she blurted out. "He was foolish enough to agree to the duel, and Charles has gone to stop him."

Eugenie sucked in a sharp breath. "Charles?"

Phoebe nodded, her expression grave. "Yes. The duel is set to take place at St. James's Park at dusk."

Niles's frown deepened. He glanced at the window where the late afternoon sun hung low in the sky. "We don't have much time. What do you need from me?"

"Charles asked me to seek you out," Phoebe explained hurriedly. "He believes Warwicke will be of some use to him in stopping this."

"I can send word to Warwicke at once, but I can't promise he'll arrive in time," Niles responded.

Phoebe's voice trembled as she pleaded, "Please. You must do something. I cannot imagine what I would do if something happened to Philip or Charles."

Eugenie's chest tightened, her world spinning for a moment. What if Charles was hurt trying to protect Philip? Or worse—what if he was killed? A cold wave of terror swept through her, but another, stronger feeling quickly followed it.

Determination.

She could not stand idly by while Charles threw himself into danger. She had to do something. She had to help him.

Niles turned to her. "Eugenie, will you inform Tanner that I must speak to him at once?"

Eugenie forced herself to nod, spinning on her heel without another word. But as she stepped into the hallway, a plan was already forming in her mind. It wasn't a good plan. But it would do.

She reached the butler and made the necessary request, then rushed up the grand staircase, taking the steps two at a time.

Throwing open her bedchamber door, she marched straight to her wardrobe.

Alice, who had been tidying the room, looked up in confusion. "What are you doing?"

"I need to change," Eugenie announced, pulling open the wardrobe doors. Her fingers skimmed past silks and muslins before settling on what she sought—men's clothing.

Alice's eyes widened. "Why are you changing into men's clothing?"

Eugenie laid the garments on the bed, turning to face her maid with unwavering resolve. "I need to help Lord Bedford."

"With what?"

"Stopping a duel."

Alice's eyebrows shot up. "I beg your pardon?"

Eugenie clenched her hands into fists to keep them from shaking. "His cousin is caught up in a duel, and Lord Bedford has gone to stop it."

Alice folded her arms. "And why, exactly, do you need to be involved?"

Eugenie met her lady's maid's gaze. "Because I could never forgive myself if something happened to Lord Bedford."

Silence hung between them.

Finally, Alice sighed. "Can I talk you out of this?"

"No."

With another heavy sigh, Alice stepped forward. "Fine. Turn around. I'll start with the buttons."

Eugenie turned, exhaling slowly as Alice's fingers worked at the fastenings of her gown.

Her nerves were raw, but there was no time to dwell on them.

A sudden thought struck her. "I should take my muff pistol."

Alice froze. "I do not think that is wise, my lady." She resumed unfastening the buttons. "Besides, have you even thought this through? How do you plan to get to the duel?"

"I'm going to ride my horse."

Alice's fingers stilled once more. "But you haven't ridden since your accident."

"I know," Eugenie admitted, swallowing her unease. "But it's the only way. The traffic this time of day would make it impossible to get there in a carriage."

Alice made a frustrated noise but continued helping her dress. "And what about your brother? He will be livid when he finds out."

"I have no doubt, but I will deal with him later. First, I must ensure Charles is safe."

Alice paused. "Charles?"

Eugenie winced, realizing her mistake. "I mean Lord Bedford."

A knowing smile played at Alice's lips. "You two are calling each other by your given names now?"

She didn't reply, but the warmth rising in her cheeks was answer enough.

Alice shook her head. "It's about time." She finished adjusting the clothing and stepped back. "Since I can't convince you to stay where it's safe, I might as well help you."

Eugenie moved to sit at her dressing table, and Alice reached for some pins, quickly twisting her hair back.

"Will you wear your wig?" Alice asked.

Eugenie considered it before shaking her head. "No. It might fly off while I'm riding."

"Then at least wear a cap."

"I can agree to that."

"Good. Perhaps that way, you'll go unnoticed."

Rising, Eugenie crossed the room and pulled a pair of Hessian boots from her wardrobe. She slid them on, then retrieved her small muff pistol from her reticule.

Alice watched Eugenie, disapproval clear on her face.

"Wish me luck," Eugenie said as she turned for the door.

"Do I have a choice?"

Eugenie stopped and turned back around. "Just promise me you won't tell my brother where I've gone until I have ridden off."

Alice pursed her lips but finally relented. "I can agree to that, but you must promise to be safe."

"I will," Eugenie promised before slipping out of her bedchamber.

Moving swiftly, she descended the servants' stairwell, ignoring the curious glances from the household staff. She entered the kitchen, then slipped out the back door into the fading sunlight.

With purposeful strides, she approached the stables, her heart pounding. One of the older grooms, John, looked up in surprise.

"Ready my horse," she ordered.

John stared at her in disbelief. "Your horse, my lady?"

"Yes. I wish to go for a ride." She forced her voice to remain steady, though her nerves crackled beneath the surface.

John hesitated but, after a long pause, gave a small nod before disappearing to do her bidding.

Left alone in the stables, Eugenie stepped towards the first stall, where her horse, Sir Spotticus, lay dozing. "Sweet dreams. I shall be back shortly."

After a few excruciatingly long moments, John finally returned, leading the brown gelding towards her. He held out the reins. "Are you sure, my lady?" he asked, his voice laced with concern.

Eugenie wrapped her fingers around the reins, her grip tightening with resolve. "I am. This is something I must do."

"Would you like me to accompany you to..." He trailed off, clearly unsure of what exactly she was setting out to do. "... to wherever it is that you're going?"

"No," Eugenie said firmly. "I will be all right."

John moved to place a mounting step by the horse's side. He then extended his hand towards her. "Allow me to help you, at least."

Eugenie inhaled deeply, steeling herself against the wave of trepidation that washed over her. It had been over three years since she had last ridden—a long three years filled with the memory of her fall and the pain that had followed. She had vowed never to mount a horse again.

But she had no choice now.

Charles needed her.

"My lady?" John prompted gently.

Eugenie opened her eyes, staring down at his outstretched hand. A simple gesture, one of assistance, but it felt like an admission of weakness.

"I do not need assistance," she said. "I can do it on my own."

John tipped his head in acknowledgment. "As you wish," he murmured, stepping back, though she noticed he remained close, watchful.

Turning to the horse, Eugenie placed her foot in the stirrup and gripped the saddle horn. Her heart pounded. Would she fall again? Would this time be worse? Would she—?

No.

With a firm breath, she hoisted herself up and settled herself into the saddle. The gelding shifted beneath her, but she quickly adjusted, gripping the reins and steadying herself.

She had done it.

"I will be back shortly," she said, her voice steadier than she felt.

John merely gave a slow nod in response.

Taking another breath, Eugenie encouraged the gelding forward. As she moved towards the stable doors, her confidence grew with each step. The familiar rhythm of the horse's gait, the feel of the reins in her hands—it all came back to her, piece by piece.

She could do this.

She *had* to do this.

Reaching the open air, she paused for only a moment before urging the horse into a run, wondering why it had taken her so long to return to the saddle.

———————

Charles's sharp gaze swept over the open expanse of St. James's Park as he searched for his cousin. The park, usually bustling at this hour, was eerily quiet, the hush of impending violence hanging thick in the cool evening air. Then, in the distance, he spotted Philip.

His cousin stood at the far end of a clearing, feet planted unsteadily, a pistol in his grip as he stood a short distance away from his opponent. Charles breathed a sigh of relief. He had arrived in time. The duel hadn't commenced yet.

Without hesitation, Charles urged his horse into a run. The pounding of hooves echoed through the stillness as he closed the distance. He didn't slow until he was mere feet from Philip, pulling his horse to an abrupt halt and swinging down with practiced ease.

Philip turned, startled, his brow furrowing in confusion. "Whatever are you doing here?"

"I've come to put an end to this madness," Charles said, striding towards him. "What the devil are you thinking?"

Philip gave an infuriatingly casual shrug. "I came to teach Mr. Kingston a lesson."

Charles clenched his jaw and looked heavenward, seeking patience. He then turned his attention to Mr. Kingston, who stood a few paces away, his expression a mask of unwavering resolve. Beside him, his sister shifted uneasily, wringing her hands together as she cast nervous glances between the two men.

"This duel ends now," Charles declared, his tone brooking no argument.

Mr. Kingston shook his head. "I demand satisfaction, my lord."

"And you shall have it," Charles countered. "I will personally see to it that Philip takes responsibility for his child."

Miss Kingston stepped forward then, her eyes wide and pleading as she grasped her brother's arm. "Please, Henry. Don't do this. I couldn't bear it if something happened to you."

Mr. Kingston's chest puffed out with self-importance. "Nothing will happen to me. I am an excellent shot."

Philip scoffed. "As am I."

Something in the way Philip slurred his words made Charles snap to attention. His keen gaze flicked over his cousin, taking in the slightly unfocused eyes and how he swayed slightly on his feet.

"Are you drunk?" Charles demanded.

Philip lifted a hand, blinking as he attempted to count on his fingers. "I may have had one or two drinks before I came." He paused, waggling three fingers. "Or was it three?"

Charles swore under his breath. "You are in no condition to duel."

Philip waved a hand dismissively. "That's not true. I tend to think best when I'm a little bottle-weary."

Charles turned his glare to Mr. Kingston. "You intend to go through with this, knowing full well my cousin is inebriated?"

Mr. Kingston considered him for a moment before saying, "I will agree to drop the duel under one condition." His expression turned calculating. "That you, Lord Bedford, marry my sister."

Charles's brow lifted in incredulity. "That is not an option."

Miss Kingston gasped, her face draining of color. "What are you doing?" she asked, turning to her brother in horror. "That isn't what we discussed! I don't want to marry Lord Bedford. I don't even want to marry Mr. Ellsworth."

"But you would be a countess," Mr. Kingston argued, as if that should outweigh all else.

Charles's patience was hanging by a thread. This was turning into more of a debacle than he had anticipated. And if he didn't put an end to it soon, there was no telling how far it would spiral.

"I am not going to marry your sister," Charles said firmly.

Mr. Kingston's expression darkened. He lifted his pistol, the barrel now aimed directly at Philip's chest. "Then your cousin will die tonight, and his death will forever weigh on your conscience."

Charles's mind raced for a way to settle the situation. He needed time. "Where are your seconds? The doctor?" he asked, glancing around.

"There was no point in them being here," Mr. Kingston replied. "We are dueling to the death."

Charles stiffened. "You are breaking the sacred rules of a duel by sending your seconds away." His frustration mounted. The entire purpose of seconds was to mediate, to ensure that dueling etiquette was upheld—not to turn the event into outright murder.

Mr. Kingston remained unbothered. "My only concern is that Mr. Ellsworth pays for what he has done to my sister and the disgrace he has brought upon my family."

A small, shaky voice cut through the tension. "What if I told you that Philip isn't the father of the baby?" Miss Kingston asked, her hands pressing against her stomach.

"What are you talking about?" Mr. Kingston bellowed, his grip tightening around his pistol.

Looking entirely unsure of herself, Miss Kingston rushed to explain, "I attended a ball and I made the unfortunate mistake of taking a turn in the gardens with Mr. Steele."

A muscle in Mr. Kingston's jaw twitched. "Mr. Steele is a known rake," he said, his voice laced with barely contained fury. "What were you thinking?"

Miss Kingston wrung her hands together. "I wasn't thinking. He took advantage of me and then left me. Philip happened upon me afterward and helped me."

Mr. Kingston's lips pressed into a hard line. "You are lying."

"No, I am telling the truth," Miss Kingston said, her voice resolute. "When I discovered I was increasing, I panicked. I was terrified. And I—" She exhaled shakily. "I named Philip as the father."

Mr. Kingston shook his head. "I don't believe you. You are merely trying to protect Mr. Ellsworth."

"For once, I'm innocent," Philip declared, smirking. "I've bedded many women, Kingston, but your sister is not one of them."

Mr. Kingston didn't lower his pistol. "This changes nothing. Either Lord Bedford marries my sister, or I will kill Mr. Ellsworth."

"Henry," Miss Kingston pleaded, stepping closer. "Didn't you hear me? Philip is not to blame."

But Mr. Kingston's expression remained hard. "These are lies," he spat. "All of it. I know that Mr. Ellsworth visited you at our townhouse on multiple occasions. Did you think I was daft? That I didn't know what went on under my own roof?"

Miss Kingston's voice wavered. "Henry, please. He was just trying to help me. Nothing more. You have to believe me."

"But I don't believe you," Mr. Kingston spat out. "You lied about everything else. Why is now any different?"

Charles took a measured step forward, placing himself between Philip and the gun's line of fire. "I won't let you shoot my cousin."

Mr. Kingston's grip on the pistol didn't waver. His eyes burned with unrelenting anger. "Then you will die tonight," he declared, cocking the hammer back.

The sharp sound of hooves pounding against the ground drew their attention.

Charles turned his head sharply towards the noise. A rider was fast approaching, hunched low over the horse's neck, their cap pulled low over their face. But even through the shadows, he knew instantly who it was.

Eugenie.

She rode with purpose, her posture fearless as she reined in her horse with practiced ease. As soon as she dismounted, she moved swiftly and came to stand before him, her hand pulling free a muff pistol, leveling it at Mr. Kingston.

"No one is going to die here tonight," she declared. Her voice was clear, sharp, and left no room for argument. "Lower your pistol."

"You first," Mr. Kingston snarled.

Charles edged closer to her, his voice dropping low as he demanded, "What are you doing here?"

Eugenie kept her gaze locked on Mr. Kingston, her pistol steady. "I thought you might need my help."

"There was no need," Charles replied. "I had it handled."

Eugenie's lips twitched in dry amusement. "Is that so?" She gestured towards the pistol still trained on him. "Then why, pray tell, is a gun being pointed at you?"

Mr. Kingston interjected, "This will all end if Lord Bedford agrees to marry my sister. We could all walk away from this."

Eugenie shook her head. "I'm afraid that is impossible because Lord Bedford is marrying me."

Silence fell.

Mr. Kingston huffed. "You?"

Eugenie nodded firmly. "Yes."

"But you turned me down," Charles said. "Multiple times, in fact."

"I did," Eugenie admitted. "But I have since changed my mind."

Charles stared at her, searching her face for any hint of falsehood. There was none. He wasn't about to argue, but curiosity burned inside him. "Why?"

"Do we have to discuss this now?" Eugenie asked, keeping her sights on Mr. Kingston.

"Yes," he said. "I would prefer it."

A long sigh left her lips, and then, finally, she turned to meet his gaze. "Because I love you, Charles."

His breath caught.

And he had never felt so utterly unmoored in his life.

"I have tried to deny it. I have tried to ignore it. But I am unable to do so," Eugenie continued, her voice softer now, yet filled with unmistakable conviction. "I honestly have no idea what's going to happen next or how things are going to work out. All I know for certain is that you make me happy and that is all I need."

Charles could only stare at her, stunned by the weight of her admission. She had never been so honest, so vulnerable before. He said the only thing that he could. "You rode your horse here for me," he said, astonishment thick in his voice.

Her eyes never left his as she replied, "I did. I couldn't stand by and do nothing—not when you were putting yourself in danger."

A strange, overwhelming sensation flooded through him—pride, admiration, and something far deeper. He took a slow step forward, positioning himself beside her. "What you did was reckless and foolish," he murmured, his fingers grazing the sleeve of her coat, "but..." He let out a slow exhale, as if coming to terms with the depth of his emotions. "But I have never loved you more for it."

Eugenie's eyes went impossibly wide. "You love me?"

A slow, steady smile curved Charles's lips. "I do," he said, his voice thick with emotion. "Hopelessly." He swallowed hard before adding, "One kiss. That is all it took for me to know."

A brilliant smile broke across Eugenie's face. "I feel the same way," she whispered.

Charles leaned in slightly, lowering his voice as if only for her ears. "I don't think I could love you more if I tried. But then you smile, and my heart expands, making me realize—" His fingers brushed against her hand. "There is no end to how much I can love you."

A sharp, irritated voice broke through the intimate moment.

"This is all very sweet," Mr. Kingston interrupted, his scowl deepening. "But Lord Bedford will be marrying my sister. And that is final."

Miss Kingston let out an exasperated breath. "Henry..."

Before she could finish, a loud, commanding voice rang out from a short distance away.

"Lower your weapons!"

Charles turned his head swiftly towards the sound.

Emerging from the darkness, Warwicke strode towards them with an air of authority, his overcoat billowing slightly as he moved. Behind him, two men in red waistcoats—clearly

Bow Street Runners—trailed closely, their expressions grim and unwavering.

Mr. Kingston straightened, his grip on his pistol tightening. "Who are you?" he demanded, his bravado slipping just slightly.

Warwicke closed the distance in a few quick strides and wrenched the pistol straight from Mr. Kingston's grasp.

"I'm someone you've made very upset," Warwicke stated, inspecting the firearm before tucking it away.

Mr. Kingston looked utterly gobsmacked. "You took my pistol."

"Yes, because you don't need it anymore." Warwicke gestured towards the two Runners, whose gazes were locked on Kingston with the patience of men accustomed to dealing with foolish offenders. "My friends here are ensuring that this duel doesn't proceed."

Mr. Kingston narrowed his eyes. "This is between me and Mr. Ellsworth," he declared.

"Not anymore," Warwicke said. "Or have you forgotten that duels are illegal?" He studied Kingston with barely concealed irritation. "Where are your seconds?"

"Mr. Kingston sent them away," Charles offered up, folding his arms.

Warwicke clicked his tongue in disapproval. "Then it's a good thing we arrived when we did. This isn't a duel; it is an execution."

"But I demand satisfaction," Mr. Kingston said, though the words now lacked the burning conviction they once held.

Warwicke's expression turned steely. "If any harm befalls Mr. Ellsworth or Lord Bedford," he warned, his voice carrying a dangerous edge, "you will answer to me."

Mr. Kingston swallowed hard, the fear evident in his expression.

"Do I make myself clear?" Warwicke asked, his tone brooking no argument.

After a long moment, Mr. Kingston finally gave a stiff nod. "Yes."

"Good."

"But what about my sister?" Mr. Kingston asked, his eyes flicking towards Miss Kingston, who still looked shaken.

Warwicke looked uninterested. "I suggest you remove yourself to the countryside for a while," he said dryly. "Preferably after you are released from prison for the attempted abduction of Lady Eugenie."

Mr. Kingston's face paled. "I did no such thing."

"The two men you hired turned on you, naming you as a co-conspirator," Warwicke said. "You should have never done something so foolish."

"I would do anything for my sister," Mr. Kingston declared.

Warwicke placed a firm hand on Mr. Kingston's arm. "Well, I daresay you will change your tune after spending some time in Newgate," he said. "It is time to go."

With that, the matter was settled.

The tension in the air slowly began to dissipate, but Charles barely registered it. His mind was still reeling—not from the duel, nor from Kingston's empty threats, but from Eugenie.

From her words.

From her confession.

From the fact that she had risked everything for him.

And he knew, without a shadow of a doubt, that he would never let her go.

20

N ow that Charles was safe, Eugenie could finally breathe again. She slid her muff pistol into the pocket of her jacket as her eyes followed Mr. Kingston as the Bow Street Runners led him away. And now, she wasn't sure what to do.

Should she simply mount her horse and return home? Pretend this night hadn't changed everything? Could she do that after what Charles had confessed?

He loved her.

And she loved him.

Yet, as she turned her gaze to him, she realized his expression was not one of joy, but of something else entirely—disapproval. His lips were pressed into a firm line, his brow furrowed as if he were trying to make sense of what she had done.

She clasped her hands in front of her. "Are you upset?" she asked cautiously.

"Yes... no... I am not quite sure," he admitted. "You rode all the way here, dressed as a man, and stepped in front of a pistol that was being pointed at me."

Eugenie forced a smile. "That is all true." She took a step closer. "But I love you."

His expression softened at those words. "And I love you, too," he murmured. Then, shaking his head, he added, "But you shouldn't have taken such a risk. Not for me. Not for anyone."

"I would do anything for you," she said earnestly, "even ride a horse."

That, at last, earned the reaction she was hoping for. His lips curved into a smile. "You rode a horse for me."

"I did," she confirmed, a playful tone in her voice. "So you should be a little nicer to me."

He chuckled. "You make a good point."

A throat cleared nearby, and Eugenie was suddenly reminded that they were not alone. She turned to find Philip standing there, arms crossed over his chest, his gaze sweeping over her with open curiosity.

"You are wearing men's clothing," Philip remarked.

"I am," she replied.

Philip tilted his head, a smirk tugging at his lips. "Trousers suit you."

Charles, however, was less amused. "Go home, Philip. Your mother is worried sick."

With an exaggerated groan, Philip asked, "When will she realize I am an adult?"

"Perhaps when you start behaving like one," Charles retorted.

Philip rolled his eyes. "I don't know why you're upset with me. I was only trying to do the honorable thing with Miss Kingston." He threw his hands in the air. "It's not my fault she was increasing."

"Yes," Charles said flatly, "but your 'honorable actions' nearly led to your death."

Philip huffed. "I am a far better shot than Kingston."

Charles leaned in slightly, wrinkling his nose. "Yes, but your breath reeks of whiskey. I don't think you could even shoot straight."

Puffing out his chest in pride, Philip declared, "I could. I have discharged my pistol in far worse states."

"That is not something to be proud of," Charles muttered under his breath.

Philip made his way towards his horse, untying the reins with casual ease. "I don't know why you worry about me so much. I will be fine."

Eugenie watched as Philip mounted and rode off, the easy swagger in his posture at odds with the night's events. She could tell, just by looking at Charles, that his cousin's reckless-ness troubled him more than he let on.

Charles ran a hand through his hair before turning back to her. "Now, where were we..."

Before he could finish, a tall, broad-shouldered man stepped into view. His presence was commanding, and a long, jagged scar ran down his right cheek, lending him an air of danger.

"You are lucky I arrived when I did, Bedford," the man said, his voice deep and assured.

Charles turned to him with an expression of gratitude. "That I am." He gestured towards Eugenie. "Lady Eugenie, allow me to introduce you to Baron Warwicke."

Eugenie's eyes widened slightly. "Lord Warwicke." The infamous war hero. The man so many in London whispered about with both admiration and fear.

A faint smile touched Warwicke's lips, softening his other-wise severe features. "My lady," he said, inclining his head. "It is a pleasure to finally make your acquaintance. I am a friend of your brother's."

Eugenie found herself smiling in return. "I have heard much about you."

Warwicke looked amused. "Most of it isn't true," he remarked before giving a polite bow. "If you'll excuse me, I have something to attend to."

As Warwicke walked away, Eugenie's gaze lingered. So that was the man everyone spoke of in hushed tones.

Charles's voice broke through her musings. "When should we marry?"

Her eyes snapped back to him. "As soon as possible."

A slow grin spread across his face. He took a step closer. "Tomorrow, then?"

"But that would require a special license."

Leaning in, his voice dropped to a low murmur. "I am not opposed to such a thing, assuming it is agreeable to you. I won't do anything you aren't comfortable with."

A warmth spread through her chest. "I would marry you today, tomorrow, or any day thereafter." Then a teasing note entered her voice. "But aren't you worried our marriage will cause a scandal?"

Charles's lips twitched. "What's one more scandal?" He lifted his hand to tuck a stray curl behind her ear. "All I know is that when I look at you, I see the one I love. The one I need. The one I'm meant to be with."

"Well," she whispered, her gaze flicking to his lips, "if you are sure..."

"I have never been so sure of anything in my life."

Then he kissed her.

It was not a chaste kiss, but one filled with raw emotion, with the depth of all they had been through. It left no room for doubt, no space for hesitation. With every touch, every lingering caress, her worries melted away. He was her future.

When the kiss broke, he pressed his forehead against hers. "From the moment I met you, I knew I didn't want anyone else. Even when you challenge me at every turn. It will never change. I just want you."

A thunderous voice cut through the intimate moment. "Eugenie!"

Eugenie sighed dramatically. "My brother has arrived to ruin the fun."

Charles straightened as Niles stormed towards them, his expression stark with disapproval.

"Save it, Bedford," Niles said. "I saw you compromising my sister. I do hope you two are engaged."

"We are," Charles confirmed.

"Good." Niles reached into his jacket and pulled out a folded document. "Elsbeth convinced me to secure a special license for you two. You'll be married tomorrow."

Charles lifted a brow. "I... thank you."

Niles turned his piercing gaze on Eugenie. "And what were you thinking, Sister? You can't go around donning men's clothing and breaking up duels."

"But it worked, didn't it?" Eugenie countered.

"This time," Niles responded.

Eugenie looped her arm through Charles's. "You can't lecture me anymore, Brother. I am about to be his wife."

Niles looked unimpressed by her admission. "I am your older brother. Lecturing you is my birthright."

Charles chuckled. "I have to side with Westcott on this."

Eugenie gasped. "Traitor."

He squeezed her hand. "That doesn't mean I love you any less. But I think we should retire the men's clothing for now."

She pretended to look put out. "Very well. But only because you suggested it—not Niles."

Not looking the least bit amused, Niles asked, "Shall we go home before it grows too late?"

"I can agree to that," Eugenie said. "But I have to do one thing first."

Niles exhaled in wary resignation. "Which is?"

Without another word, Eugenie turned towards Charles

and, in one swift motion, rose on her toes and pressed her lips against his, knowing words were no longer enough to express what he meant to her.

When she dropped back down, she said, "There. That is all I wanted to do."

Behind her, Niles groaned audibly. "Eugenie..." he grumbled, rubbing a hand over his face as though she tested his patience beyond reason.

She turned to face him with an air of defiance. "You cannot be upset. We are getting married tomorrow."

Niles muttered something under his breath before replying, "And your wedding cannot come soon enough." He gestured towards the waiting carriage. "Come, I had your horse secured to the back of the coach. Let us return home before you think of something else to do that will give me more gray hairs."

With a final glance at Charles, Eugenie took her brother's arm and allowed him to lead her towards the carriage. The coachman helped her inside, and she settled across from Niles as the door shut with a decisive thud.

As the carriage lurched forward, Niles leaned back and crossed his arms over his chest, his eyes assessing her carefully. "You rode your horse here." It wasn't a question, but rather a statement of fact.

Eugenie met his gaze evenly. "I did."

"I know what it must have taken for you to do such a feat."

"So you know why I had to do it," she said.

He nodded. "I do. And I must admit..." He let out a reluctant sigh. "I do not fault you for it. I would have done precisely the same thing if Elsbeth had been in trouble."

Eugenie let that settle between them for a moment, the quiet understanding, the mutual respect. Then, as the coach rattled over the cobblestone streets, she admitted, "I love him."

"I know," he said, his tone edged with humor. "In fact,

everyone seemed to know that—but you. It was painfully obvious."

"You have no objections?"

"None," Niles replied. "I do believe that you and Bedford are good for one another. And I know that Mother and Father would have been proud of you."

At the mention of their parents, Eugenie felt a sudden tightness in her throat. Her eyes prickled with unshed tears. "I hope so."

"This is all I have ever wanted for you," Niles said, his voice softer now. "To find love and to be loved in return. It is no less than you deserve."

Eugenie bit her lower lip as she found herself confessing, "I worry that if something happens to Charles, I will lose a part of myself—just like Grandmother did when her husband died."

Niles's expression grew thoughtful. "I used to worry about the same thing," he admitted. "But then I realized that I cannot predict the future. None of us can. And love... love is something I would not want to live without. Not anymore."

She considered his words before saying, "I agree."

"Good, because I am out of advice," he said. "And, quite frankly, I cannot take you seriously while you are dressed like that."

Eugenie reached up and pulled the cap from her head, placing it in her lap. "You should see me with my wig on."

Niles rubbed his temples as though she were giving him a headache. "I suppose I shouldn't be surprised that you had a wig made."

Eugenie simply smiled and settled back into her seat. For the first time in a long time, she felt utterly, wonderfully content.

Charles exited his bedchamber and strode down the corridor, his footsteps echoing softly against the polished wood floors. Today was his wedding day.

It still felt surreal—this realization that, in just a short while, he would stand before a parson and bind himself to Eugenie for the rest of his life. But there was no apprehension, no hesitation. Only certainty.

He had finally found his match, a woman who both challenged and completed him. A love that transcended words. His heart now belonged to Eugenie, and he had no objections.

As he descended the grand staircase, he spotted his mother waiting in the entry hall, holding the morning newssheets in her gloved hands. The way she pursed her lips told him she had something to say.

"Your engagement made the Society page," she announced, holding up the newssheets.

Charles frowned and reached for it. "How in the blazes did that happen?" He unfolded the newssheets, his eyes scanning the article. The name at the bottom of the column made his stomach twist.

Mr. Fairchild.

Which meant Miss Winslow had wasted no time in breaking the news. But how had she learned of his engagement so soon? It had only happened last night.

A curse slipped from his lips as he crumpled the newssheets in his fist.

His mother lifted a brow. "Does it truly matter?" she asked, unruffled by his irritation. "You will be married soon enough."

"But how did she..." He cut himself off before he could say too much. As much as it frustrated him, he could not reveal Miss Winslow's true identity.

His mother's keen eyes didn't miss a thing. "She?" she repeated, tilting her head in interest. "You know who this Mr. Fairchild is, don't you?"

"I do," he admitted. "But I am not at liberty to say."

"Then I won't pry."

He eyed his mother curiously. "That doesn't sound like you."

She laughed and reached for the newssheets. "I am simply too pleased about your upcoming nuptials to concern myself with gossip. That trumps all else."

Charles leaned in, pressing a kiss to her cheek. "I will see you at the chapel."

"I do think it's rather silly that you insist on traveling with Eugenie," she mused. "Do you truly think she will change her mind?"

"It is a risk I am not willing to take," he replied, half-joking, half-serious.

His mother shook her head with a knowing smile. "Then go, and hurry. I am quite eager to welcome Eugenie into our family."

Charles tipped his head in acknowledgment before turning towards the main door.

As soon as he stepped outside, he spotted Addington, Wilton, and Alcott standing near the waiting carriage. They straightened upon seeing him, wide grins spreading across their faces like schoolboys up to mischief.

Addington stepped forward first. "We came to wish you luck on falling prey to the parson's mousetrap."

Charles smiled. "How generous of you."

Alcott moved to stand beside him, his expression entirely too serious for comfort. "Here is my advice," he said, lowering his voice as though imparting great wisdom. "Run. Do not marry. Stay a bachelor forever."

Charles chuckled. "That is terrible advice, considering I'm actually looking forward to marrying Eugenie."

Alcott shuddered dramatically. "Then it's too late for you. There is no saving you now."

Wilton glanced heavenward. "Leave Bedford alone. He's much more tolerable with Lady Eugenie in his life. You two are just jealous."

"Why would I be jealous?" Alcott huffed. "I prefer bachelorhood. It is safe. Predictable. No wife to answer to."

Wilton gave him a knowing look. "But you do have a sister that you answer to."

Alcott grunted. "That is true. I should marry her off to the Duke of Clarence."

"The duke is old enough to be your sister's grandfather. Perhaps even her great-grandfather," Addington stated.

Charles, amused by their bickering, shook his head and turned towards the carriage. "As enlightening as this conversation is, I need to depart for my wedding if I wish to arrive on time."

Wilton pressed his lips together, but the humor in his eyes was unmistakable. "We tried, but Bedford is too far gone. He is a man in love."

Alcott made a face. "Love? What a foolish thing to succumb to. A wise man marries for mutual toleration."

"You should write poetry," Wilton quipped dryly.

Alcott held up his hands. "Laugh if you must, but when I marry, it will be a practical decision—not some sentimental nonsense."

"How romantic," Addington muttered.

A footman opened the carriage door, and Charles stepped inside. Before the door closed, he glanced at his friends. "I do hope I will see you all at the chapel."

"We will be there," Wilton assured him. "Perhaps spending time in a chapel will do Alcott some good."

"I attend church," Alcott revealed. "My sister makes sure of it."

"Yes, but do you listen to the sermon?" Wilton asked.

Alcott's smirk widened. "I listen... enough."

With that, Charles settled into his seat as the carriage door shut behind him. He exhaled slowly, a sense of quiet anticipation settling over him. By the time this day ended, Eugenie would be his wife. And that was all that mattered.

A short time later, the carriage rolled to a jerking stop in front of Eugenie's townhouse. Charles pushed open the door before the footman could assist him and stepped out onto the pavement. He took the steps two at a time. Before he could lift a hand to the knocker, the door swung open as if the butler had been expecting his arrival.

"Good morning, my lord," the butler greeted, stepping aside with a formal bow. "Do come in."

Charles nodded his thanks and strode into the entry hall. Almost immediately, he spotted Elsbeth waiting near the grand staircase. She wore a knowing smile, her hands clasped before her.

"It is entirely unnecessary for you to escort Eugenie to the chapel," she said, amusement lacing her tone. "I would have ensured she arrived on time."

"I know," Charles admitted, not the least bit apologetic. "But now that Eugenie has agreed to marry me, I want to spend every waking moment with her."

Elsbeth's smile softened. "I am glad you have finally come to terms with your feelings."

Before he could reply, the sound of light footsteps drew his attention to the corridor. Eugenie stepped forward. The silver fabric of her gown shimmered in the soft morning light and a delicate headpiece adorned her blonde curls. And in that moment, he knew he would always think Eugenie was the most beautiful person he had ever seen for as long as he breathed.

Charles didn't even realize he was moving until he was suddenly in front of her. "Are you ready to get married?" he asked, unable to hide the eagerness in his voice.

If Eugenie noticed his enthusiasm, she didn't seem to mind.

A radiant smile spread across her lips. "I am." She lifted the folds of her gown slightly. "Do you like my gown? It was my mother's."

Charles studied her, taking in the exquisite detail of the fabric, but more than that, the emotion in her voice. "It is lovely," he said.

Her eyes grew moist. "I just wanted my mother to be part of my wedding, even in some small way."

Charles reached for her hand. He curled his fingers around hers, squeezing gently. "I did not have the privilege of knowing your mother, but I imagine she would be very proud of the woman you have become." He held her gaze, allowing his sincerity to shine through. "Because I know I am."

"Thank you, Charles. That means more than you will ever know," she acknowledged.

The deep chime of the long clock in the corner rang through the hall, marking the hour.

Elsbeth turned towards them. "It is time."

Charles took a small step back and offered his arm. "Shall we?"

Eugenie looped her arm through his as she replied, "I would ask if Sir Spotticus could come to our wedding, but Niles has already expressly forbidden it."

"I do not think horses are allowed in chapels," Charles said.

"You make a fair point," she conceded.

A familiar voice came from the corridor. "Bedford makes a good point," Niles remarked as he approached. "But didn't I say the same thing?"

Eugenie turned towards her brother, arching a brow. "Yes, but Charles says it with authority."

Niles stopped beside his wife, shaking his head with exasperated affection. "She is all yours now, Bedford."

Charles didn't hesitate. "I will gladly take her." His gaze met Eugenie's, full of love and certainty.

"You say that now," Niles said with mock seriousness, "but wait until you see her hat collection."

Eugenie rolled her eyes. "You know you'll miss me."

Niles's teasing demeanor faded, and his expression turned more solemn. "We will," he admitted with emotion in his voice.

Charles led Eugenie towards the waiting carriage, each step bringing him closer to the moment when she would be his. And he, irrevocably, would be hers.

The thought sent a thrill through him—a sensation both grounding and exhilarating. He had always believed himself to be a man of careful plans and of calculated decisions. Love had never been part of that plan. But then Eugenie had arrived, upending his world with her sharp wit, her unshakable spirit, and the warmth that had quietly woven itself into every corner of his heart.

He hadn't been prepared for her.

But love did not come with a warning. It did not announce itself politely or give time to prepare. It arrived like a force of nature, unstoppable, unrelenting, and undeniable. It changed everything. It made him question how he had ever lived without it.

Now, as he helped Eugenie into the carriage, her fingers warm in his grasp, he knew with certainty—she was his unexpected forever. And he would never want it any other way.

EPILOGUE

Six years later...

Eugenie sat at her writing table in the corner of her drawing room, the tall windows overlooking the rolling green fields of her country estate. She dipped her quill into the inkwell, her fingers steady despite the slight ache from hours of writing. With a final flourish, she finished her latest article for *The Morning Post*.

As she set the quill down, a familiar feeling of satisfaction washed over her. Sometimes, she still couldn't believe that this was her life—that for the past six years, she had been a contributor to one of London's most respected newssheets. Though Society might label her a spinster turned wife, she wrote about her life as a young mother rather than dwelling on the years she had spent unmarried. Fortunately, her children supplied her with a wealth of material to fill every column.

A voice interrupted her thoughts. "Are you finished?"

She turned at the sound, a smile forming as she took in the sight of Charles standing in the doorway. He held their one-year-old son, David, against his chest, the boy's chubby fingers curled into his father's cravat. David's dark curls, so much like his father's, stuck up in disarray, and his bright blue eyes darted around the room, full of curiosity.

"Yes, I shall post it today," Eugenie replied as she rose from her seat.

"Wonderful," Charles said as he strode into the room. "Then perhaps you can take this little rascal off my hands. He seems to have an inexhaustible supply of energy today."

"I would be happy to," Eugenie said as she went to stand beside her husband. "Where is Mary?"

"She's at her riding lesson," Charles answered, placing David on the ground. "I suspect she'll be there all afternoon. I have never seen a child more besotted with horses than she is." He paused, giving her a knowing look. "Well, besides you."

"I do love horses, and I am grateful to you for getting me back in the saddle."

He raised a brow. "Although, your trick riding days are over."

She laughed. "For good reason."

Charles wrapped his arms around her waist, pulling her close. "And how are you faring today?"

"Well," she said, relaxing into his embrace. "Niles and his family should be arriving soon."

Charles groaned dramatically. "I am not looking forward to my three nephews invading our peace. Those boys are downright unruly."

Eugenie shook her head with a fond smile. "Yes, but Niles and Elsbeth manage them well enough."

"That they do," Charles admitted. "But I still wince every time I see them climbing trees at breakneck speed. They seem to have no fear of injury or—heaven forbid—death."

David, growing restless, tugged at Eugenie's skirts. "Up," he demanded, lifting his arms expectantly.

Eugenie bent down, gathering her son in her arms. "It is nearly time for this little one's nap."

"My mother was hoping to put him down," Charles said. "She enjoys reading him stories and indulging his every whim."

"I have no objection to that," Eugenie said with a grin.

Charles smirked, lowering his voice conspiratorially. "Then perhaps we can steal a moment alone. You've been so busy writing that I have felt most neglected these past few days."

Eugenie feigned shock. "Neglected? Surely not."

With a flirtatious gleam in his eyes, Charles leaned in and brushed a kiss against her lips. "Dreadfully so. Perhaps you might make it up to me?"

"Some alone time would be lovely. But we'd best hurry if—"

Before she could finish, the main door burst open. The thunderous arrival of three boys shattered the quiet, their boisterous shouts echoing through the house.

"They have arrived," Eugenie said.

"Is it too late for me to hide?" Charles muttered under his breath.

Moments later, Niles stumbled into the room, looking utterly disheveled. His usually neat cravat was askew, his dark hair thoroughly mussed, and his expression one of pure exasperation.

"Never again will I ride in a coach with three boys," he declared, dropping his satchel unceremoniously onto the floor.

Eugenie raised a brow. "Didn't you say that last time?"

Niles threw his hands in the air. "I did! And each time, I come closer to the brink of madness."

Behind him, Elsbeth entered, looking as fresh as if she had stepped out of a leisurely stroll rather than endured a chaotic journey. "You poor, poor earl," she teased, patting her husband's arm. She then turned her attention to David, beaming. "And how is my handsome nephew?"

David responded by reaching for her.

Elsbeth scooped him up from Eugenie's arms, pressing a kiss to his chubby cheek. "Oh, you have gotten even cuter since I last saw you!"

"That was only a few months ago," Niles pointed out. "Give the baby back."

Ignoring him, Elsbeth sniffed David dramatically. "Mmm, he smells like baby."

Niles sighed. "You'll have to forgive my wife. She's been talking of nothing but babies lately. She insists we must try again for a girl."

"There is nothing wrong with having more children," Eugenie said.

Lifting a brow, Niles asked, "Have you met your nephews? We had to hire a separate nursemaid for each of them because one was simply not enough."

Eugenie grinned. "Where are they now?"

"I had their nursemaids take them out back to run off some of their energy before supper," Niles said with a dramatic sigh. "But I, personally, could use a nap."

Elsbeth handed David back to Eugenie before slipping her arm through her husband's. "Come along, Dear. I shall escort you to our bedchamber, you poor old man."

After they departed, Eugenie placed a hand on her stomach. "I do hope this next one is nothing like her cousins."

Charles studied her. "You think it's a girl?"

She shrugged. "Perhaps, but I won't complain if it is a boy."

He took a step closer, resting his hand atop hers. "All that matters is that you and the baby are healthy."

"Should we tell everyone at dinner tonight?"

Charles nodded, a smile playing at his lips. "I think that would be perfect. My mother will be thrilled."

"If it's a girl, I was thinking of naming her after my mother. And if it's a boy, Arthur."

Charles's eyes softened. "You truly mean that?"

"I do," Eugenie said. "I never met your father, but through your stories, I feel as though I know him."

Emotion flickered across his face. "Just when I think I couldn't love you more, you surprise me."

"Well, it is only fair since you have given me so much," Eugenie said. "I was once scared of loving you, of giving up my freedom. But by loving you, my heart was set free."

Leaning in, he pressed his forehead against hers. "There is no one else for me. In this life and the next, it will be me and you. Always."

She closed her eyes, allowing herself to sink into the warmth of Charles's embrace. Nobody had ever made more sense to her soul, nobody but him. For she had waited her entire life to find someone she could be with in silence, feeling wanted, appreciated, and loved, and when it finally happened, she knew why it was worth the wait.

But before she could lose herself completely in the moment, a tiny, insistent movement in her arms disrupted their closeness.

David wriggled against her chest, his little body squirming with restless energy. He pushed against her shoulder, letting out an impatient whimper.

Eugenie chuckled, shifting her grip as she pulled back slightly. "It seems someone is unimpressed with our sentimentality."

Chuckling, Charles took him from her arms. "Very well, my son, you have my full attention. What is it you require? A kingdom? A pony? The moon itself?"

David clapped his hands together, then grabbed a fistful of Charles's cravat and tugged.

"I believe he simply wants his father," Eugenie said.

Charles pressed a kiss to the top of David's head. "Then he shall have me. Though I do hope he will allow me at least some time alone with his mother in the near future."

"You were the one who wanted children," Eugenie quipped.

"I do believe it was a mutual decision."

The sound of glass breaking echoed throughout the main level.

Turning towards the doorway, Eugenie said, "It would appear the boys have made it inside now."

"Heaven help us," Charles muttered.

Eugenie placed her hand on his arm. "Let us go greet our nephews."

As they walked hand in hand out of the drawing room, Eugenie couldn't help but smile. This was her life now. And what a perfect life it was.

The End

**He returned from war hailed as a hero, but a stranger to himself—
and to the wife he never knew he had.**

Dominic Stevens, Baron Warwicke, comes home bearing the physical
and emotional scars of battle. Haunted by fragmented memories and
burdened by duty, he's stunned to learn he has a wife—a woman he
does not remember marrying.

Dorothea rejoices when Dominic comes to remove her from her
brother's abusive household. But the man who stands before her now
is colder, harder... a shadow of the husband she once knew. Still, she
is determined to reach the heart he has forgotten, believing the man
she married is still there, merely buried beneath the pain.

Intent on seeking an annulment to free them both, Dominic fights his growing feelings for the gentle, resilient woman who refuses to give up on him. But when danger threatens Dorothea's life, Dominic must confront not only his past but also the possibility that the love he thought forever lost in his life may be the very thing that saves them both.

ABOUT THE AUTHOR

Laura Beers is an award-winning author. She attended Brigham Young University, earning a Bachelor of Science degree in Construction Management. She can't sing, doesn't dance and loves naps.

Laura lives in Utah with her husband, three kids and her dysfunctional dog. When not writing regency romance, she loves skiing, hiking and drinking Dr Pepper.

You can connect with Laura on Facebook, Instagram or on her site at www.authorlaurabeers.com.

www.ingramcontent.com/pod-product-compliance
Lightning Source LLC
Chambersburg PA
CBHW060856250626
47159CB00008B/2760